Always Magnolia

Dianna Dann

Wayward Cat Publishing

Always Magnolia

Some of us can't blind ourselves, can't rest in the fog, or dance in the rain. We are the ones who remember.
--Jericho Slater (?-September 15, 2014)

1.

I was there the day you nearly drowned. You were battling a riptide of rage, like you do, and as soon as I saw you storming through the scrub to the lake I knew something bad had happened. I wouldn't find out what until the day after you walked away from me on the railroad tracks west of the junkyard, and disappeared. Anyway, you walked right up to Putty and shoved him into Kyle–threatened to take his truck and put it in the lake. And Putty put his hands up and was saying, "Anything you want, man. Anything." Because that's the way it always was with you and Putty; he'd do anything for you and I guess you knew that and that's why instead you took Ron's motorcycle and popped a wheelie off the little pier and we all saw what happened. We were all watching it the whole time but just didn't want to see.

It's mostly death that triggers you. It cuts you deep on the inside and your upset shows itself in violence instead of tears. You shot a rabbit once, at the junkyard, and the next day you beat up Randy White. When Mr. McCormick, lot fifty, died in his sleep and we all stood and watched the EMTs wheel his body out of his trailer on one of those rolling beds–we were all twelve that summer–a few days later you hit Casey Lawrence in the back with a shovel and chopped down the tree by the pool with an ax you stole from the Old Twins, lot twenty-nine. And all anyone talked about was how you stole the ax when you could have got one from the junkyard any time you wanted. When the trailer park mama cat, Ringo, was hit by a car–we were older that year, but it's blurry in my memory–you took a sledgehammer to Pat Dunn's bicycle a few days later. She didn't do anything about it; it was Bobby Jack Beaumont, after all. The darling of River Front Trailer Haven. You were loved and pitied and hated and feared and everybody knew that when something died...you would find a way to feel it in a way none of us could understand.

The bike fell on top of you as you hit the water and we all stood frozen for a few seconds, digesting it, and then the boys ran out into the lake, their gangly legs flailing up and over the surface trying to get to you. They dragged you out and you vomited in the sand and you couldn't stand up by yourself. You started thrashing around, glaring at all of us like a wild animal trapped in a cage. You wanted to know what the hell was going on and they tried to tell you. You vomited again and again and crawled through it.

"What is this?" You were saying. "What happened?"

Finally you sat up and went empty, like your body let you drain out of it, and then you were crying and mumbling and everybody panicked because they didn't know what to do with that. They put you in the back of

2

Putty's pickup and drove you off to the junkyard and I was left standing on the muddy shore watching, because Ruby didn't want me to be within fifty feet of you. It wasn't legal or anything. Ruby said I could make it legal, said I could get an order of protection or something like that. It would say you couldn't be around me and I told her that was nuts.

They wanted me to come along. They waited for me to get into the truck. But I couldn't do it. I was thinking of all the other times you got into trouble, and I was the one to help, and it was sad that this time it would have to be someone else. But Ruby would say you brought it all on yourself. That's what she'd say, whether it's true or not.

You fell out of a tree when you were seven and broke your arm and the only one you'd let touch you was me. You leaned on me and I had my arm around you as we walked as fast as we could to the junkyard with you screaming in my right ear the entire time. Nobody cared that you cried then. We all agreed we'd have done the same. And then with your arm in a cast, you sat on Willa Fogarty's lap, she was lot fourteen until she had to go live with her daughter in Houston, eating cookies, over at the picnic tables by the pool. Everybody wanted the chance to comfort you, but I was there first.

When you were ten you almost suffocated after hiding in a refrigerator at the junkyard and you couldn't get the door open from the inside. You were lucky Kyle thought to look there first, but you came out screaming, flushed and sweating. You dropped to the ground and wouldn't let anybody near you but me. And I was the

3

only one to stay with you, patting your back, when your dad came out and shot his gun into the air.

When you picked a fight outside the middle school and ended up against seven other kids, Kyle and Putty had to drag you out before they killed you, or so they tell it. We missed the bus because of it and had to walk home along U.S. 1, and you leaned on me the whole time. We were fourteen that year. The shoulder of my best blouse was stained with blood from your nose and it never came out. But you didn't cry that time. You'd stopped with the crying by fifth grade. So, I get that everybody was scared when you nearly drowned and the tears started flowing. But they knew I couldn't help you; not this time. I wasn't supposed to be with you anymore. I wasn't the one.

We all grew up together at River Front Trailer Haven. Every one of us. Putty Coot—Harold really, but he'd hit you if you called him that, and you never did—started mowing lawns before he was in high school and he has a solid business that includes landscaping; his uncles own that nursery on U.S. 1. Kyle Bickell works at the bar down the way and spends most of his time getting into some kind of trouble or other. You'd know all about that if you could remember. Mary Stahl got married last year and has a baby. Ron Wilson, whose bike you drowned, was the only one of us to go to college and he came home a year ago to start up an aluminum siding business with his brothers. As for me, well, Celia told me the bait shop was mine, while Ruby would get the laundromat. You worked the junkyard with your dad. You and I used to joke that we were no different from the filthy rich, inheriting our family businesses. But I understand now

4

that you might not want to take over the junkyard after all.

Putty was your best friend until that day at the lake. If you ever remember, maybe you'll understand it, but I don't. Ruby says they were all scared and I told her sure, I could see Kyle–he's a drunk jerk-off most of the time anyway–and Ron, who, to be honest never really liked you, and even Mary. She liked you well enough, but I can see how your behavior could scare a person off. But not Putty. He was supposed to be like a brother to you. He was the one who made sure everybody stuck by you after you hit me last year. Because there was something wrong in your head, he told us. You didn't know how to relate in this world with its sickness and pain. That's what he said. In a speech like. And we all decided he was right, even me. You couldn't help yourself and we had to stick by you, we had to stick by one another, all of us, no matter what. Because we were the trailer park trash nobody else wanted. Us against the world and all that. And then you go a little bit crazy and Putty is gone. They were all gone. But me.

It was because we were always together, the half-dozen they called us, that I couldn't see forcing you to stay away from everybody just because we had a problem, you and me. And I didn't want to lose my friends, either, so I told Ruby I wouldn't do it–go to the judge, I mean, and get protection. And even though the time had long passed, the bruises all healed–Ruby took pictures when I was too upset to stop her but I found them and burned them–Ruby still worried, still told me to be careful when she knew you'd be around, still warned me you'd kill me one of these days. She's a good mom, if a little overprotective. And just so you know, she doesn't believe you did anything wrong and she hopes you'll come home soon. Honest. But I don't think she'll want you to come home to me. Not yet. She still watches me, sideways like.

Anyway, the boys, and Mary, carted you off to the junkyard and I was standing next to your vomit and I picked up the keys out of it. Three little keys. One of them was tiny, like a luggage key. Celia had one, that time she went up to Tallahassee to see my great Uncle Cyrus, she borrowed a suitcase and it had a tiny little lock on it with a tiny gold key. And Ruby said, "Ma, what you got to lock it for?" Because Celia was riding up with my Aunt Jewel and who would care if Aunt Jewel saw her underwear? But Celia said, "It's there. Why not use it?" She used this same logic with pills and cigarettes, and drinks younger men put in front of her when she went down to Sandy Jakes; but don't you be thinking my grandma is a drunk or anything. You'd know if you could remember. You love Celia, almost as much as I do.

The other two keys were small too, but thicker. You vomited the keys on the sand, Jack. Do you remember? I should take this opportunity to apologize for not giving them back to you right away. But I didn't know. I didn't understand. I know it might not make sense to you, but I was afraid if I gave them back, you'd remember everything all at once and our lives would be the way they were before and I'd have to stay away from you like Ruby wanted. And I was afraid of the truth. Because who swallows keys and then vomits them up again? I washed them off in the lake and carried them home. And when

Ruby came in from work, the first thing I said was, "Bobby Jack nearly drowned at the lake today."

She dropped onto the sofa, kicked off her sneakers and said, "Don't do it."

"Don't do what?"

"Let him be."

My face burned hot. She knew.

2.

You'd lost your mind and the story spread all over the trailer park within hours like this: Bobby Jack had ruined Ron's bike, nearly drowned, cried, and said he didn't live at the junkyard, and Mr. Beaumont was not his father. It was true enough. You acted like you didn't know Putty or Kyle or any of us. All of that, just from almost drowning.

Old man Pinkerton, lot seven, said it wasn't possible. Amnesia needs a trauma to the head. And so far as anyone could tell, it was the chest. You got the wind knocked out of you by the bike, is all. But Henrietta Cleary, lot twelve, said psychological trauma would do the trick. And then an argument erupted over whether or not nearly drowning was psychologically traumatic enough to do it. But Doc Fred, lot nineteen, not a doctor, said when you woke up from nearly drowning, you wouldn't have known you'd nearly drowned, so how could it have traumatized you? At which point Celia, lot five, my grandmother, hit him with her peacock feather and told him he didn't know his ass from a hole in the ground. Mr.

Haverty said you didn't nearly drown anyway; there's no such thing. You drowned, he said, just not fatally. Mrs. Cleary rolled her eyes and sucked on her lower lip and that was the end of that nonsense. Finally they all went back to their beers. All the while, sitting out there at the picnic area with us, Ruby was glaring at me and nodding and I couldn't tell if she was thinking, "Yes, Maggie's a good girl and won't get herself tangled up with the likes of Jack Beaumont again," or "Yes, Maggie's in trouble."

But you weren't Jack Beaumont anymore, that's the thing. Ron told me you spent the first day wandering around the perimeter of the junkyard like you were looking for a way in and your father was yelling at you, telling you to make up your mind, come back inside or run away. Nobody could fault Mr. Beaumont. And talk was already going around about your mom and how, obviously, the apple doesn't fall far from the tree. Do you remember your mom? Celia was already organizing a bake sale for both you and your dad—kept saying, "Poor Digger." Because your dad wasn't to blame. He was a good Christian man, stuck by your mom longer than most would have, so Celia always said.

The day after that, you wandered around the trailer park and up to U.S. 1 and along the little plaza and back and forth in front of Pebble Sands Convenience Store and Hair Salon, mumbling and rubbing your face. You'd gone batshit crazy, if you don't mind my saying it, and everyone was worried, Ruby most of all.

"Stay away from him," she kept saying. "I don't like it. It looks dangerous."

And I said I am, I am. And I was. I put a black rope

through the holes in your keys and wore it around my neck. The keys hung much lower than my gold cross, the one my grandmother Hanson gave me, and Ruby and Celia just assumed it was another one of my necklaces, maybe the one with the cat charms on it or the sunflower, so they didn't notice. But I could feel the keys against my skin, tucked into my cleavage under my bra, and it was like I had a secret. I felt guilty about it and wondered why secrets were always bad.

I was at work at the bait shop later that day. I'd walked through the rain to get there and sent Celia off for her lunch break. Thunder rattled the glass door and wind sometimes whistled through the slender opening at the jamb. Only the hard core fishermen were likely to stop in, so I was alone and you know how, when it rains, everything is darker and brighter at the same time? Looking out the back window at the field, I was marveling at how deep the greens were when I heard the bell jingle, and being as it was dark and stormy and maybe I was already a little spooked, when I turned around and saw you at the door with a gun, I screamed.

You understand, don't you? I thought you had a gun. Bobby Jack Beaumont—nearly drowned, clearly crazy— with a gun. You'd come to kill me—followed me from the trailer park in the storm to murder me. In that split second, before I realized what it actually was, I thought, great, I'm going to die at the bait shop and my body will stink with the smell of shrimp and seaweed for eternity. Not exactly as I'd planned. Not that I'd planned my death; but after you hit me, and Ruby went on and on about how if I took you back, you'd beat me again and again, and it would get worse and worse, until you'd finally kill me, I guess maybe I'd begun to figure my death would have you involved in it somehow.

I only realized you were holding an umbrella when you turned and left the store. When the electricity went out I almost wet myself and started bawling and ran to lock the door behind you. You probably heard the bolt hit the jamb and I felt bad about it. But honestly, Jack, what kind of crazy do you have to be to walk through a rainstorm and never open your umbrella?

Ruby came in a while later from the laundromat to check on me—said I was right to lock the door; but she didn't know the real reason I'd done it. And the power clicked back on and we laughed at how when I was a little girl, she and I would lock ourselves in the bathroom during thunderstorms, light candles, and have tea parties. You couldn't tell you were in a bathroom so much in the dark, except for the smell.

Do you remember my mother, Jack? Ruby Hanson. She's got that tired, wrinkled face fifty-five year old women get when they have their first baby at fifteen, marry an abusive man at seventeen, have two more children, none of whom turned out all that well, and smoke themselves near to death because of it. But she was a beauty when she was young. I've seen pictures. She rode in a parade once, on a float, with a sash and a crown. She was Mrs. Tangerine, or something like that, and pregnant with me at the time, she tells me. And I pretend I can see myself in her eyes, in the picture. But I can't really.

I think she knew when I was eleven—about you.

That's when she started talking about statistics. She quoted them like she knew what they were, and like they were true. Women who have children too young have daughters who do the same thing, she said. It's a statistic. Go look it up. Women who are abused by their husbands raise daughters who get muddled in abusive relationships, she told me. When I was *eleven*. She kept telling me. Right up until the day you hit me. She must realize it's a statistic because there's not a damn thing you can do about it.

My father is Bishop Hanson; you remember him I'm sure. He left before I was born. And he left again when I was two. And again when I was six. He kept leaving and coming back until I was twelve, almost thirteen. Then he left for good, sort of, except for the day you hit me. Ruby sometimes says he's evil.

"But, Magnolia, baby," she'd say on especially hard days. "If he showed up right now, walked through that door, I'd...well, you'd have your father home. For a while, anyway." She'd sip her beer and slur her words. "It's a statistic, you know. Abused women...they always take 'em back."

I'm just saying. And on my way home from work that night all I could see in my head was the look on your face, standing there soaking wet, dripping rain on the floor of the bait shop. There's a word for it, it means...small, open, *prey*. Ron would know the word; maybe I'll ask him. You looked so scared and Ruby would be so happy–she loves the I-told-you-sos–and so worried, to know she was right. Because I knew I was going to have to find you and help you.

3.

The last I'd heard from Ron—Putty knew nothing, or at least pretended to—after you left the bait shop, you hiked out behind the junkyard west, and hadn't been seen coming back. I couldn't sleep that night; the rain pattered and echoed on the roof of the trailer and that would usually lull me straight away but all I could think about was you, out in the scrub, too crazy to pop open your umbrella.

I closed my eyes and put my fingertips to the gold cross at my neck and whispered, out loud because Ruby says it has to be spoken to count, "Dear God, make him open his umbrella." And God told me right back that I should definitely go out to the scrub and look for you. I have to confess, I trembled with giddiness—the kind of excitement little girls get when their daddies take their hands and swing them around and around—thinking about finding you, letting you lean on me again. It had been such a long year without you—without knowing for sure.

Celia would call it Stockholm Syndrome and laugh at me—she's done it before, this past year in fact, when she caught me staring at nothing; she called it mooning. I tried to tell her mooning was something completely different but she just put her hands up and made that noise, "Agggh." Only people who smoke a lot can do that noise justice, don't you think?

Nobody really believed you abused me. You only hit me that one time, so far as anybody knows, and like Putty said, you couldn't help it. But over the past year since it happened, the incident grew and grew and became the measure of our entire relationship and nothing I could say anymore, could make you a better man for Ruby and Celia. They still love you, of course. I'm just not allowed to. "We've got experience on our side," Ruby often said and I believed her. She was my mother, after all, and mother knows best. Leastwise, mine does.

So, I calmed myself down and gave myself a talking to, told myself I was only going to help. It didn't mean anything about us. That could wait.

The next morning was hot and steamy; kids were already in the pool and Old Man Pinkerton, lot seven, was lying on one of the tattered lounge chairs in his bathing suit, gray hair all over him, oiled up and shiny. Said he was old enough now, to bake in the sun. He lifted his head and watched me walk past like he knew where I was going and I didn't care. I walked through the lots to the back gate and took Beaumont Road south past the junkyard.

You told me once that the Beaumont junkyard covers six acres of land–I thought you were trying to impress me. When I think about it now, with all that's happened, I shiver. It's surrounded by chain link fence with coils of barbed wire atop it which makes the whole thing so much worse. The sign out front reads: Junk Cars Boats

Appliances. I never thought about it, until that day, but then I wondered if that was really the name of the place. I mean on paper. Or did it not have a name? And for some reason I wondered what I'd name myself if I had to put it on paper. Descriptive like, you know? Like Junk Cars Boats Appliances. What would I be? Girl Jack Loves, I thought and smiled, absent-mindedly crossing my fingers. And then I frowned. Girl Not Allowed to Love Jack. I was going to change that; I was going to change all of it.

You remember that time we spray painted over 'boats' because there weren't any in there and we laughed about it for weeks because your dad never noticed? And after the hurricanes came through the very next year, we had to go out and paint the word in again.

There were eight dogs in all at the junkyard, but only Wilder and Manning roamed free. They used to follow you everywhere until Manning growled and leapt at Henrietta Clearly, lot twelve. You kept them locked up after that, even though some of us thought it was Henrietta's fault. She was yelling at you, pointing her finger; she put her hand on you, shoved a little, and that was that. The other dogs lived in runs on the edges of the property where they could maul intruders—if a person ever managed to get over the barbed fence and find themselves trapped in a dog run.

It's empty now, you know, the junkyard, and all sealed up—no one's allowed in for a long time; that's what the police told us. John Johnson, lot twenty-two—you remember him, don't you? Remember how none of us believe his name is really John Johnson? He has Wilder and Manning, even though Loretta Swanson, the owner

17

of River Front Trailer Haven, lots one through three, doesn't want them around. She says they're going to bite someone sure enough and we ought to have them put down. But none of us will allow it. At first we all tried to feed and water the dogs left in the runs. They're vicious, Jack. After a day or two, the county came and took them away–they'll be put down for sure.

Anyway, it was mid-summer and walking through the scrub with its sand and saw palmetto, shrubby oaks and sparse, weak pines was like being lost on an alien planet. Remember Ron used to tell us to stop calling it the scrub? What year did he start that? It was the one when he did the science project on it. He told us, "It's not scrub–not technically. It's scrubby flatwoods. See the pines, there?" And Putty shoved him and Kyle got all high-pitched and sang, "Scrubby flatwoods, scrubby flatwoods."

But Ron was persistent and you boys finally let him talk because you were bored by trying to make him stop. We should be grateful, really. It's because of Ron that we know the birds and their calls. We know the difference between the saw palmetto with its huge, rough stems snaking along the dirt, and the scrub palmetto, its fans popping straight out of the ground. Ron told us all the names of the plants–the rosemary and the stagger bush. We know what toad song is because of him. And he was the one to keep Putty and Kyle from bothering the gopher tortoises. And see how I say tortoise instead of turtle? That's Ron. We love the scrub because of him, and I still like to hike it when I want to clear my head.

That first day out, walking the quarter mile to the railroad tracks seemed to take forever. All I had was my own breath in my ears and I was so scared I'd find you dead. I kept saying to myself, "We'd have heard the shot." But would we really? Remember when we all watched that movie where those kids went off along some railroad tracks to find the body of a boy who got hit by a train? So we all went out one morning and walked for miles up and down the tracks looking for a body until we saw one of those maintenance cars coming and we ran home like we were being chased.

When I came up to the cleared corridor where the tracks snake their way along the coast, I found you sitting just up north a bit, twenty yards back, this side of the rails, against a stubby oak, with your old backpack beside you, staring west across the scrub. I was still scared, but I walked forward and you turned and when I got close I saw you were empty. You didn't jump or flinch or even look at me like you knew me. You were a blank.

I saw the things I missed the day before in the bait shop. Your face and neck were covered in black stubble and you wore a dark gray t-shirt, darker under the arms, with jeans, and your sneakers barely tied, like you could slip your feet right out of them. When I got to the tree we stared at each other for a while. I was glad for the little bit of shade and looked up and then down the tracks. You zipped open your backpack and dug around in it and pulled out that photograph I gave you–the one Mary took of me at the beach laughing, with the ocean behind me.

You held it out to me and I took it.

"That's you," you said. Real matter of fact like.

I nodded.

"Magnolia," you said.

I turned it over and there on the back, I'd written 'Always, Magnolia.'

I gave it back to you and you put it on the sand and started pulling stuff out of your backpack. "This is what I took," you said. In the pile was a half used matchbook with something written on it, a big gold hoop earring, a pair of sunglasses, a leather journal with a little lock on it, a piece of scrap paper, and a ladies watch. And a handful of keys that you sprinkled onto the sand like a waterfall. They were just like the keys I found in your vomit; I could feel them in my cleavage and I trembled. You looked up at me standing over you and said, "Do you know what any of this is?"

"No."

You were angry then, I could tell, and you picked it all back up again, sifted the sand out of it, and shoved it into your backpack and tossed the pack away from you toward the tracks. I sat down beside you then but you didn't look at me. And I figured you didn't know anything at all.

"Do you remember what happened?" I asked you.

You told me you found yourself in the trailer at the junkyard and this man was telling you to get up and get to work but you didn't know what he was talking about. Nothing was familiar, you said. But at the same time, recognition nagged at you. It was like something you wanted to forget. When you looked at the room you were in, it made you want to scream but you couldn't think of any words. And when you went into the little bathroom, you thought you'd vomit and the face in the mirror was odd and evil. Evil, you said. And the man, your father, was repulsive. That was the word you used.

The way you described your dad was like...well, you know those mirrors in the fun house at the fair and how they stretch everything or smash it up? That's what you were saying. Your dad is a large man—it's obvious you got your wiry frame from your mom, leastwise that's what Celia always said. Your dad is a half foot taller than you, balding all along the top of his head with a greasy comb over. And he's got a beer belly, it's true. Looks pregnant. We've made fun of him for years over that. But he's sweet enough; his face is warm and friendly and sure, he yelled at us a lot when we were kids and shot his gun into the air. But we were on his property. Celia said it served us right every time. A junkyard isn't the place for kids. Teenagers or young adults, either.

But when you told me about him, about how he stood there in the trailer badgering you, trying to get you to go to work, you made him sound like a giant. You said he had rolls of flesh hanging off his face and body, shiny with sweat, red and splotchy. He opened his mouth wide when he spoke and you could see his yellow, rotting teeth. And he cursed every other word. At least, when you told me what he said, you used all the words I'm not allowed to say in front of Ruby. It was like you weren't talking about Mr. Beaumont at all. Like you saw him different from how anyone else did. I tried to imagine it—if I saw your dad and didn't know who he was, would I be scared of him? I didn't think so.

"So I left," you said. "And that's what I brought with me." You lifted your shoulders and your head shook, rattling on your neck, like you were astounded at your own stupidity.

"You're shook up is all," I said. "Maybe you just grabbed whatever was near."

"No," you said. "I went around the room, digging through drawers and the closet to find it all." Here you laughed and looked at me, waiting, I guess for me to say you were nuts. But I didn't.

"You've had a trauma. Seems to me you'd act strange. Your brain's not firing right."

We sat quiet for a while. I think I was waiting for you to remember me.

"Why'd you come out here?" I asked you.

"I'm leaving. I just don't know which way I'm supposed to go."

"Well, south will take you to Miami. And north will take you up out of Florida."

You looked both ways. Then you got up and got your backpack, came back to sit and took out the scrap piece of paper. You unfolded it and handed it to me. It said Tucker Reed, and had an address in Georgia and a telephone number on it, scratched out in a frenzy of poor handwriting.

"North, then." You said.

"Who's Tucker?"

You looked at me and I could see you weren't sure.

"You're not Tucker," I told you. "You're Jack. Bobby Jack Beaumont. You live at the junkyard."

You shook your head.

I asked when you were going to leave and you said you'd wait. You knew more about Bobby Jack Beaumont than you did about Tucker Reed from Georgia, so you'd better give it a few days to see if it

22

wouldn't come back. But when you thought about Jack, and the junkyard, you said it made you shake, made you want to vomit. So you were pretty sure in the end, it would turn out you weren't Jack at all.

I didn't tell you, but I liked that. I smiled and you saw it and you even smiled a little. I'd already pretty much decided you weren't Jack, not anymore. Jack didn't sit still. Jack didn't stare out into the scrub like it was worth looking at. Jack never looked empty, but angry or mean or like he was working on something there in his head. Jack didn't use words like repulsive and badgering– because Ron taught us fancy words like that and Jack didn't like Ron. Jack wasn't scared. I wanted you to not be Jack. One day, when you remember it all, you'll understand.

You asked me to tell you about this Jack person and I said where do you want me to start and you said the beginning and so I did. And after that first day, when I had to go home, you said I should write it all down so you could remember it. You said it was gone, all gone. And if what I said was true, if that was you I was talking about, even though the story was sad, you'd want to keep hold of it.

And I said, "You haven't heard the whole thing yet."

4.

That first day I told you I had only fragments, incomplete pictures of the beginning. We were three when we met and there was no way I could parse what I really knew and remembered from what Ruby and Celia and all the other people at Trailer Haven told me. They told all of us, actually. All through those years, the residents loved to spend the evenings sitting out near the pool at the picnic tables drinking beer, laughing, and reminiscing. During winter, we'd all wear sweaters and socks and somebody would always get drunk enough to throw someone else into the pool. In summer, we all stank of generic-brand mosquito repellent and Loretta Swanson wouldn't allow us in the pool with it on. But we'd go in anyway.

They'd talk about their childhoods, and their travels, and they'd also tell us stories about when we were young, the things we did to get into trouble, the embarrassing stuff we'd like to forget, and some good stuff, too. So we remember more how they told us than we do how it might have really happened.

When you showed up at Trailer Haven in nothing but

a dirty diaper, there was talk about calling the police. Nobody had any clue who you were or where you came from. But Willa Fogarty, lot fourteen, said she thought Digger Beaumont had a kid. Said she thought she saw him drive down the road with a baby seat in the truck one time, but that was a year before.

Nobody wanted to get Mr. Beaumont into trouble, especially since they all knew about your mom, so they found another diaper and gave you a bath and fed you. Sure enough, your dad came down the street whistling like he was calling one of the dogs. He came into the trailer park and got you. He was mad and I can see him in my memory grabbing you by the arm and you crying. But Celia said it was right. You'd run away, after all, and you were such a little thing to be going out on your own. But everybody told Digger you could come visit any time, they were glad to have you, and then it seemed like he sent you over. You showed up almost every day and one of the older kids would walk you home later, to the front gate anyway. Nobody could go into the junkyard except the adults. But Celia always told them to watch you, and make sure you got to the office at least.

You were practically raised at Trailer Haven after that. Celia figured out pretty quick that you didn't need the diaper and everybody pitched in with hand-me-down clothes and shoes. And everything was fine, except once in a while, your mom would come into the park. Sometimes we thought she was looking for you, but she never seemed to be, until she saw you. Then she'd wake up, like she'd been in a trance, and say, "Bobby Jack, why are you here," and take you home.

One time, she came into the park screaming. We could hear her all the way down the road and everybody got quiet, trying to figure out what she was saying. She got closer and closer and louder and louder, until we finally saw her on the little side road coming toward the picnic tables. She was screaming, "Josiekatellen, josiekatellen, josiekatellen," at the top of her lungs, and her throat was scratchy and rough and we could tell by looking at her she was crazy.

She was bone thin and wearing what looked like a dirty sheet, with a hole in the middle for her head, spattered with blood, and mud, and little burned out holes. Underneath, it was pretty clear she wasn't wearing anything else. All the adults jumped up as she came near us and a few walked her home; she screamed the whole way. And when they came back, everybody sat around and debated what she was saying.

Pat Dunn, lot eight, said she was singing a song; she was sure she'd heard it before. Mr. Haverty, lot thirty, said no, it was probably the name of her sister up north way. Your dad had spoken of her once or twice—said at some point, he'd have to send her to her sister's. There were places up that way that would take care of her better than he could. But he loved her so and couldn't stand to be parted from her. She had lucid times, he'd tell them, times when she knew him and they were in love again.

But Ruby, my mom, she said your mom was saying names. Josie, Kate, Ellen. She was sure of it. And then there was an argument over whether or not your mom's sister could have three first names. Then Loretta, the owner I told you about before, she stood up and screamed, "I've got it." And she told everyone your mom had obviously given birth to three little girls who'd died shortly after and those were their names. From there, as Celia tells it, the craziest stories started flowing. Some had your mother as a former movie star and those were her best roles. Others decided she had multiple personalities and she was trying to communicate with them. It was a fun story to hear again and again. "You remember when Tish Beaumont came through screaming at the top of her lungs?"

There was a time they don't talk about, though. I remember it like it was yesterday; some things imprint on your brain because they're so awful. In the early evening, hazy gray, one day in winter when it wasn't so hot and most of us kids were just out of the pool and standing at the picnic tables wrapped in our towels, our teeth chattering, I saw your face before I saw her. We were seven, I think, that year. We all turned when we heard her moaning.

She was stumbling toward us, stark naked, her body covered in bruises, cuts, and sores, some bleeding. It's only a flash in my mind–there and then gone like the lights that flicker on and you see the monster in the room and then they go out. The adults took her away fast. I was too afraid to even ask about it, but Celia told me your mom was sick; she'd been hurting herself. And your dad had a hard time taking care of you, and the junkyard, and her. "Poor Digger," she'd always say. "Poor Digger."

5.

When I stopped talking I saw your face was pinched up like and I thought you must be trying to remember but you didn't. I said, "Come home," we'd find someplace for you. Mr. Haverty, lot thirty, or Doc Fred, lot nineteen. They wouldn't mind having you until you sorted it all out. But you said you couldn't; there was something cruel, in the scrub, a line you couldn't cross over; you could never go back.

"What's it like?" I asked you. "Not remembering."

You sat there staring at the dirt in front of you for a long time before you said it wasn't so much you couldn't remember but that everything in your head was moving so fast you couldn't catch anything. It was good me talking, you said. You could concentrate just on that and it didn't matter what your mind was doing, didn't matter what it was you couldn't see.

My first reaction was sadness, because that sounded so much like you, the way you were before–always looking around for the next thing to occupy your brain, like you had too much in there and you couldn't focus, or didn't want to. You wouldn't look people in the eye for more than a second. The explanation at the trailer park was that you were a natural born liar and natural born liars never look a person in the eyes. But Celia said that was horse crap.

"Horse shit," she said. "Natural born liars'll look you square in the face and tell bald face whoppers. No. It's the opposite. Jack's got a conscience. He's hiding it from us. He don't want us to know he's not a good boy."

"Of course he's a good boy," Mr. Pinkerton said.

"I know that. I'm just saying, he knows he's not perfect."

"Well say not perfect, if that's what you mean."

Being critical of you could ruin a person's standing in the park if she weren't careful. I caught on pretty early that Celia struggled between sober reality and urgent hope where you were concerned. One minute she was defending you and the next clucking her tongue and saying, "Something ought to be done about that boy."

"It's his mother," she would say in a whisper now and then. That was the explanation for all of your faults and the reason nobody paid them any mind.

But you *were* different. Before you went crazy, you were hiding all that stuff in your head from all of us. And after, you were hiding it from yourself, too.

There's a picture of the half-dozen tacked up on the cork board at the laundromat. Ruby took it when we were all about ten. She'd given us each a Popsicle and we sat on one of the picnic tables, our feet on the bench. Whenever I think about us, as a whole, I see that picture in my head. You're on the far left, the black of your hair stands out. Already tanned, you're squinting into the sunlight, frowning, taking a bite out of a purple one. Putty is next to you, already twice as big, tough and taut, always sunburned with candy apple red hair, showing his teeth in a wide grin to the camera. And Kyle, all arms and legs and ears, like a big caramel colored puppy, has one arm around Putty and his mouth is open; he's laughing loud. Then there's Mary, one hand at her neck in mid hair flip. She holds her Popsicle out, away from her, already concerned about her clothes and anything sticky. Her hair is the color of beach sand and falling straight off her head like it's melting. She's smiling, flirting, turned toward the boys. I'm next to her, my brown hair full of sweat and stuck to my face—I've got those awful bangs Ruby cut. But I'm smiling, happy, my shirt already stained orange. And Ron is beside me, plump and slathered in zinc oxide, saying something to Ruby as she snaps the shot.

We're all there, as we are now, in those younger versions. I used to look at it and laugh, but now I see we're trapped. We're caught up in the path we don't even know we're on and for some of us it'll turn out okay, but it doesn't matter. You're on a path and you can't get off; even if you know where it's going.

I walked the scrub to Beaumont Road and home where I got you some food. I stole a gallon jug of water from Mrs. Bentemyer, lot six. She's saving up for another apocalypse and has a bunch of enormous cans of food and jugs of water stacked up high in front of her trailer and covered with a green tarp. I took Celia's old transistor radio down from her closet for you; I figured you could listen to that while I wasn't with you, to keep your head clear. I thought I'd lose my arm carrying all that out to the railroad tracks, and when I got there, you stood up and looked afraid. You said I was beet red and I didn't doubt it.

That night, back at home, I told Ruby and Celia I'd found you and that you wouldn't come home. I told them I was going to go out there every day and make sure you were okay and had food and water, and to hear their reactions, you'd think I was about to prostitute myself up north by the library. Why not Putty? They wanted to know. Why not Kyle? I had to remind them that your friends were acting like you had the plague.

"What if it's all just an act?" Ruby said. "To get you back. Did you ever consider that?"

Even Celia laughed. It's been a year since we broke up—since I told you we had to break up. You were really sorry; of course you were. You didn't mean to hit me. You didn't know why you did it. But I had to do what Ruby said, for a lot of reasons. I hope you understand that now. My dad was a good man, Jack. He was just angry, somewhere very deep. He'd lost faith in himself and he drank to make it all numb, but it didn't go numb, it turned to rage and he hit Ruby too many times.

I've always thought it was funny that Ruby never left him. Not once. It was always Bishop who ran off. You see? He didn't want to hurt Ruby, just like you didn't want to hurt me. And so he kept trying to leave and stay away and it was hard for him. Ruby was a habit he had to keep breaking until it finally took.

That might be why I did what Ruby wanted. I don't think you knew you were hurting me. You couldn't concentrate on it long enough to see that what you did had any real effect on me, beyond the bruises, and they would heal. So I tried to break your habit for you. And the truth of it is, I can say it now, I knew it wouldn't take that first time. I knew. All last year, Jack, I've seen it in your face. We were still together in every way but in acting it out. And I knew one day we'd act it out again and maybe whatever it was in your head driving you mad would be gone when we did. I felt like I wasn't actually breaking up with you at all and so it didn't hurt so much.

I could see Ruby fighting with herself. She was trying to tell me to stay away from you because she thought she knew our future. She thought she'd lived it with Bishop. But she and I both remember the times she admitted she'd have him back. How could she fault me for wanting you?

One time, a few years ago, Ruby and I walked down U.S. 1 to the neighborhood where Bishop lives. We took the main road all the way down past the tracks and then turned on to his street. The sun was burning our faces and all the dirt from the roads and the barren yards was in our throats and I thought even if he saw us, he wouldn't recognize us. Next time, I told Ruby, we should push a shopping cart and act homeless and then for certain he wouldn't know us. She laughed and I laughed and we choked on the dirt and coughed and got within two houses of Bishop's, heard a screened door slam into its jamb, then turned and ran all the way back to U.S. 1.

I know she's been down that way a few times since, without me. I wonder if she makes it there. I wonder if he sees her and they talk. I wonder what else they might do. Some habits are ingrained; they run so deep they're a part of who we are and breaking them is nearly impossible. You might stop picking at that scab for a week, even a year or two, but something eventually comes along and nags at you and before you know it, you're raw again.

And as painful as it is, most of us prefer to bleed.

The next day I brought more food, two more jugs of water, and Ron's sleeping bag and tarp. He wasn't too happy about it. If you ever remember it all, try not to be too hard on Ron. When you think about it, he was always left out. You and Kyle and Putty did everything together. Ron saw you as just another one of them—harsh, cruel, drunk. Criminal, in a way. And you didn't mind it, being a part of that. So don't blame Ron so much if he didn't like you. I guess you wouldn't, seeing as you didn't like him so much either. I know you think there was something going on with us, but there wasn't.

When I came up to the tracks, you looked worn, drawn out, like you were dissolving real slow. You scratched at the black beard invading you neck like you had fleas. But once you ate and drank some more you came alive again. You wanted me to tell you more about Jack. That's how you said it—like you weren't him, even though you knew you must be. It was too much for you right then, to let it be you. I said maybe it would be better if you didn't remember everything, and I wasn't sure I could come up with just good things. There must have been good things.

I told you that for me, the years were tucked into one of those frames with thirteen spots, one for each school picture. You can see your kid grow from kindergarten to twelfth grade all at once. And when I think on our lives,

34

that's how it looks. Maybe that's why I can't think of good things. I've stuck all of it into school years and they're each overshadowed by something really bad.

And maybe it wasn't good that I told you. I mean, I didn't know at the time. I didn't understand what it was you were trying to forget. If I'd known, I'd have let you stay that way—empty. But at the time, I thought it would help. I thought if I could tell it just so, you'd know what you'd done and be sorry about it and you'd be different once you got your head back on the right way. I thought you'd be a new Jack and we'd be safe from the past. But I'm learning that there is no real safety for any of us.

"I'll tell you," I said. "But it's my way I'm telling—the way I remember it."

And you said that was okay, so that day I told you about Sunny and the first thing you did.

6.

The first time I saw Tucker Reed, I didn't know who he was. You'd been gone five days by then, disappeared north into the scrub, and we were all stunned. I told everybody I was afraid you weren't coming back but they said you'd have to, sooner or later. Ron drove me up to the police station to answer questions. I told them about the keys; I'm not sure if they believed me about the vomit, and I'm not sure what it all means—what part you played in it. I'm having trouble deciding how to feel and I'm sorry about that, Jack. You should know everyone at the trailer park is still with you, even me. Some of us are just confused and scared, that's all, and I hope you don't hate us for it.

As we left the station, going through the main lobby, I saw this blond guy sitting on a bench against the wall, watching us. He had an anguish about him—his whole body. He seemed to be asking us questions, just not out loud, and I was helpless.

I told Ron, "Everybody's looking at us, like we have the answers."

He put his arm around my shoulder and led me out of the station and down the steps to the parking lot across the street. When I got into Ron's little four-door, I looked up to the station and there he was, the blond guy, looking right at me. I couldn't get him out of my mind after that.

By that time, Ron was all I had left. Everything was ruined. Putty was the worst; I think he felt guilty and it would take some time before he realized he really had nothing to do with it—your part of it, anyway. Kyle spent all of his time working and I only saw him once in a while coming or going. And Mary just stayed away. I needed them all—needed us to be together like when we were kids. I needed them to miss you with me, to worry about you with me. But they disappeared like you did. We aren't us anymore.

But what was there to do, anyway? The police prowled everywhere. What would be the point of going out to the lake or the tracks, or even the field behind the plaza? We'd be followed. By cops or reporters. A little bomb had been dropped into the half-dozen and our friendship was over, just like that.

Celia said the others were scared of being caught up in it somehow—I mean, after what Putty told them about me and what you'd done. Nobody wanted to be blamed for something. And she looked at me different after that. I think she did blame them—all of them, even Ron. But Ron was willing to accept it. So he stayed longer—came around almost every day.

When we got back from the police station, Ron and I sat at the picnic tables by the pool with Mr. Haverty, and Old Man Pinkerton, Loretta Swanson, and everyone else who dared to come out.

"We need the police," Pat Dunn said. "The reporters shouldn't be allowed to come on this property."

"If you'd stop talking to them," Celia said. "Maybe they'd stop coming over."

"What was I supposed to do? They stick the microphone in your face and ask questions."

"Keep the gates rolled closed," Mr. Haverty said. His voice was hollow and scratched, like he'd been screaming for days, and his eyes sunk deeper into his skull. "Put up a sign. Tell 'em we ain't got nothing to say about it."

Mrs. Swanson agreed and went off to get some of the bigger boys to help.

"Doc will complain," Celia said. "He'll have to stop and open the gate and close it behind him. He won't like it."

Ron gave me a worried look. They all sat staring at the table in front of them. Nobody laughed, or winked, or nudged anybody else. Nobody had a beer or a cigarette. Jack, it was as if you'd gone and left them with a nightmare they couldn't shake.

I told them about the blond guy I saw at the police station. I don't know why I did it, but they didn't like it.

"He was pale, the way you get when you've been sick for a while," I said. "His eyes were rimmed red, like he just got finished bawling. You notice that kind of thing when it's somebody our age. Little kid, no big deal, they cry all the time." I kept going, not really talking so much as thinking out loud about it. "And I knew somehow he'd been crying about the junkyard. He wanted me to go to him and tell him something. Tell him he was wrong. But I don't know anything. None of us do."

Ruby had shown up by then and she stood there shaking her head at me. "You think we need that right now?"

"It's bound to happen more and more," Pat Dunn said. "They arrested that one man who wouldn't stand back. I wouldn't be surprised none to find him coming over here when he gets out of jail, asking us questions."

"They got no place else to look," Mr. Haverty said.

"Well, they can find someplace else," Ruby said. "This ain't our fault. We didn't do anything wrong."

She sat down with us and we all went back to staring at the table. We heard Kyle's squeaky bicycle wheel, we heard the bike land up against the trailer, and then the door slammed. One of the little ones jumped into the pool and nobody looked up to see who it was. Loretta was yelling at somebody over at the side gate.

Mr. Haverty said. "Sure we did."

7.

We had to get the bus to kindergarten and I was scared and you and Putty teased me. Back then, Putty was Harry and Ron was Ronny and I was Maggie. We walked a short way along U.S. 1 and the cars rushed past and I started crying. I kept looking back at Ruby standing at River Front Drive watching us and Putty started making baby noises and Mary laughed and you shoved me a little. But it's okay.

Mary, Kyle, and Ron weren't in our class, so Putty was the only one who saw what happened. We talked about it once, I can't remember why, when we were in high school. Mary started it and you didn't say anything. But Putty said it never happened, said she was lying and when she said I'd told her all about it, he said I was lying, too. She said the mark is still there but he didn't believe her.

"Go on and look at it," she said.

But he wouldn't do it. Do you remember that day? Mary was so angry at us, because neither of us, you nor I, would say anything. We just sat there and acted like Putty was telling the truth. I never asked him about it but now I wonder if he somehow didn't see it, after all, even though in my memory he was right there watching it. And then I thought, maybe he forgot, but how could he? I wondered then if he'd somehow convinced himself it never happened because it was better that it hadn't. I thought that was a wonderful thing to be able to do. But I think it was really all about you. You didn't remember it, so Putty wouldn't, either. He did it for you.

Do you know Putty loved you? I get that he wasn't there when you went crazy; he stayed away. But if you don't ever remember everything, you should know he loved you. He had a brother who went away when he was little. He was sixteen, I think, and went to live with his real dad, and Putty was heartbroken. Leastwise, that's what Celia always said. He latched on to you that first day at the bus stop and from then on he didn't want to be anywhere you weren't. If you ask me, Putty had decided that you were everything he wanted to be. So when you did something bad, he learned to make it not so bad, somehow. Or he just let it out of his head like you did.

We'd been in school for months by then; it was after Christmas break. Mrs. Lancaster was one of those wiry, gray teachers who really did have her glasses attached to a fake pearl chain around her neck. Mary and the others got that other teacher; she was soft and round and gave out hugs all the time and she smiled a lot. Mrs. Lancaster didn't. She kept a cup full of pencils on her desk, very sharp. We were using our own by that time, but you used those fat pencils Celia got for you. She said you didn't have the motor skills necessary to use a regular pencil. Remember Putty teased you when she said it? He made motor boat sounds and you hit him.

I saw you with one of Mrs. Lancaster's pencils that morning when we all filed into the classroom, noisy and chaotic. Mrs. Lancaster stood over the sinks at the back and didn't see it when you stabbed Sunny in the arm. She gasped and tears welled up in her eyes and when the class started and Mrs. Lancaster saw her face, she asked her what was wrong, but Sunny just shook her head.

I saw it, but like a dream, fuzzy and unreal. I thought, why would you do that? It made no sense at the time. Sunny didn't say anything to make you do it; she didn't do anything. And I decided you did it because you liked her. When you threw rocks at me that day in front of Ron's trailer, Ruby said that's what little boys do when they like a girl. They might hit her, tease her, throw things at her. When I was five or six that made some kind of weird sense. And when Bishop was home and he punched Ruby and she hit her head on the on the wall when she fell back, I thought he doesn't just like her, he loves her.

I know it's creepy to say this, but the truth of it is I was glad you stabbed Sunny. I was glad you liked her. There were some other emotions mixed up inside me, but that's the one I remember feeling the most–happy.

Mrs. Lancaster glared at everyone–that always made her look like a rat but that time we didn't laugh–and asked what happened. But nobody said anything. She sent Sunny off to the clinic because she was bleeding and everybody, even the principal, talked to her and asked her who did it but she wouldn't say.

That was the first of it–the first thing you did to Sunny. You'd found that one person you could take it all out on and you knew she would let you. And not one of us–Putty, Kyle, Mary, Ron, or me–tried to stop you. We didn't talk about it, we never told. I think it was just part of the pact. By the time we were five, we acted as an organism–like the ants building up mounds of sand crystals in the empty lot behind the plaza. If one did something, we all did it. And if one got into trouble, we all did. So we all shared in it–your rage and your violence. And we all felt the guilt you felt. When you apologized, and put your hand on Sunny's arm that day, we all apologized...for letting it happen. And Sunny told her parents she ran into the pencil; it was nobody's fault.

The next day, after school, I found you sitting against the fence at the junkyard on Beaumont Road, just beyond the open gate. You had your fists at your temples, your shoulders hunched up tight. You relaxed when I sat down beside you and you told me what you'd done.

"I hurt Sunny," you said. As if I hadn't been there, didn't know. You felt the sharp pencil in your hand and something was with you, a thing you couldn't see, that took your hand and shoved it at Sunny's arm. "Don't tell my dad."

"Will he hit you?"

You turned to me, sharp and pulled together. "My dad's good," you said. "Not like yours."

I don't think I knew until then that everybody at Trailer Haven could see into my trailer in the same way I saw into theirs. I saw the parents who smiled all the time and the parents who were drunk. I knew which kids had dinner at the same time every day with their moms and dads and which sat at the picnic tables until long after dark, hungry. But I thought I was invisible to them. Ruby and Bishop couldn't be seen, or heard.

"I won't tell," I said.

You put your hands back to your head and said, "Forget, forget, forget."

I left you there like that; I was scared. And you did forget. Because you forgot, Putty forgot. And soon we all forgot.

8.

When I told you that story, you nodded a little bit, like you had to digest it. And I asked you if you still wanted me to tell you about Jack and did you still think I should write it all down and you said yes.

"It's someone else," you said.

"It is, in a way." I said. "You're not like Jack at all."

You said maybe you weren't Jack, maybe I was mistaken. But how was that possible? And you said people have twins, what do they call them? Doppelgangers? Is that what you said? And I said if that was it, where was Jack? Jack rode the bike into the lake and the boys took Jack back to his trailer. Where was he?

And you shrugged. I could tell you knew somehow that you were Bobby Jack Beaumont and I can understand how, if you're a little crazy, it would torment you a bit, trying to find yourself inside your own head and coming up empty.

Now I know why you stabbed Sunny. I've been thinking about it a lot since you left—about all the things you did that I told you about while you were here. I wonder about what other awful things happened to you that triggered them. You should come home and tell me.

I told you then that you needed more food than what I could bring you once a day. "You should walk over to the little south plaza," I said. "It's got a Subway and a diner and some restrooms where you could wash up."

You grabbed your backpack and turned it upside down on the dirt and dumped it all out again: the journal, the paper, the earring, all that stuff. And you said, "You think they'll trade a gold earring for a sandwich?"

I got this wave of fear in me, washing over me, like a drug. The way you said it. See, the old Jack would have been mad at me. He'd have made me feel stupid. But you were gentle, teasing. I don't know, maybe that's how teasing is supposed to be with someone you love. So I laughed.

"You have money and a credit card," I told you. "In your wallet."

But you didn't bring your wallet.

"How is it," you said. "I brought all this junk and not a wallet? Or any clothes, or food, or water?"

I looked at the stuff there on the dirt and I had this flash of an idea. I thought, if I were upset, and confused, and had to run away fast, I'd take those things from my room that were important to me. A picture of you, and one of Ruby and Celia and my dad. My diary. My favorite book. And so I thought those things–a half-used matchbook, a watch, the keys–they must mean something.

I told you I'd go and get your wallet and your clothes and anything else you wanted, but you said no. You said I couldn't go back there; it wasn't safe.

"Whatever you did," I said. "You know it'll be okay. It's always okay."

You leaned against the tree and put your fingertips on your forehead and pressed them hard.

And I said, "What did you do, Jack?" I only said it because I knew you didn't know so I wouldn't have to hear the answer.

I took the empty water jug with me through the scrub to refill it at the spigot by the picnic tables, then walked back down Beaumont Road before your dad closed up for the night and let Wilder and Manning escort me to the office through the rows of junk cars and stacks of tires and wild bundles of wire that could be labeled and special lighted in an art museum. Your dad was on the front porch of the little tin roofed building, waiting for me, wearing pale denim overalls and a white t-shirt inside out. He came down the steps and hugged me, tighter than usual and I thought maybe he'd been drinking, but he didn't smell like it. Digger Beaumont was always a hugger and we joked about it sometimes. But I don't know, once you grow up, it's not as nice. Celia would tell me I was being cruel; he's an old man—he's had his share of troubles. And it's not like he was a stranger.

He said I could go on over to the trailer and get whatever you needed, said I should try to get you back home. "It's not just that I need the help." I thought maybe he wanted to say he missed you, that he was lonely there by himself, maybe that ever since your mom took off it's just been the two of you and he didn't want to let go of that. But he didn't finish his sentence, so I don't know what he was going to say.

I was in your room digging through the piles of trash and clothes, gathering stuff up when I realized he was standing in the doorway watching me. I gasped and told him he scared me and he didn't say anything, just looked at me in this weird way. I think he wanted me to warn you–tell you to come back or he was going to have to go out looking for you; but he didn't say it. He was scared, I could see it in his face. Real scared.

He held out his hand and said, "Give this to him, will you?"

Dangling off a chain, the gold heart pendant whipped about as he motioned for me to take it from him. I knew it was the same one and I was surprised to see it. I didn't take it at first. I looked up at your dad and tried to smile. He didn't know I'd seen it before. On my way out of the junkyard, I walked fast, my heart racing. I had to get away–you were right; there was something there and your dad was afraid of it, too. And by the time I got back to my trailer, I realized I'd been asking myself over and over in my head. "What have you done, Jack? What have you done?"

I wondered if it had anything to do with the shooting. But that was so long ago; we all thought that was over, taken care of. One minute I was hoping that was what it was–something simple and familiar–and the next I was worried it was something worse.

When I stood under the scrubby oak out by the tracks the next morning and gave you the heart, you rubbed your thumb over it and your hands shook. I waited for you to recognize it and say so. I got a little dizzy from wanting it and fearing it at the same time. But you
50

couldn't remember; there would have been some sign of it. I shifted outside myself somehow, watching somebody who wasn't you, holding something I knew was yours. Tiny rivulets of sweat trickled in ragged paths down the side of your face. Your black hair was shiny wet. Dark stubble shaded the lower half of your face and your neck and your dusty clothes were splotched with dark spots of sweat. You were foreign somehow, and I was trying to mold you into a version of Jack and I had the sudden urge to run, but I didn't.

"Is it your mom's?" I said.

I thought you didn't hear me because you didn't answer. You pulled open your backpack and dropped it in and sat still for a bit, staring out at the tracks. Then you grabbed the backpack and tossed it away, like it was trash. You have to know now, if you can remember, how that confused me.

I didn't tell you about your dad–that he had the eyes of a trapped feral cat, and he wanted you to come home. There wasn't anything I could do, anyway. I couldn't drag you. At some point, I figured, this would all come out and we'd figure out how to deal with it and get back to normal. I wanted to try to tell you that Celia and Mr. Haverty had everything taken care of; they would always be there for you if you were in some real bad trouble. But I didn't think I could just come out and say it and have you believe it, what with your not remembering who they were or what all you'd done before.

"First grade," you said, after you'd eaten half your sandwich.

9.

In first grade, the other kids found out we were poor and lived in the trailer park. You wonder how they figure these things out. In kindergarten we were all friends, except for that little kid who kept dunking his head in the toilet–nobody wanted to be his friend. But we all laughed together and listened to the stories Mrs. Lancaster read, and played together and fought over the swings, but still held hands and sang on the way back to the classroom. Kindergarten is kinder, isn't it? We were all too young to realize we weren't supposed to be friends with just anybody.

Suddenly, we were poor. Our clothes weren't as nice or as clean, nor were our faces. We didn't notice. And anyway, we were outdoor kids. Why huddle cooped up inside cramped trailers when we had a pool and an entire park to explore, and the lot across River Front Drive behind the little plaza, where we played ball or just ran around chasing one another? Those other kids looked like they sat still a lot. Our teacher didn't help any. I don't remember her name. She'd tell Ron, in front of the whole class, to ask his mother to darn the knees in his pants before he wore them again. And when this other girl,

Karen, I think, sitting next to me wanted to use my hairbrush, the teacher caught her and practically shouted that she might get lice. And Putty had to sit out recess because she said he didn't have the right kind of shoes. He told her his mom was waiting for a check and until then all he had were flip flops. And when we'd all stay there with him at the picnic table where he had to sit, she'd yell at us and try to make us play. We'd run off and pretend only to trickle back to the table.

The point is, Sunny was unhappy about the whole thing and about a month in, she showed up at the bus stop wearing a lacy, pale pink dress and these dainty little strappy shoes. Her hair was pulled back in a pink head band with sparkles all over it. You laughed at her and called her Pinky and took her headband and threw it in the ditch.

"Who do you think you are?" Putty said.

And Mary said, "You think you're so much better than us."

You pushed her and she landed in the dirt and went to school with a gray smudge on the back edge of her dress. Most of the dirt was on her underwear. When she cried on the bus, you called her a baby and told her she deserved it for wearing a stupid dress to school.

The other kids weren't much better and by the end of the day, she got off the bus last and tried to stay out of your way. But you weren't finished with her. It was almost as if you were the one who'd spent the whole day being picked on and you had to do something to make it stop so you tackled her and pulled her down into the ditch and, well...

54

I watched this tv movie once about a bully girl who killed her best friend and the thing that struck me was how she got the other girls to help her. They all got on her and held her down in this river until she drowned. I don't know how people do that—how they go from friends to murderers so fast and so easy.

I'm not saying you were trying to murder Sunny. But when you pushed her into the ditch and held her there, face down in the muck, and Putty and Kyle, and even Mary laughed and started chanting "Push her, push her," it made me think we were all no better than the other kids at school. And I never forgot that. I'm not the only one who figured it out, because everybody, except Mary, went through the rest of elementary school without ever trying to fit in again.

Anyway, we all walked Sunny to the pool at Trailer Haven and stood her under the little shower nobody ever uses for what it's for—does anybody even know what it's for? And she told her mom she fell into the pool trying to get a beach ball out of it. Anything Sunny brought to school that you didn't like, ended up tossed into the ditch that year.

And I found you the day after, sitting in the field behind the plaza, your knees up, with your fists at your head and you told me the story of what you did to Sunny and how you felt this thing pulling you into the ditch on top of her and this thing made you heavy. You were supposed to hold her down until she stopped twitching and then it would go away.

"I think it was inside of me," you said.

"You should tell your dad."

"I love my dad."

And then you forgot again.

10.

I understand now, after hearing what Putty had to say, why you stabbed Sunny the year before, but I don't understand why you tried to drown her in the ditch. I don't want to spend too much time imagining what might have led you to it.

The year we were six, my father left again.

My sisters are Lilly and Rose and they're a lot older than me. When I was born, Lilly was fifteen and Rose was thirteen. That shows you how long Bishop and Ruby were together. Celia says the day they met she knew they'd never get over each other. Ruby says it was Bishop's first day at school, in the eighth grade, when they became inseparable. Well, that's not the right word, really. Ruby says she never looked at another man again, not since that day he walked into home room and sat next to her. But Bishop was never quite as committed to the whole thing. Ruby was pregnant with Lilly the next year and dropped out of school. The first thing Bishop Hanson did, she tells me, when he found out he would be a father, was hit her in the face and strangle her until she passed out; then he broke up with her and started dating some other girl. Nearly tore her apart, she says. But it wouldn't be the last time.

When she was pregnant with Rose two years later, he dropped out too and they got married and went to live with his mom just down south. Bishop was a mechanic, when he was working, and Celia had already bought the laundromat so Ruby worked there and left my sisters with my Grandma Hanson. And soon enough, Ruby and Bishop had a little house all their own up against the railroad tracks.

The fifteen years between Lilly and me being born were not good. Celia got this word once, from the dictionary, or heard it on the television or something. Tumultuous. She kept saying it over and over again like she liked it and it was a good word. She said that's what those years were, said my parents fought a lot and it got to the point where Ruby stopped trying, because it never turned out her way, but with bruises instead. Ruby doesn't tell it exactly like that.

Celia bought the trailer here in River Front Trailer Haven when Ruby was pregnant with me and when Bishop hit her this one time, in the stomach, that was it. She was done, she said. She was going to leave him and move in with Celia. But she never did. I still remember sitting at the little table in our tiny kitchen last year after you hit me and I was still crying and holding a piece of meat to my face and Celia and Ruby smoked cigarettes and we all drank beer—me too, even though that was what started the fight that got me hit—and they were both trying to make me understand why I had to leave you.

Ruby was telling me how much she loved Bishop, how she knew he was the man for her, if she could have exorcised that demon in him, figured out where he got it from and expelled it, everything would have been perfect.

"But I should have known," she said. "You can't get rid of other people's demons; only your own. And maybe my demon was Bishop, just like yours is Jack."

But I wasn't hearing it the way she was telling it. She'd been with Bishop since she was fourteen years old, forty years. And at the first test of him, he beat her up and ran off with another girl, but she still thought he was the right one. I was sitting there thinking she should stop talking, because she wasn't telling me to stay away from you. She was telling me to keep going, keep going, because if I could just figure out what it was that was making you hurt me, everything would be wonderful.

When I got to the bait shop for work that day, after I told you about the first grade, Ruby came down from the laundromat and stood at the counter picking up sinkers and floaters out of the little singles baskets and weighing them in her hand. She didn't look at me and I leaned over on the counter and asked what was wrong. But I knew.

"I heard you been out there to the tracks again is all," she said.

I thought for a bit, not sure what to say. If she could have seen you, I think she'd have felt better about the whole thing.

"He's not the same," I told her. "He's not Jack at all. He's calm and thoughtful. He's scared, too. I can see it."

She raised her eyebrows and smirked.

"What?"

"He can be scared, sleeping out in the scrub by the tracks. Meanwhile his dad is worrying his self into a heart attack. The whole lot of us is worried. I don't see why he can't get his self together at home."

"He'll come home," I told her. "Just give him some time. I been telling him about himself. Telling him stories about when he was little."

Here she looked at me. "Stories," she said.

I nodded. She shook her head and left. I don't know where I got the idea, but it seemed to me she only partly wanted me to leave you alone. But she went after it again that night after work, at the trailer. Celia was there and we sat in the living room eating dinner—we had spaghetti and sauce in those deep ceramic bowls you like, holding them up to our chins and twirling with our forks and trying to keep the sauce from putting more stains on the couch.

And Ruby just up and said, "What happens when he remembers everything and goes back to being Jack?"

And I said, "I don't think it'll be that way."

"Why wouldn't it?"

"It's like you said with Daddy—how it was a demon what got him. And if you could get rid of it, everything would be okay."

"What does that have to do with anything?"

"I'm just saying, I think Jack's getting rid of it now, whatever demon it is that's got him."

Celia was giving Ruby the eye, mentally telling her to say something else and finally, Ruby said, "You know it don't work that way. You don't want to make my mistake, honey. You don't want to waste your life on it."

I snorted, a laugh but not exactly, and said, "Like you aren't still walking down south to see Daddy."

Ruby went all red and looked at me like I'd betrayed

her and Celia acted like she didn't know what had been going on.

"How do you expect Maggie to be strong if you ain't gonna be?" Celia said.

"Maybe I don't expect her to be. Maybe I expect her to be just like me." You could hear this sinking sort of sadness in her voice. It wasn't anything new, trust me. I'm willing to bet that hollow cooing, like the mourning dove, settled into her regular speech sometime after Bishop hit her the first time.

Then the two of them argued about it and I was let alone. It served Celia right, you know. Since the first day you came into the trailer park, she fought for you. Yes, she criticized, she questioned, she suggested discipline, and once even considered calling social services, so Ruby says. But she never did, because the truth of it is she was your champion. And it wasn't right of her to expect Ruby to tell me to end it with you, to stop loving you, or thinking about you, or wanting to be with you, when she spent all her time telling everybody you'd turn out fine with enough love and support.

But Celia knows what she's talking about. You're going to be just fine. If you'd come back to us.

11.

The next morning, I was over at the spigot by the pool filling up water jugs to take them out to you when I saw Mary drive by on her way to her mom's trailer, so I walked down to see the baby. She was loaded up with a diaper bag and a portable play yard and a bag of rattles and soft, bright fabric shapes, and still balancing Romy on her hip.

"Let me," I said, taking the bouncy little thing all done up in pink.

Mary smiled at me and told me I should come on in. I felt awkward and dirty following her. Even as she struggled with all the baby stuff, her body floated and her hair swung soft off her head. She wore a tight skirt and high heeled sandals and pale brown lipstick. It wasn't so much that she didn't belong there with me, in the trailer park, as it was that she knew it.

Her trailer is still the same and walking in and smelling the lemon cleanser took me back to the days we'd all go over when she was sick and sit on the floor of her room telling her it wasn't any fun at the pool anyway and she wasn't missing anything. We'd always leave soon after and agreed her trailer was too clean. There was never any leftover pizza in the refrigerator and macaroni and cheese on the stove, like at Kyle's trailer. There weren't cats everywhere like at Ron's. And no stacks of magazines and crossword puzzle books and wires from the television and game systems like at Putty's. My trailer was plain messy and we liked that because we knew we didn't have to wipe our feet or be careful touching anything.

Mary set up the little play yard and I put Romy in it and we sat on the couch. I perched on the edge, with my knees together, because that's what Mary did. Her mom was in the bedroom, getting dressed. I didn't know Mary got a job and her mom was going to start watching Romy three days a week. I let her tell me all about it. And she said she'd decided to go into nursing.

"When did you decide that?" I asked her.

"A few days ago."

We didn't say anything for a while and it was easy because of Romy. We could have sat there on her mom's couch for hours not saying anything to each other because Romy would smile or laugh or shake her rattles. It reminded me of you wanting to be distracted and I thought maybe you just needed something to look at that would make you forget anything bad. A lure of a sort, like Romy.

"How is he?" She asked me.

"Confused."

"I heard. Still, it was nice to see you all, even if the day ended badly."

I couldn't help chuckling. So many of our days ended that way. But we kept doing them over and over again.

"What do you think happened? What made him mad?"

I shook my head. "She looks like you," I said of Romy.

Mary got up and pulled an old photo album from a shelf under the end table. She opened it and showed me pictures of her when she was a baby and as she grew up. There was the trailer park twenty-five years ago—twenty, fifteen, and ten years ago. We watched Ruby and Celia, the Stahls, Mr. Pinkerton, and Pat Dunn—all of them—growing plumper and grayer, and weary.

"I need to have a photo album," she said. "Eric is saving up for a real nice camera and a photo printer and we're going to have real pictures. Like the ones Doc Fred used to let me print at his place, remember?"

"There's Jack," I said.

We were all there. In the pool, eating ice cream, dressed up for Halloween. Mary and I sat very still and looked at our own faces looking back at us. Our younger eyes weren't innocent, like you'd expect. Instead they stared at the camera, almost begging, even over smiles and silly poses, worry shaded them, and I wondered what we were trying to say to the future—what were you trying to say, Jack?

"It's funny," I said. "I don't remember your mom taking all these."

She rolled her eyes and closed the book. "I do. It was embarrassing."

Mrs. Stahl came out from the bedroom and squealed at Romy, picked her up twirled her around.

"Don't make her spit up, Ma."

"Magnolia," she said. She pulled me into a half hug and Romy got a fistful of my hair.

"You should stay and help. We can take her to the pool."

"No pool," Mary said. "You promised."

Mrs. Stahl winked at me. "I did."

Mary held the door open and I went out ahead of her thinking she'd grown up and I hadn't. I wondered if I should have pulled away sooner, like she had—started early on. Maybe I'll never grow up if I stay at Trailer Haven with you. Ron and Putty have their own work and moved away years ago. Even if Kyle still lives here, he has a job that takes him away. And Mary left last year. You and me, Jack. We're stuck here—you at the junkyard and me at the trailer park—and now I don't know if you'll ever come back and if you don't, it'll just be me here alone.

Out front, at her car, Mary turned to me and asked about you again. Is he violent? He's not hitting you, is he? What do you mean he's staying out there? It rains practically every day. And finally, she sighed and said, "You're still crazy about him, aren't you?"

"In a way."

"In a way? What's that mean?"

I shrugged. "When you've loved somebody your whole life, you can't just stop. It's changed, though. Different."

"You'd go off with him this very minute if he asked you. Don't lie. You're always lying."

"I am not."

"To yourself you are," she said. "About Jack."

I wanted to argue, to defend you, but Mary and I had

already said all the things we could say last year. She thought if a person said a thing enough times the other person would change, but it doesn't work that way. I wonder how long it will take her to figure that out.

"Are you happy?" I said. "With Romy and Eric, I mean?"

She nodded, but she didn't smile big like I thought she would.

"What is it? What's wrong?"

"It's nothing, really." She ran her fingers over her right ear, pushing her long sandy brown hair behind it and smiled at me—it was a teary sort of smile, the kind you don't usually see on Mary. "It's just that. Oh, God, I'm going to get all profound like Ron does."

"Well, I don't mind. What is it?"

She leaned back on her car and crossed her arms against her stomach. "Sometimes I feel like I've been chasing life for so long, you know? And every time I think I've caught it, and I can relax and be happy, I find I'm running again. And honestly, Mags, I'm not sure anymore if I'm chasing something or running away."

I wanted to say there's plenty to run away from, but I didn't. I said, "Maybe that's all life is."

"Oh, my God," she said. "What did Ron do to us? We're talking like philosophers."

I didn't see what Ron had to do with it, really, and why it ought to be a silly thing to wonder what life was about. But when she changed the subject real quick, I realized maybe it is, to some people. Maybe that's why Ron never fit in. Nobody wanted to figure life out, because maybe that was impossible and people don't like impossible things.

"Do you ever wish you hadn't done it?" She said.

I know what I wanted to say to that, and it wasn't profound at all, but I couldn't say it. Instead, I told her what Ron told me, and what he's told me a dozen times. "You can't ever regret doing what's right."

"Did you ever tell Ruby or Celia?"

I shook my head. "You didn't tell anybody, did you?"

"No, never."

"I appreciate that."

"It's not my story to tell. You don't have to stay here, you know," she said. "You don't have to work the bait shop."

"What's wrong with the bait shop?"

"I'm just saying." Her voice was tight with frustration. "If you're hanging around for him. Don't. He's not worth it."

"It's Jack. How can you say that?"

"He's nuts," she said. "He's insane. Like his mother. You know that. We all know it."

"That can be fixed."

"At what cost?"

I didn't know what that meant. "He loves me; I'm sure of it."

"Come on, Maggie. He told you he loved you once in, what? Third grade?"

"It was more than once, and he doesn't have to say it at all."

She put her hands on the sides of her face, like she was trying to talk to a stupid person and said, "Oh, my God, you really have issues. What he's done to you isn't

68

love. It doesn't come close. It looks more like hate, if you ask me."

"Well, hate isn't the opposite of love," I said.

"Ron again."

"Don't blame Ron. He doesn't think Jack loves me either."

What you should remember about Mary is that she was always better than the rest of us. We used to joke about her normal life and her normal parents and how awful it must be to grow up like that. We'd laugh, but it was sad, you know? I mean, sad for her. Because she was part of us, but never *really* part of us.

But now that I'm looking back on it all, I realize each of us had one thing that kept us outside the whole, didn't we? We were a body, connected, and yet still separate. I know now that you can be a part of people's lives without loving them, or even liking them much.

I grabbed her and hugged her tight and almost cried and I think she did too. I was still sure that we would, all of us, stay friends forever. And even if that isn't exactly how it's turning out, when you get home, we'll all be here. You'll see.

"Don't worry about me," I told her. "I'm going to be fine. Jack too. It'll be okay."

I watched her car make its way out of the park and then turned to see her mother standing at the door holding Romy. She smiled at me like she always did and I could see the pity.

12.

When I went back out to the tracks later that morning, you were sitting there under the spindly little oak with all that stuff from your backpack in separate groups on the dirt. I touched my chest when I saw the keys, making sure the rope was hidden under my shirt. A hot wind picked up and the deep blue southwestern sky promised to cool the scrub for an hour or two. I looked down at you—your hair was shiny black, especially around the edges, wet with sweat. And you looked up at me and smiled. I'm pretty sure that was the first time, since you nearly drowned.

"What is it?" I asked you when I sat down under the tree.

"They're different." You pointed at the first group— the watch and the matchbook and the keys. "I keep seeing these in my mind in the same place."

"Where?"

You shook your head. "I'm not sure. A dresser I think. It's messy and there's a lot of stuff, but I just get this flash, this instant sort of recognition and then it's gone."

"You mean, that's where they were when you put

them in the backpack to leave?"

"No. I got it all out of the room I was in. Different places. The keys were in the top drawer of the dresser, under a pair of shorts. And the watch was in the corner, on the floor, underneath a bag of weed."

"You didn't bring the weed?"

I laughed a little and you said, "I didn't even recognize it at the time. Anyway, when I think about them, or...when they come to me, in my head, when I'm not thinking anything, I don't see them where I found them that day; I see them other places. Places where they belonged when I took them the first time."

"And those?" The earring and the sunglasses were on top of the leather journal with the locked clasp.

"Those are harder," you said. "I'm pretty sure I stole them."

"You didn't steal all of it?" I was confused and I think you were too.

"No, not really. These," you pointed to the first set with the watch and keys, "were in the trailer before. That's right. They were there where I was, someplace close. But not in the room where I put them in the backpack. And I didn't steal them. It's like...they're mine, somehow. But not."

"So, you took them from one place in the trailer and brought them to your room–Jack's room. And on the day you forgot, you gathered them up and brought them with you."

"Yes." You seemed to breathe a little easier then, like things were starting to make sense. But they really weren't, were they?

72

"And these things," I said, pointing to the journal with the sunglasses and earring on it. "You stole from somewhere else, not in the trailer."

"Yes," you said.

"Maybe from the trailer park...where I live."

You weren't above stealing, if you recall, which maybe you don't. When we were little, you'd steal candy from the Pebble Sands Convenience Store and Hair Salon. You got caught a few times before Mr. Peterson banned you from the store. Celia talked to him and he let you come back in, but he'd follow you around staring at you; you didn't care. You'd ask him about his wife and his kids and his dog, and he'd start telling you stories, all while you kept pocketing candy bars. It's a wonder he ever caught you at all.

When you got a little older, you started stealing money. One time up north you bumped some guy who'd just left the teller machine and helped him pick up his twenties. You were gone before he could count them. You took Putty and Kyle down south where you broke into this old man's house–Kyle's uncle, I think it was–and took the five thousand dollars he had under his mattress. Kyle and Putty had their shares spent within a week or so, but we never knew what you did with yours. You must have stolen money out of every trailer on the lot except mine and I'm not even sure about that.

"Why would you steal one earring?" I asked you.

You shook your head. Then you picked up the journal and said, "I should break this open and read it."

We both sat there for a bit while you looked at it and I tingled with guilt, wondering if one of the keys dangling between my breasts would fit the lock. For a brief second, when I saw your face, I thought you knew I had the keys and you were waiting for me to admit it. But I couldn't do it. I never thought of you as the type of person to write in a journal until I saw you there by the tracks looking empty and confused, so I thought it might be yours and if you read it, everything would come back to you and you'd go home and nothing would change. So I kept quiet.

"What about the paper?"

The scrap piece of paper sat by itself, folded and tucked into the sand just a bit to keep it from blowing away in the breeze. We both knew what it said, the name and address, written in a panic—an urgent message, lost now and waiting.

"That was given to me," you said. "I think."

"You think?"

You shook your head. "I can't see it, exactly, so much as feel it. I feel my hand taking it. It's shaking."

"The note or your hand?"

"My hand. I should remember it, but I can't."

"It'll come back, eventually," I said. "Where's the picture of me?"

"It's in the backpack. I know where I got that."

"You remember?"

"No. But it's obvious."

It wasn't so obvious, really. Mary and I went to the beach with some other kids a few years ago. It'd been a while since she'd been separating herself from us, finding other people to hang out with. She told me she was tired of it all; it was the same thing all the time. Kyle was drunk every weekend and picking a fight with Ron and Ron would leave. Then you'd find something to rage about and you'd push Putty around and Kyle might try to get in the middle and you'd hit him in the stomach and he'd vomit. Putty would call Kyle a drunk and someone would always get left out in the scrub by the lake and have to walk nearly a mile back home. Mary wanted to be around normal people, she said.

When we got home she went right over to Doc Fred's and used his little photo printer so we could pass the pictures around and we sat out by the pool at the trailer park with everybody. You were there and I could tell by the way your jaw was set, hard like you were grinding your teeth, that you didn't like it. There were pictures of the other guys who were at the beach with us and I knew that bothered you. You left and headed back to the junkyard and I followed you. For a while I watched you walking, your hands shoved into your pants pockets and your head down.

I called out to you and you stopped and turned around.

"It's not like that," I told you. "It was just a day at the beach."

You said things. Like, we never go to the beach. The beach is for different kinds of people. I knew what you meant, in a way. We went to your trailer and your dad was at the stove flipping a grilled cheese sandwich on a pan; he was whistling, wearing a bathrobe, open, the ties hanging down on the sides. He had on a pair of dingy white socks. He wasn't wearing anything else and you turned me around and told him to put some clothes on. We heard him leave after we went into the bedroom. He took his grilled cheese sandwich and went outside in just his bathrobe and socks and I remember wondering where he was going, but you were still mad so I forgot about it.

I gave you the picture. I said, "Look at it. Look at the sky and water. And there's a sea gull flying there, behind me."

And you asked me if you could keep it and I said you could and I wrote 'Always, Magnolia' on the back of it. I never saw it again until the day out in the scrub after you lost your mind. I thought you tore it up because it reminded you that you belonged in the junkyard and not on the beach. And I never went to the beach with Mary again. But you should go...when you come home. We should both go. Just the two of us.

"You should tell me some more," you said, out there by the tracks. "Second grade."

"That was the year you first kissed me," I said.

13.

The next time I saw Tucker Reed, you'd been gone for seven days and they were still showing your picture on the television. I'd been having a crazy dream about there being two of you. One had a long black beard and tied up in it were little gold keys. The other you was fifteen. Both of you were dragging me through the scrub to the lake. I woke up every time sweating, wanting to scream that I was sorry, that I wouldn't do it again, if you'd just come home.

Tucker was in the Pebble Sands Convenience Store and Hair Salon. I'd gone in for a candy bar to take to work with me and I stopped and stared at him when I saw him standing there looking at the granola bars. He recognized me, I think. This time he looked better; he even smiled a bit.

"Keep away from those," I said, pointing to that one box that never sells. "They've been here forever."

He picked out a different kind. "Crazy around here, isn't it?"

I nodded.

"I suppose it's tough," he said. "On the locals. I mean, all the attention."

"Yes."

"I'm not a reporter or anything."

"I know." I picked up a chocolate bar and he followed me to the register. I rang the bell and tried not to look at him while we waited for Dougie.

"You get used to the smell, I guess." He said.

"What?"

"The smell."

"Oh. Yeah, I guess. It's the hair salon."

He nodded. I felt stupid. I think his eyes were watering from the chemicals.

"Kills your appetite a little," he said.

"Hey, Maggie." Dougie Peterson came in from the hair salon, his spiked hair tipped in pink. He eyed Tucker warily for only a second and wiped his hands off on his navy blue apron before ringing up my candy. "How're you holding up?"

"I'm fine."

I didn't want to talk about it. Everybody was acting like I'd rubbed arms with the devil and survived and I wanted to scream at them that we all had, hadn't we? Once Dougie gave me my change I left the store in a hurry. I'd almost forgotten about Tucker until I heard the bell over the door in the bait shop and jumped. I jump every time now, since you left; I may never get used to it again.

He apologized for startling me and I said, "It's not you; it's the bell."

He wandered around the shop looking at the tackle and the nets and the souvenirs in the spinner racks.

"You going fishing?" I asked him.

"No. I'm just wasting time. Is that okay?"

I nodded. Sure, if you want to hang out in the bait shop, be my guest. But I kept my eye on him. He said he wasn't a reporter and after seeing him crying in the police station, I took him at his word. But why was he hanging around the plaza? Shouldn't he be down at the end of River Front Drive with the rest of the gawkers? Or up north at the hotel with all the desperate people, waiting, ignoring the police who kept telling them to go home until they knew anything for sure. The news ate it up though; you wouldn't believe it. Kept putting those poor people on television so they could tell their stories and then acting like it had something to do with us when they didn't know any more than we did.

Tucker was over at our freezer case staring down at our ice cream sandwiches. I sat up on the wood stool and opened Jericho's book and tried to read it, doing my best to make him think I wasn't paying him any mind. But then he came over and stood at the counter and I could feel myself blushing as I smiled. He sighed a bit, like we'd known each other for years and we were about to get back to the conversation we didn't finish the last time we met. I remember thinking it ought to be creepy; I ought to make him leave. But it wasn't, somehow. I just knew, that's all. I knew why he was there.

"I'm Tucker Reed," he said.

I didn't even flinch, Jack. I didn't gasp or anything. I smiled. There he was, in the flesh. Tucker Reed from Georgia. I almost said it out loud and I'm glad I didn't. It was then that I realized I knew more than I told the police. I was smiling at him and wondering what I was going to do about it. I knew more than I wanted to and it made me think you were more involved than we all hoped. So far, the police aren't saying much about it—just that you're wanted for questioning in connection with it all. Everybody's divided on whether or not you should come home voluntarily or not. And Celia says those of them who think you shouldn't, must believe you're guilty. But I don't agree. It's like Doc Fred said. The cops can make you guilty even if you're not.

"What are you reading?" He said.

I showed him the book and he raised his eyebrows. "Did you write this?"

"A friend of mine did."

"What is it? Some kind of religion?"

I laughed. "No. At least I don't think so. I hope not."

"Shouldn't you know?"

"Maybe."

He laughed too, then. I gave him the book and he flipped through a few pages and smiled. "The man who is cut the deepest," he read aloud. "Knows the greatest joy." He looked up at me and said, "Do you believe that?"

I started to answer him—started to say yes, but I didn't.

"Does a baby need to cry before it can laugh?" He said.

"I don't think that's what he means."

"So tell me."

"Keep reading," I said.

He read a bit more. "When we know the evil men can do, we realize the value of the good." He looked at me again. "You don't think we can appreciate goodness
80

without evil?"

"Maybe," I told him. "At least, that's what Jericho thinks."

Turning back to the book, he shook his head.

"You don't agree?"

"No," he said. "A child who has known only love is happier than a child who hasn't."

Everything sort of fell, pulled on me like the undertow that drowns kids in the ocean. It started to make all the sense in the world. I'd been trying to find a reason for it—for your life and mine. I thought there was something we could grab on to, to pull ourselves up out of what we'd been pushed into—thought it was as simple as just not remembering it quite true. But maybe I was wrong, maybe there wasn't a light for us to find. Some people might be born to the dark and they just have to live it.

I smiled at him. "I guess."

And he said, "People need answers. They need a reason for sorrow, and pain, and evil."

But there isn't one. Is there?

I could see it on Tucker's face—he thought the same thing. It might sound strange to you that I've come to that conclusion, Jack. I remember the times we'd take your dad's truck out and you'd find someplace dark and quiet to park and we'd drink a whole six-pack of beer from sweaty wet cans before it could get as warm as the night. And I'd try to explain to you about God. God doesn't allow the bad, I'd say. You'd frown and shake your head and get angry.

"He's omnipotent. He can do anything. If he doesn't

stop a rape or a murder, he's allowing it."

"No, no," I'd say. "It's not like that. He's just waiting for us to turn to Him."

But you never understood. You could only think God was as vicious as the people who did awful things. And I don't know, maybe you were right about the omnipotent part. But maybe there are things we just can't know and maybe we'll figure them out in another lifetime, or better, in a heaven, if such a beautiful place like that can exist with people in it.

And I'm not saying that because I've decided there isn't a reason for the horror I've had to digest, that God isn't a part of the world. I'm not saying that at all. I'm just saying, Jack... When you come home we can take Celia's car and you can drive us out somewhere, anywhere you want. We can go to the cemetery and do anything you want there. We can go to the beach in the dark, or over to Orlando to watch the planes take off from the airport. Remember you told me once you wanted to do that? Anything you want. And you can tell me anything you want about God and I'll listen. I'll stop talking at you about it, and only listen.

If you'll just come home.

"Why did you come here?" I asked Tucker. He didn't seem surprised or angry at the question.

"I'm looking for my sister," he said.

14.

The summer before second grade we discovered the tracks. We'd started hiking farther and farther from Trailer Haven. We walked up and down U.S. 1, looking for money—we usually found some—and exploring the neighborhoods north and south of the park. We walked by my dad's house lots of times and I never said anything. One time he was standing out front smoking a cigarette watching us and I waved. Mary giggled; she might have thought he was just some old man I was waving to.

We'd walk all around the edges of the junkyard, teasing the dogs until your dad came out to the fence and shot his gun off. He told us if we didn't stay away from the property, one of these days he'd shoot at us, instead of the sky. But we all knew he was joking, just trying to keep us safe.

One day Mary said she heard a kitten, somewhere behind the fence, near one of the sheds out back. Ron said it must have been a hawk. A red-shouldered hawk, I think.

"They wail like a woman in trouble," he said.

Nobody laughed at him or shoved him. I think we

were all remembering the day out in the scrub when we heard one and he told us about it and he was right. It echoed with suffering and pain and loss—a mother, somewhere far, grieving.

"It was a kitten," Mary said. "Not a hawk."

I didn't want to say anything, but seeing as Ron's trailer was filled with cats, I figured he'd know better than Mary. We all stood quiet and still, trying to hear it but you wouldn't give us any time. You kept saying you didn't have any cats. Anyway, the dogs wouldn't stop barking so we never heard what Mary heard. I don't think you know, but Mary and I used to walk out there by ourselves sometimes hoping to see one. We never did.

Then one day Putty said if you walked west far enough, you'd get to the other ocean so we set out to find it. Once we got to the railroad tracks we stopped, mostly because we liked them. We sat on the rails and the ties and talked about what we'd do if a train came along, who'd be the last one to run.

"We should always come here," you said. "Every day."

You wanted to stay out there, live there. We all thought the junkyard was the best place to live. We wanted to go in and look at all the stuff, climb the mountains of rusted out appliances, walk the rows of weather worn engines, washing machines, and television sets, sneak into the sheds and see what treasures we might find, or sit in the junked cars and pretend we were driving across the country. But you said it was an awful place.

I remember us out by the tracks, at every age. Kyle when he was nine or ten, always sat inside the tracks facing south, his caramel skin glistening with sweat. And even back then he had that tired look, like his eyes never wanted to fully open, as if he was already drunk. I can see him there with a beer, as a teenager, smiling and laughing at something somebody said. And Ron sat cross-legged and hunched all the time, like a toad, looking down at his hands and whatever it was he was twisting around in his fingers–grass or a twisty-tie he'd picked up on the trail. Ron was always thinking, wasn't he?

And Putty wouldn't sit still. At eight, he's running north and south on the track calling on a train. And I see him at nineteen walking along the rail, his arms wide, keeping balance. Sometimes he'd jump up and down where he stood. Up and down, like a spring. He had too much energy and not enough to do with it.

I have to wonder if any of us have really changed.

One weekend after school started we'd all gathered out by the tracks when you suggested we get some rope and tie Sunny down. We'd leave her there, you said. "Come on." You grabbed her, pulling her toward the rails. You didn't have any rope, but she was scared just the same. The others laughed when you pulled her up onto the tracks and tackled her. Straddling her, you told her you'd sit there like that until the train came. "People will think we killed ourselves on purpose." Sunny started crying and it only made you laugh. "Don't you want to die?" You said.

Then Kyle said, "Did you hear that? Was that the train?"

And we all heard it–far in the distance. A rumbling and then a horn. You whooped and said it was time to die. And Sunny started screaming. It echoed all around us after each shriek. It surprised all of us, you most of all. You fell trying to get off her and you and Putty and Kyle started to run but she just lay stuck on the tracks screaming so you had to go back and get her.

"We were just joking," you told her.

And we all agreed we didn't really hear the train. We waited a while, listening, like we did for the kitten that time, making sure no train was coming. But again you couldn't keep quiet, you kept on and on about it. There was no train, it was just a joke. But Mary shoved you and took Sunny off toward home.

That was when you kissed me. We were on the trail and for no reason at all you came up beside me, put your arm around my shoulders and kissed my cheek. Then you ran off laughing. That was the last time I remember you laughing, Jack. I mean in that joyful, easy way. The last time you were fun without there being a sadistic edge to it. That year, the bad part of you took over. As if you'd been fighting it, and it won.

Mr. Haverty said it was because that was the year all the other boys started shooting up and you stayed small. He said the same happened to him when he was a boy; he had to fight harder and yell louder just to be equal. But Mrs. Cleary, lot twelve, said it was just the way you were meant to be.

"Take a look at Digger," she said.

We were at the pool that evening, after you held Sunny down on the tracks, and I was sitting with the adults while they watched you dunking Kyle under water.

"He's a man with a lot on his plate. He can't afford to

be cheerful."

They all waited to see Kyle's face every time you let him break the surface for air and as long as he was smiling, they said nothing.

"You're saying he learned it?" Celia said.

And Mrs. Cleary said you did. From your father and your mother. Your mother, according to the trailer park, was troubled. That was the word they used when the kids were around. And over our heads, they'd roll their eyes and twirl their fingers at their ears. We all knew what they meant. It was no wonder, in the majority opinion, you'd turned out the way you did.

But they didn't see you up close like I did. They saw you screaming, cursing, hitting, stealing. They saw an angry kid who in second grade got angrier. But I saw your eyes and I knew it wasn't anger. I didn't have a word for it then; and it had been there so long by the time you nearly drowned and it disappeared that I'd forgotten it. I know what it was now, Jack. It was fear. Overwhelming, uncontrollable fear.

Suddenly, like a flock of birds that moves together without having to talk, we all darted off to the big field behind the plaza with our squirt guns. We played water wars with the Bahia grass shafts reaching all the way up to our waists and rubbing their black seeds off onto our clothes. Mary screamed when she caught a sticker in her foot because she fell out of her flip flops and Ron led her back to the road and home. You stood, panting and sweaty, in your bathing suit while Putty and Kyle ran far off to the other side of the field, their voices echoing all around us like the hawks.

As the dusk grew into dark, I followed you home and watched you try to beat the memories out of your head. You let me catch up and told me the story.

"I tried to kill Sunny with the train," you said.

The idea just came to you–words in your mind. You'd heard them before and it was that thing. That thing that came around sometimes; it was heavy, you said. It covered you whole, and it scared you at the same time it made you feel safe. You had every detail of the story, every thought, every expression on Sunny's face, the way she tried to pull free, turning this way and that beneath you, all there in your head, clear and crisp. But I knew you'd forget it. We all would.

"I heard what they said back there at the pool. About my dad."

"They didn't mean it."

"My dad didn't teach me to hurt Sunny."

"I know."

"I love my dad," you said.

"I love my dad, too."

"I know," you said.

15.

When I got back to the trailer that morning after telling you about the second grade, the boys were sitting in the worn and fraying lawn chairs around Ruby's gurgling rock fountain. When we were young, and they'd be waiting for me like that, they'd start shouting about something as soon as they saw me. We're going out to the lake, or we're setting up a tent in the scrub, or let's go swimming. But now they were quiet and when I saw them there I stopped and almost turned around to run. Quiet is scary.

They all three looked up at me and I could see more clearly then, how they'd changed–how separate they were from one another. Putty's scarlet head shook back and forth slightly, like he was trying to talk himself out of something. His knees bounced up and down, his feet running in place. I could still see the second grade in his face–round and innocent, now hardened on the edges. Kyle stretched out in his chair straight as a board with his t-shirt pulled up to his chest, his hard middle glistening like he'd put on oil. One foot, crossed over the other, beat out a rhythm while his hands were clasped behind his head. He was smiling, lazy and hot. Ron sat hunched over his knees, scowling.

"Well?" Putty said. He got up and gave me his chair and pulled the old cooler from next to the front steps and sat on it.

"He's out by the tracks," I told them. "I been taking him food and he goes down the way to the diner at night."

"We heard," Kyle said.

"He's sleeping out there?" Putty said. "It's not right."

"I can't *make* him leave."

"He can't sit out there forever."

"Well, what do you want to do then?"

"I don't know. Something." Putty pulled his hands through his hair, leaving spikes jutting out toward the back of his head. He'd let it grow another half inch and then I'd see him nearly bald, getting out of his truck over at his parents' trailer, a cigarette hanging out of his mouth. He'd smile and rub his stubbly head with his hands. Happened so regular I could count the months by it.

Kyle let his elbows drop to the arms of the chair, closed his eyes, let his head fall back. "He'll come out of it soon enough."

"Ron gave up his sleeping bag and tarp for him," I said and they both turned to look at Ron because they were surprised he'd do it.

"He still crying?" Kyle said.

"He was just shocked that first day, didn't understand what was going on."

"And he does now?"

I didn't answer that so they knew you were still confused.

"Should we go out there?" Putty said. He stood up and started walking around our circle of chairs. "We could set up one of the tents."

"He can't set up a tent by the tracks," Ron said. "He's trespassing as it is."

"You don't know where the line is," Putty said.

"Can we not have an argument?" I said. "Not now."

"So, should we go out there?"

"Not yet," I said. "Give him some time."

We sat quiet for a long while with Kyle drinking up the morning sun and Ron pouting and Putty walking in a circle and stopping and walking back the other way around and around.

"Well, something happened," Kyle said. "Something upset him or he wouldn't have taken Ron's bike off the pier."

They looked at me, like I had the answer to that. We'd made a game of it in the last few years. We went over a lot of the stuff you'd done, trying to match it up with a death or a sorrow that happened before it. There must be a pattern, a code we could break and use to fix you. But there were a few times when we had nothing, couldn't find any reason for what you did. Maybe we were just like Celia and Mr. Haverty, trying to make excuses for you.

"Maybe nothing happened," Ron said. And he almost went further—almost said maybe you were crazy. Maybe there was no reason for your behavior, maybe there never was. It had been said before and none of us liked it.

"Remember the last time we saw her?" Putty said.

I didn't tell you that part of the second grade–not because I forgot. I still think there are some things better hidden away in our heads or made different. But maybe I should have told you.

It was right after Easter, after you'd spent the day at the trailer park and we'd just got on River Front Street and were going to walk with you part of the way home. She was running toward us, naked as all get out, and when she saw us she started screaming. Celia, Ruby, and Mr. Haverty and a few of the others came out and started ushering us back through the gate.

She was screaming for help. Help me, help me, she was saying. Mr. Haverty grabbed her, stopped her, and she pulled away from him and started batting herself in the face and rubbing her arms like she was infested with invisible bugs. She finally threw herself on the ground and started rolling around. Her screams had settled into choking sobs.

You stayed over at Putty's that night and all the grownups tried to talk to us. They were saying how she was sick and we shouldn't worry and that Mr. Beaumont was doing the best he could. And we should all be extra nice to you, because it was hard on you, too. We didn't know any different. We didn't know about hospitals and drugs and stuff back then. Whenever Ruby and Celia would talk about it, you could hear the guilt in their voices. They should have done something and they hoped wherever she'd gone to, she was getting the help she needed.

And then Celia would always say, "Poor Digger."

Your dad came by the next morning to get you and he was nice as can be and he gave us all hugs and apologized for it. He said it was his fault, said he hadn't realized she was on the edge the day before, and he forgot to give her medicine.

And Putty said, "What kind of medicine?"

Mr. Beaumont smiled, the kind of smile you'd give an eight-year-old kid when you didn't want to get too personal. He just said, "Medicine."

You know, we were only kids. If you remember it at all, I hope you know that. We didn't mean half the things we said and anyway, even you were saying them. All the boys could talk about were her boobs bouncing around as she ran up to us. You took that opportunity to grab Sunny and yank her tank top over her head, exposing her bare chest. You held her there while Putty and Kyle took turns running their hands all over her. She was only eight, like the rest of us, so Mary and I weren't quite sure what you thought you were doing.

You'd started smoking by then, and you lit up and we watched you walk down River Front Drive back home the next day. You must have held the cigarette between your lips because you did that thing you always do, with your fists at your temples, your eyes on the ground.

Now me...I thought you did that to Sunny to prove to Putty and Kyle you weren't affected at all—you couldn't care less that your mother was a nut job and ran around naked and that we'd all seen her. But your fists at your temples and your head down—that told me different, told me you were ashamed and trying to forget. It's no wonder you were on the mean side. Maybe I'd have been too, if Celia and Ruby acted like that.

When I went out to the tracks the next day, Ron walked with me a short way into the scrub. He carried the gallon jugs of water for me and asked me all kinds of nosey questions about you. Said he wanted to make sure I was okay, that you weren't hurting me. I told him it wasn't like that. I said you weren't even you anymore and he wanted to come all the way out to see for himself and I wouldn't let him. So, if you ever wonder about it, I did sort of tell them not to come out. It's not completely their fault they stayed away.

When I came up to the tracks, I stopped, a little scared, because Jericho was with you and Boxcar stood up and barked as soon as he saw me. Your spot was different, set up like a camp with blue tarps hung over some of the shrubs nearby, and a lantern and some metal dishes in a pile. You motioned me over and introduced me and you were so easy about it, I started to believe you were never going to be Jack again.

Jericho wore a ball cap and he pulled it off when he nodded hello; he had gray hair and a gray beard that littered his dark face like a thin layer of dirty snow. He had jaundiced brown eyes and more empty spaces than teeth in his mouth. The knuckles on his hands were dusted white and dry and his big toe, with a thick yellow nail, stuck out from his left shoe. Leaning against a nearby pine tree, his pack was a frame, like the long handle on one of those rolling suitcases, with rolls and sacks attached to it with worn bungee cords. He was a hobo.

You have to understand that you never would have

done what you did if you hadn't gone crazy. I mean...the Jack you were before never would have been nice to a bum like Jericho. He'd be more likely to steal from him, maybe even hit him with something. And he'd mock him. You wouldn't normally help someone like Jericho, but there you sat, sharing food with him and his dog. And smiling.

I sat down next to Boxcar and he let me pet him, wagged his tail; he looked to be some kind of Terrier mutt, the color of honey, a bit too skinny. He wore a frayed collar, tied to the oak with a long thin rope.

Jericho told me he'd come up from the south at dawn and you said he could sit a while in the shade. We looked at each other, you and me, and I knew you saw it, too. Jericho was sick. It didn't look like he'd be moving on any time soon. He'd been walking the scrub, and through neighborhoods, following the tracks north when he could. He was sleeping outside and under bridges; he walked in the rain, slept in the rain. He was hungry. You could see it in his sunken cheeks and tremors and the way he hid inside his baggy worn clothes. After a while, he lay down and slept and Boxcar walked out a few paces and sat as his guard.

"You're different," I said. "Are you okay?"

You nodded, but didn't say anything.

"You remember?"

"I just feel lighter."

I wasn't sure what that meant, but I could see it—you were happy. It's awful, when you think about it, that being happy would be unusual for you, but it was. I found myself there again, with that feeling that this was the way it would end. You'd have only fuzzy recollections of what used to be and we could move on from here, both of us forgetting. But then you asked me to tell you more about Jack. Like you weren't him at all. I should have been happy about that; it should have made me feel light, like you. But instead I got this sick feeling, this dread. And I told you about third grade.

16.

Three weeks into the school year in third grade, your mother was gone. We only knew about it because your dad came around to the trailer park and told everybody. He wanted them all to know how grateful he was for their patience and kindness. But when they asked him where she was, he said he didn't know.

"She has these times," he said. "When she's clear. When she's normal, taking her medication. And this time, I thought things would get better. But instead, she packed up and left."

Celia said he ought to call the police, what with her history and all. But your dad said that wasn't necessary. He was thinking she'd gone up north to live with her sister. He'd call later and make sure.

When he left, Celia said, "Well, he's awful happy about it, ain't he?"

And Pat Dunn, lot eight, said, "Wouldn't you be?"

Celia had to agree about that.

But as it turned out, your mother never went to her sister's house up north. Your dad came around asking them all if they knew anything, had they seen her, did they see her when she left, because he called her sister and your mom never showed up there. He was so worried Celia had to make him sit down. We didn't see your dad that much, so all the kids stood around gaping at him and trying to figure it out. We knew something bad must have happened, especially when Mr. Haverty was charged with shooing us back to the pool. I can still see you sitting there at the edge with your feet in the water and your shoulders hunched glaring at the dancing reflections of light on the surface.

When the cops came around asking questions, nobody would say much of anything. I was standing out in front of our trailer with Ruby and Celia while they shrugged and said they didn't see anything.

"She was flighty," Celia said. "It's not so surprising she ran off."

"Was she happily married?" The cop said.

Ruby's arm fell to her side and she put her hand against my stomach, pushing me back just a bit, like a warning. I never asked them about it, but I have to guess they thought none of it was anybody's business but your dad's.

And how Mrs. Wilmington, our third grade teacher, found out about it I'll never know. You missed school for at least a week because of it–your dad said you both were beside yourselves–and while you were gone, she stood in front of the class and told us all your mother was missing and we should be as nice as we could be. That's the way I remember it anyway. Putty was in our class that year and he says it never happened.

But it did happen. When I saw you again, you were

changed. You met us at the bus stop and I could tell the meanness in you had solidified–become permanent, and the fear in your eyes was overcome by rage. It wouldn't always be that way. You'd go back and forth and I was sure to get a good look before I said anything, because your mood would tell me which *you* I was going to get. Fearful Jack could sometimes say nice things and almost smile and when he was mean, he was having fun with it. But raging Jack needed only a spark and he was lost to us for a while.

When you came back to school, you were suspended before the day even started. You broke Jerry Cornell's nose. Outside the classroom, Jerry said something about your mom running off and you punched him, then grabbed his head and slammed it into the concrete walkway. Celia said if Mrs. Cornell had pressed the issue, you'd have been expelled. But the fact is, so says Celia, even Mrs. Cornell felt bad for you and she barely knew you.

The rest of the year was one bad thing after another. That was the year you took a red clay brick out of Mr. Pinkerton's garden and threw it through one of his windows and he chased you out of the trailer park. He caught you on River Front, grabbed you into a bear hug and wouldn't let you go. A lot of us stood there watching, confused.

You roared into his belly and then your breathing was hard and raspy and softening until I couldn't hear it anymore. When Mr. Pinkerton let you go, you turned and walked home; we all stood there and watched. You beat your fists against your temples and never looked back.

When Mr. Pinkerton went home, he was crying. Did you know that? I don't think you did.

The worst of it was when Sunny went missing. In the middle of the night Ruby and Celia and all the grownups buzzed about near the picnic tables and told us kids to go back to bed. They asked if any of us knew what happened to her. Who saw her last? Where was she? But nobody knew. Mrs. Swanson planned to call the police, but they didn't want her to; not yet, they said.

"But what if this is related to Tish Beaumont?" She said.

They were scared by that, but it was agreed they'd wait. Sunny might have just wandered off. Your mom might have just wandered off, too.

"You know how they are," Mr. Haverty said. And it was true enough. None of our group had yet snuck out at night, but some of the older kids did it.

Mr. Pinkerton was set to patrol the whole park, to make sure none of the children woke up and needed something, while the rest went out to find Sunny. It took a few hours. She was tied, standing, to a tree way out in the scrub, her clothes ripped like they'd been cut up with a knife.

"Nobody could get anything out of her," Celia said.

But everybody had a pretty good idea it was you who did it. The next day the whole park was there at the picnic tables talking about it. Some of them wanted to call the police or child services, but they were overruled.

"You don't send your child away because he's troubled," Mr. Haverty said.

"He's not your child," Henrietta Cleary said.

"He's as much ours as Digger's," Celia said. And she reminded them about how they took you in when you were little, how they all knew you were in a difficult situation and vowed to take care of you. And that's what they were going to do.

Mrs. Cleary tried to tell them what was best, but they wouldn't listen. Part of it was them not wanting other people, outsiders, coming around, asking questions. If the county looked at Digger and the junkyard, maybe they'd come over and look at them, too. And part of it, I think, was they just didn't want to see it.

I wandered into the scrub the next day and found you there at the tree. The rope was still on the ground, and tattered bits of Sunny's clothes lay all around. You told me what you did. You cut up her clothes and you touched her—put your fingers up inside her. Then you wrapped your arms around her and the tree, and pressed yourself hard against her and held her for so long you thought you'd squeezed the evil out of her. Then you ran away and left her in the dark.

You'd rubbed your temples nearly raw with your fists and said, "Forget, forget."

I understood then, how it was all supposed to go. You would forget; we all would. And you'd ask me not to tell your father. You loved your father.

"You're not like her," I said. "You won't be like her." But you didn't hear me. You just kept working to forget.

That's what I thought, for the longest time—you got crazy from your mom. We all thought it. And that must be why we didn't see it. It must be. We need that to be the reason.

101

17.

If you don't remember it all, even if you do, you might not understand why nobody helped you– why they didn't do anything to stop you. I wish I could say it wasn't prejudice, but I think a lot of it was. The bullies who got into trouble weren't appealing; they had braces or freckles or beady eyes or they were overweight. And they weren't quiet, never seemed to be thinking about what they did wrong. They never acted afraid. I don't know what made them do the things they did, but maybe it was because people looked at them like that and didn't just *love* them.

You were smaller than most, and the kind that even old ladies smiled at; they'd want to put their hands on your face and hair, tell everybody what a looker you were going to be when you got older. They all mistook that fear in your eyes for sadness. You'd look at the ground, frowning, instead of up at them, smirking. Everybody wanted to protect you, to keep you safe. But they didn't know what that meant, I guess.

When I finished telling you what I could bear from third grade, Jericho sat up and offered us a weak smile. "The thing about the past," he said. "Is that it's too late to do anything about it."

"You can change it," I said.

He snorted and dug a cigarette out of the pack in his front shirt pocket and lit it up. "They ain't no getting around what you done. It's best to just take it for what it is and move on from there."

"Why not forget it?" I said.

"It's you. Part of you, anyway."

"It doesn't have to be."

He chuckled, shook his head like I was stupid, and looked away. "You ignore it and it never goes away."

Well, that didn't make any sense at all. And anyway, I told him we weren't ignoring it. I was only telling you all about it, what you did when you were a kid. And he said, "I didn't say to wallow in it. Accept it and move on."

And you said, "I don't remember it."

Jericho leaned back a bit and peered at you from under closed-up eyelids. "What do you mean?"

"I forgot it."

"You got the amnesia?"

You nodded.

"And you going to let her tell you who you are?" He shook his head again and mumbled something under his breath.

You looked at me then, a little suspicious.

"I know all about it," Jericho said.

He told us he was from Texas way back when; he had a job and a family. But he couldn't get away from the thing he'd done when he was seventeen. He wondered if everybody had something like that lurking around in their heads, keeping them from being happy and I said I didn't think so.

You asked him what he'd done and he said he raped a girl at a party.

"I wouldn't have used that word at the time," he said. "I wasn't the only what did it, and the girl never told." He thought that meant he'd done nothing wrong. But then he saw her in the paper where she'd hanged herself a few years later and he started to wonder. He kept going, he said. Kept working, living, being happy. He got married and had a couple of kids, a boy and a girl. But it nagged at him. Drove him mad, until he had to leave.

"I started walking and I never looked back and I must have walked all over this country. People look at me like I'm dirt and I guess that's what I was looking for."

You were nodding; it was like you had a head full of a person, instead of being empty and lost, and you knew from experience what Jericho meant. But I didn't know. I thought about it all the way back home. I was so deep into the thinking that when thunder exploded all around me like a bomb, I jumped and ran. I could hear the rain chasing me and somewhere up ahead a seagull called out runrunrun run run run.

When I got to work later that day, Celia asked me how long I was going to do this. I told her I didn't understand what was so wrong about it and she said you'd never come home if I kept going out to the tracks. Mr. Haverty was saying they should all go out there and bring you home and I said, "Since when have any of you made Jack do something he didn't want to do?"

"Well, at least stop bringing him food and water."

"Do you want him to run off?" I said. "Because that's

what he'll do."

"He won't go anywhere. He'll sit out there until he gets hungry and come home."

And I told her you weren't a cat.

She said, "Maggie, you got to stop it. Let someone else do it."

"He's not going to hurt me."

She didn't believe me. "When are you going to stop holding on to what's not even there?"

I wanted to scream at her–tell her it *was* there, that you loved me and there wasn't anything she or Ruby could do to make me think otherwise. But they were the same as Mary, always trying to tell me it wasn't love, the things you did. It was no use trying to tell them any different.

"Just think of your mama," she said. "She don't want to lose you."

It was hard to think of Ruby. Hard to think about the inevitable. My sisters are a lot older, I told you. You never met them; they live up north where my Aunt Jewel is. They broke Ruby's heart.

Bishop went off with another woman when I was born and stayed at her place, so Ruby came to live with Celia at the trailer park. When Bishop showed up at the laundromat one day, he said he was breaking his lease on the house and moving in with his mother down the block and he was taking Lilly and Rose home with him.

Ruby said, "We'll just see what the girls say to that."

But they said they wanted to go to Grandma's. They wanted to live in a house where they didn't have to share a bedroom with their mom and a baby. Of course, Ruby was back over there with him, living at his mom's place, before I was eight months old. Ruby said my Grandma Hanson wouldn't let his girlfriend come live with them so she ran off with someone else and he couldn't go for too long without a woman around to beat up on.

By the time I was two we were all, like a real family, living over in the trailer park, lot nine, and Bishop came and went depending on whether or not his girlfriend had given up walking the streets whoring, so Ruby says. Lilly had a baby and moved up north to live with Aunt Jewel because Bishop called her a slut and told her she couldn't bring a bastard into his home. Rose moved up there a year later and that was that. Ruby hasn't seen them since.

I get the feeling I'm not allowed to leave. Maybe that's why I didn't listen, maybe there was something in me that knew what was going on, knew how it would all turn out. Maybe I was hoping you would start walking one day and I'd follow you and we wouldn't ever have to see it. We'd go up north and live with Aunt Jewel for a bit and I could get to know my sisters and find out if I look as much like them as it seems from the photos we get. And you would be the way you were there at the tracks—smiling, calm. And the past could just be however we wanted it to be.

You and Jericho were walking down the tracks from the north when I got there the next morning. You'd been off for coffees and pastries. Boxcar was tied to the tree, licking me. I gave him some water in the cracked, hard plastic bowl Jericho had for him. I could hear Jericho talking as you approached. It sounded like he was reciting something and when you got to the wiry old scrub oak,

107

you were breathing heavy and sweating, flushed and smiling.

"Jericho wrote a book," you said. "He's been telling it to me."

"What kind of book?"

Jericho dug a small leather journal out of his pack and handed it to me. It was foreign, somehow—tan, like Boxcar, but stained in places, with a cigarette burn on the bottom near the fold. On the front, he'd written *What is True* in black marker; it bled tiny spider webs off each letter, making the title look scruffy with hair. I looked up at the two of them and smiled at their scraggly bearded faces.

"Go on," Jericho said. "Look in it."

I flipped through the pages at Jericho's shaky handwriting. Some paragraphs were titled. On love. On hate. On God. On the sunrise. But most of his thoughts were random, scribbled out in a sentence or two.

"Could a full life," I read aloud, "be no more than a face upturned to the sunlight?"

"That one I got from my friend, Pete," Jericho said. "He was a simple man."

They sat down in the sand with me, and Jericho dug a hard-boiled egg out of his bag and broke it up into Boxcar's bowl before pouring in some kibble from a bag in his backpack.

"It was my first week out," he said. "I hitched up with a few fellas headed north; we'd hike by day and camp out at night. I like to thought I found my paradise. Oh, it weren't being free of my obligations or free of the past, nothing selfish as that. It was being outside in the nature all the time. Seeing it real up close. Watching the road disappear under your feet. You can see ever little rock and weed, and ever leaf on ever tree."

He took a bite of his Danish and sipped his coffee and you and I watched him, like he was a wise man and very important, and we didn't want to miss anything he had to say.

"Makes you feel small. And they don't tell you feeling small is good. Nope. Ever body says you got to be big to really be alive. But it ain't so. I wrote about that in my book. I wrote, the measure of a life well lived is not in a man's height, his strength, nor his power, but in his ability to see his own insignificance."

He nodded. Whenever he got like that, said those things that must mean a lot, he talked very proper and slow and his voice got deeper. It made us listen, didn't it? I wondered if what he was saying might not be meaningful at all. Maybe it was just the way he said it. But I know now that's silly. Truth is in the words, the ideas themselves, not in their delivery. Jericho doesn't talk like that so much these days.

"Anyway, one night we were able to buy some liquor," he said. "We sat around under an old unused bridge, built up a fire, and told one other why we were on the road. It was like a meeting, you know? Where ever body is asked to say his name and what he hopes to get out of the program or some such. And I told them about my wife and kids, and how I loved them; I loved them so much I had to leave 'em. Because I was poison. And Bill, he says, 'Bah, you ain't loved 'em. You ain't even love yourself. Can't nobody love nobody unless they loves

109

themselves.' And it clicked there for a while. I thought he was right."

"You don't think he was?" I asked him.

Now, I'd heard that very same thing from Ron last year. He came by to see his folks and stopped over at the trailer to say hi and we walked out to the road so we could talk. We left from the side gate and there you were, coming up River Front Drive, and as soon as you saw us you turned around and went back.

Ron said, "He was coming to see you."

"No," I told him. "I'm still not speaking to him."

He looked at me, his eyebrows up in that way they do when he doesn't believe me. "He was coming to see you."

I watched you walking home, your head down and your shoulders hunched up a bit and I knew Ron was right. You came to the trailer park a couple of times a week since you hit me and you'd sit at the picnic tables waiting for me to come out. I even sat with you that one time, remember? And you didn't say anything; I think you expected me to forgive you. It was always better when other people were with us. Then we could talk without having to say anything important.

"So what if he was?" I said.

Ron frowned, wilted like he was giving up. "I know you think he loves you."

"In his way," I said.

"No, he doesn't. Not in any way."

"I know he's done a lot of bad things."

"It's not even that," he said. "He's screwed up. We all know it. His mother left him, and before that she mistreated him, neglected him."

110

"Doesn't that mean we should love him more?"

"But he can't love you, that's what I'm saying. You can't love another person when you don't love yourself."

I don't think he knew what he was saying, and the way I stared at him, like my world was falling to the dirt all around me, must have made him believe he'd got through to me, because a glimmer of hope brightened his face. But he couldn't see the ripples his idea had made. From me, to Ruby, my dad, you, your mom. All around us were people who didn't love themselves, tormented by demons we couldn't bleed out. And he was standing there telling us we weren't capable of love.

I turned to Jericho, realizing I'd been off remembering and he knew it, and was waiting for me to come back. By then you were eating your pastry and you'd offered me a bite.

And Jericho said, "It worried me I might not know love at all–that I weren't up to it. But, after a while, I knew he was wrong. I loved that girl. I loved those kids. I still do. Loved 'em hard. Love is the easy part. Anybody can love. Ah, well, I suppose there are those people what are, what you call 'em, psychopaths, and such–I grant you they don't know love. But most anybody else can do it. And most of us are ruined souls. I'd warrant most ever body on the planet with half a brain has some sort of self-loathing, some shame, and disgust. But we love. No, loving is the easy part. It's what you do with it that's the problem. And so, when I figured that out, I thought I needed to write it down. I needed to remember so's I wouldn't fall prey to the likes of Bill again, and act on something that weren't true. So I found this little journal at the thrift store and ever since, I been writing down truth where I find it."

You both finished your breakfast and Jericho unleashed Boxcar so he could run off and smell the scrub. Jericho got up and dug through the big pack on the metal frame and came back to the tree with a hand fan, one that folds up, and when you pull it open there's a picture of a lady on it; she's fanning herself.

"You take this," he said.

I thanked him and fanned myself, then fanned the both of you and you smiled.

"Is hate the opposite of love?" I asked him.

"I've heard it before," he said. "Some say apathy is the opposite of love."

"Is it true?"

You looked back and forth between me and Jericho, as if we were deciding what to do with you, and you didn't like it. Jericho let out a long whistle. He pulled a dirty toothpick, split on one end, from his shirt pocket and picked at his teeth.

"No," he said. "It's like this. There's a line, see? On one end you got love and on the other, hate. And right smack in the middle, there's apathy."

"What's apathy?" I said.

"That's where you don't care a whit."

I nodded, because that made more sense than what Ron said. He said love and hate were just two sides of the same coin and to be honest, I have no idea what that means.

"Why would people say they're not opposite?"

"Oh, well," Jericho said. "Lots of reasons. Good

reasons. Nobody wants to be hated, for one thing. Easy enough to say the person in question don't hate you at all. Fact is, they care so much about you, they got to love you enough to hate you. That sort of thing. Like trying to say hate don't really exist. But it does."

I looked at you then, wishing I could just ask you—come right out with it. But you didn't remember, so how would you know? I had to figure it out myself—did you do the things you did because you hated me?

"Thank I'll write that down." He reached over and picked up his journal and opened it up, flipping through the pages to the back. We watched him scribble for a minute. "We're ready to hear the next story about Jack," he said when he was finished.

You nodded. "Jericho's going to help me figure it all out."

"How's he going to do that?"

"I'll help him practice acceptance."

It all made me wonder how we'd begun; why I'd started telling you who you were and what you did. Maybe acceptance was good.

"And you'll tell us how you're sure that what you say is true," Jericho said.

"Why would I lie?"

18.

Tucker stayed in that little motel up north a bit on U.S. 1. The one you and Kyle and Putty broke into that time a few years ago; do you remember? You got into a room in the middle of the night and hauled out the bed, a table and chair, and the television, and you set them up out in the parking lot. You told me Kyle went back in and pissed all over the walls and he was afraid the next morning, because they'd get his DNA from it and find him and he'd be arrested. And you said, "What for? Disorderly pissing?" And everybody thought that was so funny.

I wondered what room Tucker was in and he looked at me funny and told me it was six. I imagine he thought I was flirting with him–that maybe I wanted to come over to see him. But I wanted to know if he was in the room Kyle had peed all over. You should come home so I can ask you which one.

We were at the laundromat. I'd been standing out front of the bait shop talking with Ruby; she was down the way, sitting in the metal folding chair that holds the front door open. I saw him come up the road with a bag of laundry. He smiled at both Ruby and me before he went in past her. You'd been gone for eight days and it was starting to feel normal.

I went over to Ruby and whispered, "That's the guy I was telling you all about. The sad one at the police station."

"He don't look so sad now."

I told her to go watch the bait shop so I could go in and talk to Tucker. The laundromat isn't air conditioned like the bait shop is. The doors, front and back, were propped open and five big fans churned the hot air around and around in the room. Ruby had an ice machine installed and keeps big buckets of it in front of the fans on the worst days.

Tucker was standing in front of a washer, digging in his pants pocket. His thin gray t-shirt was already dark under the arms. His hair was long, just over the ears and just down the neck, and I remember thinking it ought to be the other way around. Tucker, a Georgia boy, should have cropped hair, at least on top. And you, a Florida boy, would have long hair. You ought to be the one to look like a surfer, but all you had was the dark, sun-drenched skin to show for it.

"You need any change?" I asked him.

"You work here, too?"

I told him that Celia owned the plaza and he said, "Nice," like we were rich. "You'll never starve and you'll always have clean clothes. That is, if you don't mind eating bait fish."

I said we had shrimp too and he laughed like that was funny. It was weird to see him laugh. After seeing him in the police station that first day, I expected he would never

116

be happy again. But he isn't like you, I reminded myself. He hadn't had a lifetime of pain to make him stop laughing, leastwise it didn't look like it.

"You want to maybe have dinner with me?" He said. "When you get off work?"

My mouth fell open a little bit.

"I'm staying at the little motel up the road there," he said, apologizing like. "I've been eating alone, is all. Thought you might—"

"Sure," I said. "Of course. I didn't mean to look upset. I just..." I was about to tell him I'd never been asked out on a date before, but I stopped myself in time.

It's true, though, isn't it? All of us girls, we assumed you were taking us out, or coming by, or whatever. You never really asked, did you? Even Ron never asked me to go out with him. I know you think he wanted to, and you'd be right. But we were always only friends.

I sat there on one of the folding tables while he did his laundry and he told me he was almost done with veterinarian school at the University of Georgia. I thought he looked a little young for that, but he said he was twenty-five, same as me. His mom breeds Yorkies and his dad owns a dog grooming salon and kennel called Suds 'n' Cuddles. He talked like he was nervous—fast until he realized what he was doing, then a breath, and slow for a little while. He was trying not to talk about what was going on. I didn't know if that was for him or for me, but I liked it. He told me about Atlanta and how there is a place there that has the best hot dogs in the world. And he told me about his parents' house, where he grew up and the big grassy hill out back and then he stopped talking and didn't look at me.

"How long do you think you'll be here?" I asked him.

"Until I know for sure," he said.

19.

There was a day when we were in fourth grade that had all of us going to the junkyard to look for you. You hadn't been in school for a few days and on Saturday, we decided to find you. When your father heard us coming through the gate toward the office building, he came out onto the front porch and yelled at us to stop.

"Y'all know you ain't allowed in here."

We told him we wanted to see you and he said you were out in the scrub so we walked around the perimeter of the junkyard and found you sitting up against a tree out back watching one of the dogs pace in its run eyeing you. We could smell the rot of death out there, which wasn't unusual and the boys set off to find it. But you just sat there, like you were mad.

Mary and I sat with you and watched the dog and Mary asked you what its name was and you said it didn't have a name.

"Why not?" She said.

You said, "You don't give names to things you don't want to miss when they die."

The boys came back saying the dead raccoon or

possum must be inside the fence and they wanted to sneak in and find it. They were hoping for a raccoon so they could cut off its tail. Putty already had one and Kyle was jealous. He'd take a squirrel tail if he had to, but he knew it wouldn't be the same.

You said we could sneak in, so we walked around to the front entrance and you told us we had to be quiet and if we went in one at a time and went to the left right away, we could make our way around the appliances without being seen. You went in and put Wilder and Manning in your trailer and it didn't matter if the other dogs barked; they barked all the time. We met up with you in the back and you sat on a car door while Kyle, Putty, Ron, and even Mary went around looking for it. I was trying not to look at you too much. Sometimes if I did you'd get mad and say, "What the hell are you looking at?" I could tell you were in one of those moods.

I remember thinking to myself that it really wasn't fair you would kiss me in second grade and laugh and then act like you didn't want me around. But I wasn't in a hurry. The boys started yelling and you jerked about, like you'd been daydreaming, jumped up and ran through the junk telling them to be quiet. They were over on the other side of the yard, where the rusty, locked sheds lined up against the fence, laughing; they couldn't find the animal anywhere but had found an enormous pile of nuts and bolts and screws and nails and they were throwing them at one another.

We heard the gunshot and when I turned to look at you, your face went white, like you were drained of blood. The others ran but you stood there, startled.

"Come on," I said. I took your hand and pulled at you and you ran.

Your father was cursing and he shot the gun off again. We made it to the front gate and out onto Beaumont Road, but he came after us. He was screaming at you, telling you he was going to tan your hide and send you off with your mother, and we ran and ran out into the scrub, the quarter mile to the railroad tracks and on beyond.

You'd decided to leave home for good, so even after we stopped running, panting and wheezing, wet and slimy with sweat, we kept on westward, through the pine scrub. That was how we discovered the lake. A pier reached out across it, not very far, and we figured we must be on someone's land but we never found out whose. About fifteen feet in, three signs stuck up out of the water warning us. No swimming. We decided the lake was home to a serpent—most likely the child-eating kind.

You didn't run away from home, though. You went back and when we saw you again at the pool, you wouldn't take off your shirt to go swimming. I knew what had happened, but the others didn't seem to suspect anything.

I sat on one of the lounge chairs near you and said, "Was your father really mad?"

And you said, "Wilder and Manning pooped in the trailer."

Celia came up behind you and lifted your shirt and you winced and she told Mr. Haverty to come over and have a look. When we told them what happened they scolded us for going into the junkyard.

121

"You kids have no business in there," Ruby said. "Supposing you got hurt."

"That's no cause to whip him," I said.

"I'll tell you what," she said. "If I hear you've been in there again, I'll whip you the same."

You had that glare about you, the one you get when you're so mad you might cry. I imagined you wanted to tan your dad's hide right back, if you could, and I didn't blame you.

A few days later we all walked out to the lake again to fish, carrying poles and tackle boxes, and paper lunch bags with sandwiches and chips in them. You and the boys teased Sunny because she brought a purse. It was this shiny plastic purple thing, a flat-topped triangle—a trapezoid, isn't that it? It had a kiss lock and a stiff little handle. Her dad bought it for her and told her it was called a kiss lock because the two metal knobs kiss each other when they close. She should remember him when she opened and closed it, she said.

You told her she was stupid, but she ignored you. She said the purse was only for carrying her pictures. Wherever she went, she'd have them. She snapped open the kiss lock and pulled them out to show everybody.

"Here's Daddy holding me out front of our trailer," she said. "Daddy calls me his Sunny Sunshine. Here we are in the pool."

It happened so fast, the way you stepped forward and slapped at her hands sending the pictures flying into the dirt. We all should have known it would get worse. I could almost see Mary hesitating, thinking she should take Sunny home. But she didn't. And we all started walking again like nothing was wrong.

Ron told us he knew why there were signs posted that said we couldn't swim in the lake. His mom told him a kid died already that summer from an amoeba that crawled into his ear when he was swimming in fresh water. It ate his brain inside out.

We got to the lake and stood at the shore looking at the glassy surface, the pines on the other side reflected in it, unmoving.

"Just think," you said. "Below the surface, brain eating amoebas are in there watching us, just waiting for one of us to jump in."

We walked out onto the pier and when Sunny went to the edge and looked down into the murky water, you pushed her in, purse and all. You and Putty poked at her with your fishing poles when she tried to climb out. She was gulping and struggling, and you told her to get back under the water and find an amoeba and don't come up until she got one in her brain. She managed to dog paddle past your poles, her face wild with fear, and crawl out onto the little beach. She'd lost her purse and her pictures. While she sat there for a while crying, you and Putty went ahead and baited your hooks, wondering how long it would take for the amoeba to eat enough of her brain to kill her.

Mary glared at the both of you. "Come on, Ron," she said.

But Ron didn't go. I don't blame him. He wanted to be one of the boys, not one of the girls. It wouldn't work out, but he tried for the longest time. Mary helped Sunny up and walked her home.

I found you on the pier the next day at dusk, all alone, sitting crossed-legged at the edge rocking forward and back with your fists grinding into your temples.

"Forget, forget, forget."

I could hear you before I stepped onto the pier and you stopped when you felt my footsteps behind you. I sat beside you and let my feet swing over the water's surface while you told me what you'd done and why you'd done it. You said that thing was more a part of you than it used to be. It didn't visit anymore, it lived inside you. Sometimes it was nice and sometimes it was not.

"I know," I said. And I knew you loved your dad, and I would never tell him you had your mom in you, and we would all forget.

20.

When I finished telling you about the fourth grade you were shaking your head. You said, "I don't know why I'd want to be him."

"You don't have to be," I said. "You can be anybody you want."

Jericho sputtered and said, "You can be anybody you want—what kind of nonsense is that?"

"It's not nonsense," I said. "Everybody knows it. We can be whoever or whatever we want."

"That so? How's about you jes' up and be an astronaut or the President of the United States? I never heard such high falutin' rubbish."

"Well," I said. "I don't want to be an astronaut."

"Just tell the boy the facts so he can learn to live with 'em. You can't be whole if you don't accept it all—all you done, all what was done to you, all you was given to start with, and all you threw away. You are who you are and you can't escape it."

I looked at you, and you twisted your mouth up a bit and said, "Makes sense."

"And stop with all the bad," Jericho said. "You're

only giving him half a life."

"You want I should tell nicer stories?"

"Why are you telling these ones?"

"He asked me to."

"He asked you to tell him how mean he was?"

"It's okay," you said.

We sat quiet for a while and Jericho glared at me, like I was the enemy and that was how I felt. You two acted like best pals, on a bum sleep over out in the scrub by the tracks, and how dare I keep coming over and bringing you sandwiches and water and telling you what an awful person you used to be. I shouldn't be so defensive about it; I *was* telling the bad stuff. And I had to think about why. I guess I wanted you to know the truth from me and not from your memory. I wanted you to be filled with what I said when you finally got your head back on straight and maybe you'd remember your life a shade different, set off from the reality of it by my telling it. Like second hand. Some things are better second hand– pain and loss, for instance.

"What I want to know," Jericho said, as if he had a stake in it at all. "Is what's your part in it? Where are you in the story?"

"I was right there. If I wasn't there I wouldn't know what happened."

"That ain't what I mean. You got it in your head that you got to tell him what he done, but what did you do? What was going on in your life then? You weren't all peaches and cream."

I didn't know what that meant, peaches and cream, but it sounded sweet, so maybe that was it. I never told
126

you my part of that story or any other and you never asked. I figured if you didn't ask then you didn't want to know. And who was Jericho that I should tell?

That day at the lake, when you pushed Sunny into the water and hoped she got an amoeba, I didn't do anything because Ruby was lying in bed back at the trailer with her face swollen and her arm in a sling. Bishop cracked her arm with a frying pan. I was standing in the little living room trying to make myself turn back to the television and not watch it, but sometimes you just can't make your legs do what they need to do.

It started because Ruby wouldn't tell him what happened at the pool before—when your dad beat you. It was my fault somehow. They were talking about you and the junkyard and Bishop thought he should get a gun that he could shoot into the air and I said something, but I can't remember what. Bishop wanted to know what I meant and Ruby wouldn't tell him.

He jumped out of his chair and hit her, knocking her to the floor; he pulled her back up like he always did and punched her. He'd do that again and again and Ruby told me once she tried to stand up and take it, but he hit too hard. But the more she fell the madder he got. By that time I'd got up off the couch. I meant to apologize—to say I didn't mean it, I was wrong. But I just stood there watching him hovering over her as she knelt on the ground. He twisted her left arm behind her back, reached over to the counter, grabbed the cast iron pan and, I thought he was going to spank her on the backside with it but instead, he hit her arm and I heard the crack. Ruby screamed and panted a few times and then fainted and

Bishop looked at me, rolled his eyes, tossed the frying pan to the floor and said, "Go on and get your grandmother."

When I got home later that night after work, I asked Ruby about it. I asked her what I said that day when I was nine to make Bishop so mad, and she said, "Maggie, honey, it beats the hell out of me."

Celia and I burst out laughing and Ruby didn't get it at first, but finally, her eyebrows went up and she laughed so hard she almost puked out her soda. And then we got real quiet. Celia was giving me sideways looks from the kitchen table while I was eating crackers on the couch. I knew she wanted me to leave so she could scold Ruby about going over to see Bishop. I told her she ought to get to bed, it was getting late, but she said she was just fine. Ruby noticed—she knew what Celia was up to. She was trying to watch her program but sitting too still, like she didn't want to look at her mom.

"I'm going out," I said.

"What for?" Ruby said.

"I want to."

I didn't wait for her to say anything else, didn't look at her. I was betraying her again, leaving her alone with Celia. But as I was closing the door behind me I saw her heading to her room. There are just some things we don't want our mothers to keep on about. Smoking and drinking, sure. Not wearing your seatbelt, that sort of thing. But when it comes to loving a man, we ought not have to fight for it.

Kyle was out by the pool smoking. He sat on a bench, leaning his back against the edge of the picnic table. A big plastic cup without a lid was beside him. I took the bench
128

of another table across from him. He slapped at his arm.

"Bad tonight?" I asked him.

He shook his head and took a drag from his cigarette. "It's a trade-off, ain't it? Do I stink of repellent or do I get eaten alive? Some days, it's just easier to be eaten alive."

I smiled and he was quiet for a bit.

Then he said, "We're the only ones left."

"Jack's still here."

"He ain't been here for a year at least."

"But he's still here."

"I'm talking about more than where everybody lives."

I never thought of Kyle as the type to ponder on things like that. But I do remember Celia telling me once that he was more than he pretended to be. And I asked her why would anybody in his right mind pretend to be a drunk. All she said was that one day maybe I'd be smarter.

"Looking at it that way," he said. "Jack was never really here at all."

"What are you talking about?" I rolled my eyes, but I did want to know.

He lifted the cup to his mouth and took a few long sips, drew his other hand across his lips without burning himself with his cigarette and then held the cup out to me. I took it and drank. I could smell it was rum and Coke before it hit my lips. Strong with rum. He waved it back at me when I offered, so I kept it.

"You ever hear of those people with a bunch of personalities all living in one head?"

"Sure," I said.

"Well, I don't buy it. Not at all. But I do believe everything changes us. Every little thing. And depending on our genes, you know, the DNA, we change in a certain way. I could get bit by a dog when I'm nine and be fine. Another kid could get bit and end up a serial killer."

I chuckled and lifted the cup to my mouth again.

"I'm exaggerating," he said. "But you see my point."

"Not really."

"Jack was born. And who he was born to be got sidetracked by every little thing."

"You don't think his mother's crazy was in his genes?"

He shook his head. "No. I don't know. I'm no doctor."

"But if we're all changed by every little thing, then none of us is who we were born to be and none of us has been here since forever."

Kyle's mouth opened wide into that smile of his that charmed us all. "Damned if you ain't the logical one all the sudden."

"Yeah, but maybe I'm exaggerating too. I mean, we're all changed by every little thing, but most of us, say, aren't changed all that much. Most of us go on to be who we were born to be."

"But not Jack." He pointed to me with his cigarette. "And you've proved my point."

I drank some more. He finished the cigarette, stubbing it out on the bench, and took the cup from me. We slapped at our arms and knew we had to go back inside and the more we knew it, the more we didn't want to go. It was just like summers when we were kids—at our trailers we were alone; and we didn't like to be alone.

"You don't think we can get past it?" I said. "The stuff that changes us? You don't think we can be whoever we want to be?"

He lit up another cigarette, squinting at me over the flame of the lighter. "No," he said.

"But why not?"

He leaned back again and rested his elbows on the table behind him. "Because we're just animals."

"Don't say that."

"Okay, okay; don't go religious on me," he said. "But we act like animals–creatures who take to habit like sugar. We get in ruts; we hunger after comfort however we can get it and no matter how the comfort or the cure hurts us, makes us worse off than ever, we stick with it because the unknown is scarier than what we got and anyway, the rut is deep."

"I guess."

"I ain't saying he can't change. I'm just saying most of us don't. And it ain't right to go around telling us we could if we wanted to when the truth of it is, wanting it ain't enough. Working for it ain't enough. Hell, fighting for it ain't. There's too much, sometimes...too much to overcome."

I thought of Ruby then and I had to suppose Kyle was right. If I kept on about it, I was saying she could have left Bishop if she really wanted to. She could have had a better life, if she'd worked harder for it. But a defect twisted things up in her head, or her heart or soul– something wouldn't let her break free.

"Kyle," I said, almost whispering because maybe I

was afraid.

"Magnolia," he said.

"Do you think he ever loved me? At all? Do you think maybe he still does?"

He breathed deep, in and out, a sly smile at his lips. "It was always you," he said. And then he drew it out, like a sad song. "Always Magnolia. Only Magnolia would do."

I reached for the cup and he gave it to me. "And for me always Jack."

"Don't you ever look back on it, though, and wonder if maybe something was off? For him, obviously. But I mean, for you?"

I shook my head and returned the drink; it was nearly empty now.

"You don't wonder that you're just following the script you got from Ruby?"

I chuckled again. "You been hanging out at the laundromat reading the ladies' magazines?"

"I'm a bartender. You got to know this stuff."

"Do they really talk to you?"

He nodded. "Week nights. Nothing but the old and the lonely."

"I figured you'd understand," I told him. "About me and Jack."

"How so?"

"You know what it's like to love something that ain't necessarily good for you."

He winked, got up and smashed his cigarette butt into the dirt with his shoe, then leaned over and kissed my cheek long and sweet, his hand on the other side of my head. "If you only knew," he whispered.

132

I watched him walk down the main road beyond the pool in the dark, disappearing between the glows of porch lights. He tipped the cup to his mouth and emptied it.

21.

The next day I didn't get out into the scrub until after lunch because I worked the bait shop that morning. When Celia got there to let me leave, she dug her cigarettes and lighter out of her pocket and tossed them onto the counter next to the cash register and said, "Let me ask you something."

I took off my apron and gave it to her and as she pulled it over her head she said, "How long has Ruby been walking over to Bishop's?"

I could feel the heat rising in my face. "What do you mean?"

"Now don't pretend you didn't say it. A few days ago. You said she was still walking down to Bishop's."

I nodded.

"How long?"

"Forever."

She lit a cigarette and slid herself up onto the wood stool. "Don't that beat all?" I started to leave, but she said, "Did you know my Ma named all her children after diseases?"

I smiled. "No."

"She did. Luke, for leukemia. Cyrus for cirrhosis. Al

for Alzheimer's and Melanie for melanoma."

"What about you?"

"Celiac's disease."

"Is that real?"

"It is. I looked it up once, in the dictionary at school. Ma told me her family suffered a history of death and despair. She said they did everything they could to ward off the evil, but it hit 'em all just the same. It's a wonder any of 'em lived to have children. So, my Ma decided to stop running from it–to look death in the face and say 'bring it on.'"

"Did it work?"

She drew in a puff from her cigarette and let the smoke out of her nose before breathing it out her mouth. "You ever met your Great Uncle Luke?"

I shook my head.

"No. And you won't neither. He died when he was twelve of leukemia. Cyrus is a drunk who'll die of cirrhosis and Melanie died of cancer four years ago. I'm waiting on the Celiac."

I didn't believe her–not one bit. "And Al?"

"I don't know; I don't talk to him anymore. The point is what's coming is coming and you can't ward it off with a potion or a spell or a name. There's so much in the world we can't control and so little we can and it's best you stop worrying about what you can't."

"You mean you," I said. "You can't control Ruby."

"And you can't control Jack."

"I'm not trying to."

"I know it don't seem like that to you. Not now. But isn't that what this is all about? You going out there to help him, telling him your stories."

"I'm telling him the truth."

"You can't control this one, Mags. You can't fix him. And when he does come around—and he will—nothing will be any different."

"You don't know that."

"They don't change," she said. "Your mama goes to see Bishop, after all this time, because she still thinks it'll be all right in the end. But it won't—the end came the first time he hit her but she can't see it. You've got to accept that Jack is the way he is, now and forever, and if you want to be happy, get out of his way."

"It doesn't have to be like that."

She sighed and shook her head.

"What about love?" I said.

"Ah, what is love, anyway? Is it supposed to hurt? Are you supposed to be scared all the time?"

"Are you saying Bishop doesn't love Ruby? That Jack doesn't love me? Is that what you're trying to say?"

She looked at me for a few seconds, like she was sorry. But she said, "All I know is, love isn't supposed to be like that."

"Maybe love isn't supposed to be any way at all. Maybe it just is."

"All right," she said. "Love just is. It don't have the power to change Bishop, or Jack. So what's it good for?"

"You don't mean that."

Her shoulders fell and she put her cigarette to her lips but didn't take much of a drag. "I don't know what I'm saying anymore. I'm tired, Maggie. I've watched Ruby go through this most of my life. You know that? Most of my life. And I don't want to live the rest of it watching the same thing happen to you."

I left the bait shop by the back door so maybe Ruby wouldn't see me, but she was standing behind the laundromat, the door propped open with a concrete block. She was smoking a cigarette and she tossed it and stepped on it when she saw me.

"You going out into the scrub again today?"

"Yes, ma'am."

She lifted her face to the sunlight and squinted. "Did she say anything about me?"

I didn't respond; I just stood there looking at her and she finally turned to me and shook her head. "It ain't as bad as all that," she said. "But you shouldn't have told her. It raises her blood pressure."

"Well, he hasn't hit you, at least."

"Don't get sassy with me."

"I'm sorry," I said. "I'm just—Celia and me, we're both worried is all."

"You should talk."

"You know, I'm tired of you two thinking Jack is the same as Daddy. He's not."

"Nobody's the same." She took in a long breath and pushed it out quick. "Okay," she said. "I'm sorry, too. I know we're stuck. Messed up. In the head, maybe. In the heart."

"Speak for yourself," I said. "Me and Jack aren't like you and Bishop. Bishop's just mad. At himself, at life, probably at God. He blames everybody else for his troubles. But not Jack. Jack wants to do better."

She didn't even hear me. She said, "When's the last

time you talked to your dad?"

I shrugged and looked away.

"You ought to go see him."

"Why don't he come see us?"

"Look what happened last time."

She was talking about you—about that day you hit me the year before. Ruby said it was the end. The end of it all. She'd never see him again and she'd never let him near me again; it was over. But she never remembers those sorts of feelings very long.

"You don't make no sense," I told her. "Celia's right. You keep saying it's done but it never is. You said he had to stay away from me and now you want me to go see him."

"He's still your daddy. Anyway, it's been a year. Ain't it time to forgive and forget?"

"You forgive him every time."

She started to cry then, putting her hands on her face. "I'm sorry," she said.

When I got out to the railroad tracks, I found you sitting cross-legged, leaning against the scrub oak with Jericho squatting in front of you, nodding. As I got nearer, Jericho held out his hand to stop me and I saw your eyes were closed. I could hear you, your voice choked and hollow. You were saying words—urgent, breathless. Cold, you said. Wet. Vomit. Chains, dark, clammy, sweat, blood, burns, camera, loud, chains vomit scream pain burns. You slapped your hands against your face and scrambled to your feet knocking the old man onto his backside. He sat there watching you pace back and forth hitting the sides of your head with your fists.

"What happened?" I said.

"He's all right," Jericho said.

I was angry, I have to tell you. I would have told you then, but I knew you wouldn't want to hear it. And I didn't know but maybe I was wrong. The way I saw it, Jericho was a bum—a stranger. He had no business messing with it, no business trying to make you better. But he said he was just the man to do it.

"Sometimes a person needs somebody who's not familiar with the situation," he said. And then, "Hold up now." And he took out his journal to write it down.

Anyway, once you calmed down and took the sandwich I brought you, Jericho said he was trying to get you to grab hold of the images racing around in your head.

"It started out pleasant enough," he said. "But then it got dark."

"If you got stuff all jumbled up," I said. "How do you know you're seeing what happened for real, or something you saw in a movie or on television?"

I know I've been plenty scared of the television. I saw this movie once where dozens of girls were running and screaming and trying to escape a bad place and of them climbed a fence with sharp spikes on the top and she couldn't get herself over, she wasn't strong enough, so she sank slowly onto them and died. I still have nightmares about it, Jack. So, how do you know? It's dangerous, isn't it? To be trying to grab stuff from your brain before you remember. Shouldn't you leave it be?

"Talk to me," you said when you sat down with us. "What's next? What grade?"

"Fifth grade," Jericho said. "Maybe something nice this time."

That scared me. I wasn't sure I remembered anything nice, anymore, and it seemed to me that was a kind of amnesia, too.

"Just tell me what happened," you said. And I did.

22.

In fifth grade, you said you loved me.

You beat up this kid in P.E. a couple months into the year and you got suspended and then they put you in some kind of counseling program. I overheard our teacher telling another that getting a student out of the regular classroom is like climbing a ladder in a hurricane. They were trying to put you into the special class with the kids who spit on people. I got the idea those kids would end up in jail before they were old enough to drive.

When you got back into class, Putty said he told you that all you had to do was hold it in during school. He said he'd take care of everything if you could just keep it together until you got off the bus. And you did. Putty was there the whole time; he never missed a day of school unless you did. Everything got better for you. You learned to fade into the background.

One weekend we were out in the empty lots behind the plaza digging holes and your dad's truck rumbled down River Front from U.S. 1. Kyle stopped to look and asked you who that was, with your dad, and we all turned to see a woman sitting next to him in the front seat. You said you didn't know and the boys started making fun, saying your dad had a girlfriend and you were going to have a stepmother.

"I am not," you said.

And Mary said, "Sure, why not? He'll probably get married again."

"His dad is still married to his mom," I said.

"But she's gone," Kyle said. "Nobody knows where she is."

"If she's gone seven years, your dad can say she's dead and get married again." Putty said.

"He's not getting married," you said.

I thought you were scared about it, but everybody went on digging. We'd all brought treasure to bury. It was your idea. They'd done a time capsule at school and you said the best thing to do is bury the thing that means the most to you–something you really don't want to give up. You said that's the only way you can grow up. You had to be able to lose what you can't live without. That way, you'd learn you *could* live without it–you didn't have to have anything at all to keep going.

None of us followed the rules; I knew I hadn't. You said we all had to put our things into the holes and tell everybody what we were sacrificing. Mary went first and had a gold chain with a pink unicorn charm on it. I told her she shouldn't bury that and she said of course she shouldn't, that's why she had to.

I buried a teddy bear I had when I was little. I told everybody I thought I'd have it forever and I even cried a little when I shoveled the dirt over it. But I didn't think about it again after. I cheated. I chose the stuffed animal I knew I could stand to lose.

Ron buried a bag of collectible coins. You said it wasn't special and he said it was the most valuable thing he owned. Kyle buried an old skate board; I'm sure he did it so he could dig the biggest hole. Putty buried his raccoon tail and you didn't say anything about it. And then you stood by your hole and told us you were burying your mom.

You pulled the gold heart pendant out of your pocket and held it up by the chain. Then you dropped it into the hole and covered it with dirt. We all stood quiet for a while. It was a horrible thing to say you were burying your mother. And I was confused. You were saying she was the most important thing in your life, the thing you couldn't live without. But she was a crazy woman who neglected you and let you run around in a dirty diaper and let Celia and Mr. Haverty take care of you. Then I thought maybe you thought she'd infected you so you had to get rid of her. I wondered if you made up the whole game just to do that.

Then Kyle said, "Well that was stupid. What do we do now?"

We left our shovels in the dirt and walked out past the junkyard to the railroad tracks and sat between the rails. You and the boys smoked cigarettes and Kyle swore he stole a snake from the pet store but you didn't believe him. He said you should come over to his trailer and see it, but you wouldn't do it. You accused him of lying.

"Why didn't you tell us before?" You said.

"I didn't decide to tell anybody until just now."

But you said you weren't going to his trailer to see a

snake that probably didn't exist. It would turn out to be a fake, or after you got there, Kyle would say he was joking and try to pretend he never said he stole a snake.

Then he said you were scared of snakes and you got up and started hitting him. Ron made you stop and then he and Kyle left with Mary. Putty walked along the tracks south, said maybe he would walk all the way to Miami and I asked you about your mom.

"Do you think she's all right?"

You said no.

"Do you miss her?"

You shook your head. "She was crazy."

The next weekend, Mary came and got me at my trailer; she was crying.

"They're all gone," she said. She took me out to the lot to where our shovels still lay in the dirt and all the holes were dug up and our treasures were gone. "I didn't take them," she said. "I swear."

Her mom told her she had to get the necklace back so she came out and dug up her hole, but she couldn't find it, so she started digging them all up and everybody's stuff was gone. We decided Kyle had done it and we found you boys over at the dead end on Beaumont Road behind the trailer park and you all said you didn't have anything to do with it. We all went back out and dug around in the lot but the stuff was gone.

And later that day, you were sitting with Wilder and Manning just outside the front gate of the junkyard while everybody else was eating dinner and I sat with you and told you I was sorry about your mom's heart and you said you loved me.

You said, "You're the one who understands."

The sun was behind us and the fence cast a slanted shadow on the dirt road in front of us and we were warped and leaning and I remember thinking there were parts missing somewhere and I didn't know if I'd misplaced them or you had. And the thought came to me, maybe because of Bishop and the way Ruby tensed up whenever he pulled a beer out of the refrigerator.

"Did your dad hurt your mom?" I said.

You got mad. "Why would you say that?"

I said I didn't know and told you about Bishop. I was at the little kitchen table in my trailer trying to do my math and he was helping me but he was drunk and didn't know what eight times seven was and he broke his beer bottle on the table and hit me with it and Ruby got in front of him and told me to run.

I showed you where he hit me and you said it would bruise.

"It's good he didn't cut you."

"Ruby gets hit," I told you. "Instead of me. Did your mom do that?"

You said no. She did it all herself and your dad wouldn't let you see most of it. And you said you loved him. "He's the best dad anybody ever had."

I said I loved Bishop, too.

It was much later, when the school year was almost done, that you hit Sunny in the face. We were all walking out in the scrub and you'd brought the dogs, and Wilder jumped up on her and she screamed and cursed at you. She said, "Why do you have to bring your stupid dogs everywhere."

147

Everybody thought that was dumb and said so. You didn't bring them everywhere. You left them home most of the time. But Sunny was always saying stuff like that—stuff that was wrong. And you told her if she didn't like the dogs she should go on back home and she said your dogs were monsters, just like you.

So you hit her.

She fell, landed on her butt, and sat there with her mouth open staring at everybody and nobody moved—we were stuck like that for a while, but not because we were shocked. We were tired. Mary got her up and walked her home. She didn't even bother to glare at you or shove you.

It was suggested that Sunny deserved it. Ron said you weren't supposed to hit girls and later that day, out by the pool, we all had an argument about it and ended up agreeing that if girls could hit boys, boys ought to be able to hit them. But when she turned out to have a black eye, Sunny told her mom a girl she met at the park down the way hit her. Because everybody knew it was okay for a girl to hit a girl.

And you told me the heavy thing wasn't even talking to you now—you were doing it all by yourself. But you would forget.

23.

You'd dug the gold heart out of your backpack and were looking at it when I finished telling you about fifth grade.

"Did I steal it all?" You said.

I didn't know. I don't think any of us ever saw that stuff again, but there was your gold heart, still on the chain. Jericho was shaking his head. He got up and said you two ought to walk down the way and get something to eat and wash up. You went with him and I watched the two of you for a while, waiting for you to turn and look back at me, but you didn't.

The next morning I opened the bait shop for Celia. The sun steamed the moisture in the air and we were hoping for rain. Even with the air conditioner, the store was hot. I had the big fans running and the little one on the counter by the register, too. It would look like rain all that day; nothing would come of it but a muggy mess of sticky, suffocating breezes.

Your dad came in. He was wearing little shorts and a tank top and sweating, his face flushed; he'd walked all the way from the junkyard. He smiled at me, and I tried to smile back, but it was tempered with a sadness I didn't understand. He stood at the little counter looking around the store, rubbing his head with his hand, leaving his comb over in wisps of gray hair sticking up on the edges of his bald spot.

"Did you give him the heart?" He asked me.

I said I did.

"Did you tell him he ought to come home?"

I couldn't remember if I'd told you or not, but I nodded.

"I should go out there," he said.

"I don't think that's a good idea."

"Did he say I did something? Is it because of me?"

"No."

He just stared at me. He wanted more, so I told him what I'd been thinking. I said, "You know he's been in trouble his whole life. Maybe you don't know all of it; we don't tell our parents every bad thing we do." He chuckled a little bit at that. "I think something's happened, that's all. He's done a bad thing and it scared him. It made him take the bike into the lake. And now he's forgotten it all."

"He ain't said what he did?"

"He can't remember. Maybe he won't ever remember."

He was quiet for a second or two and then said, "Maybe that's best."

"Nobody blames you," I said.

His eyes twitched for a second and I thought he and I were thinking the same thing. It was what everybody ended up saying every time you got into trouble. It all went back to your mom. How could a kid be straight when he starts out with a mother like that? And I could see the guilt in your father's eyes. I could hear Celia in my head; she was saying, "Poor Digger."

I suppose I was always too young to consider it, but now I see that, for the trailer park anyway, your dad did the right thing. If he'd had her locked up, they'd have said he was heartless. If he kicked her out, left her on the streets, they'd have called him criminal. He did good by keeping her and trying to make the best of it. It ruined you, they all realized, but they couldn't fault your dad for it. I haven't asked them what they think now. Lately when they sit out at the picnic tables by the pool, they skip the reminiscing. Every memory is now suspect, layered with doubt. And Celia watches me. When I say something now she's thinking, wondering what's true and what isn't.

"You did the best you could," I told your dad.

He dug the charm out of his pocket and handed it to me. I recognized the flat silver oval—attached to one of those chains made up of little balls—with the word promise pressed into it. I'd be telling you about it the next time I saw you.

"Would you give this to him?" Your dad said. "Tell him he should come on home. Everything will be okay if he just comes home."

When I got out into the scrub that afternoon, you and Jericho were gone. I sat with Boxcar under the oak and fed him some bologna. Then I let him off his leash and watched him sniff out places to pee. You and Jericho came up from the south carrying open beers and you had the six-pack in your other hand. Jericho saw Boxcar and started yelling.

151

"What the hell you go and do that for?"

He limped over and chased Boxcar around cursing at me the whole time and I looked at you as you came up under the little tree but you didn't seem to notice what was going on. You sat down in the dirt next to me and put the cool can against your forehead while the old man screamed at me. Dark clouds angered the sky in front of us and I said a little prayer for rain; I knew it would make Jericho sicker, but you were weakened by the heat—it was sweating the life out of you.

Having caught Boxcar and chained him again to the tree, Jericho sat and glared at me. "You ain't got no right to let my dog go without asking."

"You shouldn't have a dog. You can't even keep him fed."

It was true. The dog was lean, like Jericho, and hungry. He'd probably gained a few pounds in the days I'd been bringing sandwiches and you'd been buying them both meals in town.

"That ain't your concern," the old man said.

"And Jack and me aren't yours, so why don't you just move on?"

"This here's a free country and I can do what I like. And I don't hear Jack telling me to move on. You want he should stay out here all by hisself when you ain't here?"

We were both looking at you but you stared out to the railroad tracks and beyond at the coming storm. Finally, you said you remembered something. You'd caught hold of it in your head.

"It was that story you told," you said to me. "About

that girl, Sunny."

I was scared then, but I told myself I should have been prepared for it. How often does a person lose his whole lifetime of memories and never get them back?

And Jericho said, "What was it?"

You told us you saw yourself sitting in the trailer at the junkyard—on one end the sofa, staring at the television but it wasn't turned on. Mr. Beaumont sat in his boxer shorts and tank top, drinking a beer. He was angry—talking to you about Sunny and you were confused.

"What about?" Jericho asked you, when it seemed like you weren't going to say any more.

You shook your head. "I'm not sure. I told him I was just trying to see what it was like."

"What *what* was like?" Jericho said.

"I don't know. I just said the words. And the man said, 'it don't work that way. You don't do that to the people you know.'"

I was relieved and disappointed at the same time. I was going to ask it, but Jericho did it first.

He said, "Why would you remember that?"

And I said, "Maybe that's all his brain will let him have."

You looked at me funny then, like I knew something I shouldn't but you couldn't figure out what. I don't know why I said it. Maybe by that time I'd convinced myself you'd blocked it all out for yourself. You'd decided you couldn't live with the things you'd done and you wanted to forget them. I knew it would all come back to you at some point; it had to. And I wanted to make it easier to forget again, once you came around and had your life back. I thought that was the answer to the bad things—learn to forget them. I didn't realize there was something worse, something you had to forget just to be sane.

Jericho tried to have you do that thing again where you close your eyes and say the words that the flashes of memory bring to you, but you sat still and quiet instead and finally said you couldn't get hold of anything. You wanted me to tell you another story.

"And this time, don't leave anything out."

I started to say something. I wanted to know why you thought I was leaving stuff out. But Jericho was eyeing me and I thought maybe I'd leave it alone. And anyway, I had a good story to tell for sixth grade and I was glad your father helped me remember it.

24.

That night, still on the eighth day you were gone, Tucker Reed met me in front of the laundromat and drove us down south to a little pizza place. We didn't say much. I caught him looking at my chest once and he blushed and swore he was looking at my cross. His sister wore a cross, he said. But she left it at home—it was too precious a thing to risk losing. He asked me how strong was my faith and I said it was like climbing uphill, but Ruby says the struggle makes us stronger. He smiled. It was one of those smiles I'd seen on your face sometimes. Knowing and kindness, pity, and hope all wrapped up in it.

After dinner, he drove us to the motel. We walked next door and bought a six-pack at the little store and took it to his room. We sat at a little round wobbly table in oversized padded dining chairs, in front of the air conditioner with the curtains open so we could watch what he called the bums and hookers walk past and we drank beers. He asked me a few questions, did I go to college, did I like working at the bait shop, did I fish, but eventually he got around to telling me about her.

Nobody could hold her back. Jessica was a free spirit.

He said it's a family legend that she ran around naked for the first four years of her life. Refused to wear clothes. And once she started, she didn't like anything to match, except for the purple.

"She had an entire purple outfit," he said. "The first time she wore it to school in fourth grade, our mom was shocked. She'd managed to find everything in her room that was purple. Even showed us her underwear, purple. And Mom said 'If I'd have known you were going to wear all the purple at one time, I'd never have bought the socks and underwear.' And Dad was worried she'd get bullied for it. He kept saying, 'Are you sure you want to wear it?' But she did."

"Even her shoes?"

"Yes, even the shoes. But she'd colored those with a marker." He laughed. "She always did what she wanted to do."

He told me she never did what any of the other girls were doing, or liked the things they liked, and you'd think it would make her an outcast, but somehow it didn't.

"She was really nice, and funny. People wanted to be around her."

He kept talking about her in the past tense, like she was dead and I didn't stop him. He said she was smart, too. Valedictorian of her class in high school. He told me all about sports and trophies and jobs and she started to sound unreal. I hadn't sipped my beer in a long while—I'd been watching him and he finally trailed off and stared at his fingers as they peeled the label off his bottle. Then he chuckled and shook his head, guzzled the beer and wiped his mouth.

"I've made her too perfect, haven't I?"

"She is or she isn't."

"That's not the way it is at all."

He turned in his chair and kicked off his shoes, then got up and pulled his wallet out of his pants and tossed it over onto the bed. He started to sit again, but instead, went to the wallet and opened it up. He came back to the table and put a picture on it.

"That's one I brought for identification."

Jessica wasn't what I'd expected at all and I think it showed on my face. I picked up the picture and stared at if for a long time. I imagined her as a girl version of Tucker. Straight blond hair, thin, symmetrical face with those straight, dominant brows, and the green eyes. But Jessica had short, curly brown hair and her face was wide, her cheeks pudgy. I could see what he was saying when I studied her. She had this smile, this look to her brown eyes, that said she was honest, that she'd never tease you, or hurt you.

"What did you mean?" I asked him. "About it not being that way?"

He took the photo from me and looked at it for a few seconds before he put it on the table and leaned the chair back, balancing it on two legs, rubbing one hand through his hair.

"She was my idol," he said. "For a long time. And everybody said she was the best big sister a guy could have. But she wasn't perfect."

I almost sighed with relief.

"She wouldn't want it that way. She'd want me to remember all of her."

"You don't know she's gone," I said. But my voice was losing its certainty.

"She's been gone for ten years," he said.

25.

Things started to change during the summer before sixth grade. Putty was working, mowing lawns. An older girl moved in to River Front Trailer Haven and she and Mary got to be friends, but she didn't want the rest of us around. Her mother would drop them off at the mall up north a ways and they'd shop all day without buying anything. They never invited me along. Kyle's dad was arrested and his mom took him off to Orlando to live with his grandmother for a while. We didn't see him again until the next year and by then he was a drunk. And you were spending more time with your dad on the weekends–helping with the junkyard and riding out with him making pickups. Some days when we were all together, except Kyle, we'd trudge out to the lake or the tracks, or walk down U.S. 1 until we found something to do. But most of the time it was just me and Ron at the pool or watching television.

We'd sometimes see you and your dad in the truck, heading to U.S. 1 on a Saturday morning. Every once in a while there would be a girl with you on the way back to the junkyard and we'd always promise to tease you about it, but we never did. We'd forget it by the time we saw you again. We told Celia and the others about it once and they winked and smirked.

And Ron blurted out, "Why would Mr. Beaumont bring his date to the junkyard?"

The adults all laughed.

Pat Dunn, lot eight, said, "I think it's sweet."

It was sweet, really. Celia and some of the other women got together and went to Mrs. Swanson, the owner, and asked her if there wasn't an empty lot available for half price. They planned to go over and ask your dad if he wouldn't like to move off the junkyard and into the trailer park. They said they'd offer to help him fix up a nice trailer where he'd be proud to have a lady over. But I don't know if they ever talked to him about it or not. Either way, you two never moved over there.

Mr. Haverty summed it up perfectly. He said, "He's a junkyard man. It's written all over him."

Now that I'm writing it down, I'm trying to imagine you as a junkyard man and it's not working. I wonder if your dad ever saw that–if he knew somehow you'd never be like him. He tried to make you fit into his mold, but it wouldn't take. I wonder if he kept trying right up until the end. Is that what happened?

Anyway, the ladies of Trailer Haven were alarmed. They spent hours out at the picnic tables trying to figure out a way to talk to your dad, to tell him if he wanted a relationship, he shouldn't bring the woman home to see the junkyard so soon. He had to let love blossom first, they said. A lot of love, Celia said. It would take heaps of it to overcome the sight of all that junk and those awful trailers and sheds. He had to drive her around in one of the old sedans he had over at the yard, not the truck—heaven knows the truck's not the thing. He had to buy a suit or some slacks and dress shoes. He could meet the lady at the flea market, they said, but he shouldn't take her back there, wearing his overalls, for a date.

"Maybe he doesn't want a wife," I said one day and they all stared at me with their mouths open.

"A man needs a wife," Pat Dunn said.

"Maybe he loves Jack too much to give him a stepmother." Because of course, everybody who watched Disney movies knew stepmothers were evil.

They laughed at me. "It don't work that way," Celia said. "Adults need companionship; that's all there is to it."

When school started again you were fine for a long time. And then one day in January, you came up to the bus stop pale and sickly. Dark circles hollowed out your eye sockets and you stood dazed and unsteady. You wouldn't talk to us and Putty put his arm around you and walked you away a bit; he stuck by you all that day as best he could. I heard you vomited after lunch and went to the clinic, but no one could reach your dad so you stayed there all afternoon. But you weren't on the bus home, so I guess he came and got you.

We didn't see you for a while after that and I kept asking Putty about it and he said you were sick. When you showed up again at the bus stop on a Monday, you were wearing one of those ball chains soldiers have their dog tags on, and Sunny went to lift the charm off your chest and you shoved her off you. Then you grabbed her and flung her to the ground and kicked her. She scuttled away from you like a crab and Putty stood in front of you, making sure you stopped.

We were all scared. And Putty reminded you that you had to hold it together once you got on the bus and you said you were okay. You apologized to Sunny and she said she only wanted to look at it. You pulled the chain over your head and handed it to her. She showed it around to everyone at the bus stop and we all wanted to know where you got it from.

You said your dad found it and gave it to you. It was part of your pact. We didn't know what that meant and you said, "Me and him. We stick together."

Ron laughed a little and I think that just made you dislike him more. But I knew what Ron was thinking because I was thinking it, too. Your dad probably found a woman to marry him and he gave you the charm to make you feel better about it. Even if Putty did say later that it was sissy. He never told *you* that, of course. But he said he'd never wear a necklace.

He did though, didn't he? Do you remember when he had that girlfriend in eleventh grade and she made him wear the gold chain with half a heart on it? You were good enough not to laugh at him to his face.

When I saw you later, you took my hand and looked at the back of it, rubbing my knuckles with your thumb.

"Why do I hurt Sunny?" You said.

"The thing inside you makes you do it. It's a demon."

"A demon?"

I nodded. "My dad's got one and it makes him hurt my mom. He loves my mom."

"And I love Sunny," you said.
But you would forget.

26.

That's it?" You said, when I was finished.

"What do you mean?"

"He didn't do anything terrible. Just knocked her down."

It was startling, again, the way you talked about yourself.

"There now, see?" Jericho said. "It ain't all bad. Ever body grows up."

"What's that mean?" I asked him.

"Youth is fleeting; it does not define a man. But what a man does with the scars of the past make him who he is."

I wanted to be cruel and ask the him why, if the bad doesn't define us, wasn't he back home in Texas being the right sort of man? But I was looking at you, instead, and you were staring off at the railroad tracks again. I tried to tell myself you were only watching the storm, but I got the feeling you were remembering something and I wished you wouldn't. I wished you'd never remember and I wished I could stop telling you stories.

Then you turned to me and said, "Does it get better after that?"

"Maybe we should stop."

"What for?"

"I don't want to tell any more."

"You have to," you said. You were angry; there was desperation in your eyes and it scared me. "You have to keep going."

"Why?"

"I have to know."

"You'll remember," I said. "Soon, it'll all come back."

"No, I want you to keep telling me."

I looked at Jericho, thinking he'd help me; he'd be on my side. "This is bad, isn't it?" I said. "I shouldn't be telling him."

"Well, now," the old man said. "Seems to me you started something and it won't be right to stop, just like that. Especially with him wanting to know."

I sighed and then I heard the rain. We all looked up at the same time to see a gray curtain of water moving toward us.

"Quick," you said.

Jericho told me to get up and he grabbed Boxcar, while you pulled one of the blue tarps off the rosemary bushes and laid it out on the ground. We all sat on it and pulled the back of it over our heads and watched the wall of rain coming toward us.

"It's beautiful," Jericho said.

When the first drops hit we held the tarp farther onto our heads but still watched until the downpour pelted us and we pulled it all the way over, tucked it under our legs, and sat on the edge. Boxcar moved to your lap and licked me before turning around and swatting my face with his

166

tail. He whined and Jericho calmed him. The downpour roared in our ears and we struggled to breathe in the hot moldy plastic air.

Jericho yelled over the din. "They say happiness isn't ours because there is no rain, but that it is ours when we learn to dance in it. But there's no shame in longing for sunshine." Then he started singing a slow sort of song that could have been a prayer.

After about ten minutes, the rain settled to a sprinkle and we tossed the tarp off us and sucked in big gulps of steamy fresh air until we were dizzy. I asked if I could have one of the beers. We'd left them out in the rain and now they were spattered with mud. You twisted a can out of the plastic ring and pulled the tab for me. I took a sip and shuddered; the beer was only mildly cool.

"You want to know about seventh grade then," I said.

You both nodded and I looked at Jericho. I tried to tell him, with my eyes. I wanted to warn him somehow. He carried that book and quoted from it a lot and he believed he'd found the truth that everybody was searching for and saw himself as a prophet. He thought he could help you.

"In seventh grade," I started. "You were drinking almost every weekend–Kyle had come back from Orlando a drunk and you and Putty took it up with him. Your dad was paying you for the work you did at the junkyard. He paid you a lot and you said he had three extra refrigerators in one of the sheds and you paid him to get you beer–all the beer you wanted."

We went to the middle school that year. One weekend in April, we walked way far south to this nice neighborhood where they had a park with a pond and a playground. Kyle stole a bottle of rum from his dad and we drank it with sodas we got at the Pebble Sands Convenience Store and Hair Salon. Kyle taught us to drink a little out of the soda bottle and then pour in some rum and drink a little more and the more we drank, the more we were left with just rum.

Mary vomited while she was swinging and then laughed and vomited again. Then you made Sunny smoke from your cigarette and she didn't vomit and I think you liked that. But on the way home, while Kyle and Putty played chicken with the cars on the highway, you put your arm around my shoulder and whispered in my ear that you loved me.

The next morning we were all sick from drinking the rum. The adults thought something was going around and none of us ever told the truth. I remember it because the police came by again and you had just come over to my trailer to see where I was. Mr. Haverty and Celia stood out there with you and when I heard the voices, I came out and sat on the front steps, wrapping my arms around myself to keep steady.

The police were talking to you; you looked so small and thin and they towered over you. And Celia was saying, "I don't think you ought to ask the boy questions without his father here."

They said it was nothing, just routine. Your mom's sister asked that her case be reopened and they'd come around to see if there was any new information. They asked you about her. Was she happy, did you know where she'd gone, did she say anything to you when she left?

You were saying, no. No, I don't know anything. I don't know. And Celia put a stop to it.

"He told you already," she said. "He don't know anything about it."

After the police left, you stood there for a bit, staring off into nothing and then you said, "I hope they don't bother my dad about it."

"Does he still miss her?" I said.

"When he remembers."

"You're a good boy to worry about him," Celia said. "But he's a grown man; he'll be fine."

"I love my dad." It sounded hollow, like you were distracted and saying it from memory.

Celia said, "Of course you do. Your dad is a good man. Don't let the cops scare you one bit."

And Mr. Haverty said, "That's right. What they do, you see, is dig at people until they confess to things they didn't even do. Why you should see some of the stuff those cops do."

"That's enough," Celia said.

"Never talk to the cops, son."

"I said that's enough."

I got up and followed you over to the picnic tables and you said, "My dad says the same thing."

"What?"

"Don't talk to the cops."

I nodded even though I wasn't sure. Everybody was uneasy all day and the adults gathered around the tables with us whispering about your mother.

"What do you suppose ever happened to her?" Pat Dunn said.

"If she wanted to disappear, she did a good job." Celia said.

"Maybe she walked out into the river. Did anybody ever think of that?" Mr. Haverty said.

And then they all shushed one another and glanced at you.

A few weeks later, we all walked over to the junkyard to get you and we knew something was wrong as soon as we turned onto Beaumont Road. It took us about thirty yards before Kyle figured it out.

"The dogs aren't barking," he said.

You weren't out front, so we wandered around the perimeter and found you out in the scrub digging a big hole. The dogs' bodies, three of them, bloodied and stiff, lay together on a blue tarp nearby; it had a rope knotted into two of the grommets on one side.

We all stood there, staring, and you went back to digging. It took some time before we could speak.

Putty said, "What happened?"

"I shot 'em," you said.

"Why?"

"Tired of the noise."

You raged inside, I could tell. Your jaw was set so hard I thought it might crack. You wouldn't look at us or the dogs and when you finished digging, you tossed the shovel to the ground, grabbed the rope and hauled the tarp over to the hole. The dogs slid in with a heavy thud.

"Your dad'll just get more dogs, won't he?" Ron said.

"You think he'll get puppies?" Mary said.

They all sat in the dirt and talked about what sorts of dogs would be the best for junkyarding and mauling strangers, but I watched you fill in the hole and beat the dirt with the back of the shovel. Then you flung it away, another one left out in the scrub to rust, and turned toward home.

"It didn't make a damn bit of difference," you said, when I caught up with you. "It only made it worse."

27.

When I finished talking, you were up and walking back and forth in front of us— Boxcar at your heels—kicking up sand occasionally. You shoved your hands into your jeans pockets and hunched your shoulders up like you were in pain. You seemed yourself, then—you were Jack.

"Aw," Jericho said. "It ain't as bad as all that."

But you wouldn't look at us; you took a few extra steps and kicked at the base of a scrub palmetto, setting its fans waving.

"Why you got to tell him bad stories?" Jericho said. "There's got to be some good. Tell him something good."

You stopped then and looked at me. My breath caught in my throat. Your eyes weren't empty, you didn't look blank. I thought you knew me, but you were tired and didn't want to fight anymore. I knew that look, but I didn't know if it meant anything.

"You were a good friend," I said. "*Are.* You are a good friend."

I told you and Jericho about the times you helped out Putty and Kyle—with their school work, fixing their bicycles, giving their families refurbished stuff from the junkyard. You always had a tool to share with Mr. Haverty when he needed to fix something in somebody's trailer. And I told you about Peter Callahan, lot sixteen, and how when he was six and learning to read, you would sit with him at the picnic tables and listen to him while he read books out loud and you'd tell him what a good reader he was.

"See there, why don't you tell those sorts of stories?" Jericho whined. "The nice things he done?"

"You're a good person, Jack," I said. "But you didn't lose your mind because of the good you did. I think you did something bad and it scared the life out of you. Whatever you did, whether it was a long time ago and it's been nagging at you, or just a few days ago, you're going to have to figure it out and come around and then we can fix it."

"Well, you ain't helping by making him feel like he's bad," the old man said.

"Leave her alone," you said.

Jericho was hurt, I could tell. He tugged on the rope to drag Boxcar away from you and back to him and offered the dog some water in his plastic bowl. I sat there watching him lap it up, splashing onto Jericho's dirty cotton pants. I thought you understood—you knew the crazy in your head had to be caused by something bad and you were trying to find it in the stories.

The two of you decided to walk to the plaza and wash up at the gas station again so I went home. I felt heavy, like the tired in your eyes had infected me. I wanted to lie down and put my pillow over my head and make it all go away. I hadn't thought of it that way until then—I was
174

making myself sick in telling it all. It was worse, I think, because you weren't absorbing any of it. I was trying to give these memories back to you and you wouldn't take them.

Anyway, Ruby would say the same as your dad—about not talking to the cops. She'd told me plenty never to call them and when I did, I got into trouble. One time when Bishop beat her senseless and then went into the kitchen and got a knife, I screamed and fell on top of her and begged him not to kill her. I was ten that time and I'd heard them arguing about some money he thought she was going to give him. He grabbed me by the arm and pushed me into the back bedroom.

"I'll tell you who I'm going to kill," he said. "You, if you come out of this room."

Ruby's phone was on the bed, so I called. By the time the police showed up, Bishop was gone. He'd cut off all her hair and she stood on the front steps, the door wide open, her hands smoothing out what was left of it, her upper lip split and bleeding, telling the cops it was nothing. She'd fallen out of the shower and hit her face on the toilet. She'd already hit me with a belt and warned me to keep my mouth shut so I was sitting on the couch inside. I could see one of the cops peering through the doorway at me. He smiled and I turned away.

"Don't ever do that to me again," she said after they left.

She went into her bedroom and I went out to the picnic tables where all the neighbors talked in whispers and patted me on the back and said these were personal matters, adult matters, and I shouldn't get involved.

"But he had a knife," I told Old Man Pinkerton. "He was going to kill her."

"Of course he wasn't," he said.

"Don't you worry about that," Mrs. Cleary said. "They got troubles but...don't you worry about that."

When I got home from the scrub that day, still thinking about the story I'd told, about the dead dogs and the shovel sliding into the dirt, Ruby was getting ready to leave. Her face was all painted up and she smelled like the sickly sweet jasmine that bloomed all over the trailer park at night.

"Where are you going?"

She sighed. "Don't argue with me. I'm going to see your dad; I don't know if I'm coming back tonight."

I made a face. I couldn't help it; dread and fear mixed up with disgust are the sorts of emotions that come out somehow, whether we want to hide them or not.

"Well, you went and told Celia," she said. "So why should I try to hide it anymore?"

"Did he invite you?"

"What is that supposed to mean?"

She knew what it meant. She'd accused me of the same, plenty of times. "You never wait for Jack to ask you," she'd say. "He don't ever have to make an effort."

"What about your statistics?" I said.

"What are you talking about now?" She was standing in the kitchen, putting two packages of steak into a flimsy plastic grocery bag.

"Women who have children young, have daughters who do the same thing," I said. "Women who are abused by their husbands have daughters who are more likely to get into abusive relationships."

"Stop it." She took her bag of steaks and her pack of cigarettes and went to the door.

"Women are more likely to be killed by their husbands than the other way around."

She was at the door, ready to step out, when she laughed. "Well, of course they are," she said. "Men are stronger than women." She hesitated and I thought maybe she'd decided to stay home. "He's changed," she said. "He's older now. You'll see."

"But you said they don't change."

She shook her head and looked at me like I'd disappointed her. And then she left.

I was in my room that evening when Celia came home. She wanted me to come out and eat a sandwich, but my head was throbbing. I fell asleep and woke up at four. I found Celia in the kitchen getting ready to go and open the bait shop.

"Your mom ain't here," she said.

"I know."

"She's with Bishop, isn't she?"

I nodded.

"He isn't changed," she said. "He won't. It'll end up same as always." She pulled her gray hair behind her head and wrapped it up in a scrunchie. Patting me on the cheek, she said, "You don't have to be like your mother, you know."

"We can't help turning out the way we do."

"Nonsense. You're in control of your own destiny."

"I don't know." I sat down at the little table and sipped the orange juice she'd poured for me. "Seems to me we get on a path and there's not much we can do to stop it. It's like a train barreling down the tracks. We don't have enough braking power and anyway, there's only one way to go."

"That's no way to look at it."

"And if the path is a bad one, and you don't know anything different...how is a person to overcome it?"

"Then how do you explain Ruby? She didn't start out on a bad path. I did right by her."

"Why do you think it was you?"

"Everybody knows it's the mother who ruins the child."

"What about her dad?"

Her face fell into a frown and she put her hand to my cheek again and this time held it there, her thumb stroking my chin. "I see what you're saying," she said. "But I still mean it. You can turn out any way you want to."

When I got back out to the scrub, Jericho was saying, "Love is both a blessing and a curse, and if you can stand the curse, you'll find it true as any truth that can be known." And I was going to tell you that didn't make any sense and you should be careful what you believe. But it sounded profound–it sounded true. I decided I'd ask Ruby about it, but I'd forgotten what he said by the time I got home that day. And when I found the quote later, in his book, I didn't have to ask her. Because I was sure I understood it.

I sat down just as he was finishing his quote and he was looking at me and smiling like he'd said something really important and I ignored him on purpose. I feel bad about it now.

I said, "None of this matters all that much. What happened before, it's gone. The future is all that's important, and you can turn out any way you want to."

Jericho frowned.

"I know you don't think it's so," I said. "And maybe you're right about some things. I can't be an astronaut–at least I don't think I can. But that doesn't mean I can't turn my life in a new direction. Maybe some people can't." My voice faded and I looked at you, hoping you would understand what I was trying to say. But I suppose if I didn't know what I was talking about, you couldn't either.

"Almost," Jericho said. "If you accept who you are, and what you done, you can make the best of it. But there's always going to be that core–that center formed way back when, whether it be in your biology or in your upbringing–the very essence of who you are. That, you can't change. That, you got to learn to work with."

"But people *can* change," I said.

"To a point."

I'm learning we can live our whole lives with contradiction. Some things can be true and not true, true for you and not for me, true when we want them to be and not true when we don't. That might be one of those things we have to accept.

You were tired, and full but not with understanding; at least, you said you still couldn't remember. You had pieces but not enough to make a picture. When you would stare off to the tracks and frown, it seemed to me you had some pictures and you just didn't like them.

179

"Well, go on then," Jericho said. "Eighth grade, ain't it?"

"Tell me the bad stuff," you said.

"Why?"

"I don't know. Just do it."

That softness you'd had in the beginning, that—what is the word? The way you looked like you needed me, like you were lost, it was being siphoned off somehow and that sharp edge of yours was starting to come back. I couldn't tell you, honestly, if I was glad or not. But I knew I would never be able to tell eighth grade exactly right because of it.

28.

We were all you, in the eighth grade. I mean, we'd started acting like we kids from the trailer park were what the other kids thought we were: tough, mean, hard—like you. Even Mary, pretty as she was, had a raw anger about her and she was learning to use it, setting herself apart, demanding attention. We'd walk the halls side by side and everybody had to scoot around us—they were afraid of us, of you and Kyle and Putty, anyway, and the rest of us by association.

That year, your dad brought a girl to the trailer park block party. He'd been a few times in years past, sitting just a bit separate from everybody else, far enough to seem shy and close enough to get in on conversation when somebody would try. And everybody would always say, after he left, that it was so good of him to try, for your sake. But that year, he surprised them all.

Rosaleah was much younger than she ought to be, so Celia said after the two of them left. She wore very short shorts and a gray tank top that I was sure was supposed to be white, with a red bra underneath it, peeking out over the neckline, its straps clear as day on her shoulders and back.

"If that's the fashion these days," Ruby said later.

She had tattoos on her arms and legs and one of a butterfly on her neck just under her right ear. Her nose, lip, ears, and one eyebrow were pierced. She didn't talk much, but when she did, she'd nod and smile and then look at your dad as if she needed his approval. She was a little slow, like she was more relaxed than a person ought to be, the way you and Putty got when you smoked pot. She wasn't at all the way I thought she should be. Her outside didn't match her inside, and the way she kept looking at your dad, I guessed that was what love did to a person.

The boys, even Ron, spent much more time sitting with the adults that year and they stared at Rosaleah like they were hungry. I caught your dad smiling at them once and he winked at me. But you didn't like her. You didn't have to say anything. You sat over by the pool in a lawn chair glaring at her and your dad most of the day.

A week or so later, at the bus stop, Kyle asked you about her, wondered if your dad was going to marry her. You glared at him and wouldn't say anything. We never saw her again. I told Celia about it, and about you staring at her like you wished she would leave and not come back. She said you were normal enough, but I thought it was sad and told you so a few days later.

"Why don't you tell your dad it's okay to get another wife?"

"We're not going to talk about my dad anymore," you said.

And we didn't.

At school, a girl named Corey started following you

around and trying to be our friend; she even wanted to ride the bus home with us one time. You ignored her most of the time, but Mary saw the two of you behind the school once with your hands on each other. You kept telling Corey to leave you alone and Mary said, "As long as you're making out with her behind the portables, she'll stick around."

After that, you made her go away. And she stayed gone, until the dance at the end of the year. We had to get dressed up for it. Mr. Haverty and Mrs. Fogarty pitched in with our parents to get us dresses and suits and fancy shoes at the secondhand stores and Mrs. Swanson did all the hemming and tailoring. Mary said we looked good, but Kyle said we were trying too hard to be like everybody else.

"We should wear the clothes we have," he said.

"Nobody's wearing the clothes they have," Ron said.

Celia drove us all over in Old Man Pinkerton's van and dropped us off at the school and when she picked us up at midnight, she knew right away something had happened. She drove home, looking at us in the rearview mirror a lot of the time. The straps were ripped off my dress, my updo was down, and there was mud all over me. Mary's dress was ripped up the sides, she was still holding the seam together with her hand. The butterfly clip in her hair was barely hanging on. She'd been smart enough to stay out of the mud.

The boys sat quiet, tiny smiles on their lips. Even Ron couldn't help himself. You were the only one not smiling, but then, that was to be expected since the whole thing started with Corey dumping you.

It was almost as if the girl had planned it. Corey was there, dressed in this slinky tight pink thing and she went straight for you as soon as we walked into the gym together. She pulled you out onto the floor in the dimly lit room and started dancing and you went along. She knew you wanted her. Maybe she thought you telling her to go away was flirting. Maybe it was. She had her hands on your face, down your shoulders, on your hips, pressing herself up against you and swaying, and you were wrapped up in it, I could tell.

We lost sight of you for most of the night, catching glimpses now and then of you and Corey at the snack tables, sitting up on the bleachers, wrapped around each other on the dance floor. About the time the lights started going up, a ripple flowed through the ocean of teenagers; a tide drove us all toward you and Corey and she was laughing at you and calling you trash and saying she wouldn't go out with you even if you took a shower. I'd pushed my way through to see you standing there, your fists balled up tight at your sides, your jaw taut, ready to strike at her. But Mr. Lew, the principal, and some of the chaperones plowed through and made us all 'disperse.'

Outside, I caught up with her over in the grass by the sidewalk and jumped her. Mary, too. It didn't last long. Long enough for a little crowd to hide us from the chaperones, and for us to pull Corey's dress down and expose her breasts–not on purpose, honest–but not long enough for us to get caught. Corey limped away, carrying one shoe, and turned to you as she passed.

She said, "Getting the girls to fight for you, very classy."

And they all laughed at us. All of them. The boys didn't mind so much, but Mary started crying before we got to River Front Drive.

"They don't matter," I told her. "They're nothing."

"It's not them," she said. But what else could it have been?

Later that night you snuck Sunny into the junkyard. You wrapped silver duct tape around her mouth, tied her hands together and cut her clothes off. Then you dragged her over to the fence where one of the guard dogs tried to get at her. It leapt at the chain link, growled and barked itself hoarse, froth and saliva hitting you both in the face and you were close to her ear, whispering, "So loud, so loud. No one can hear you screaming."

As soon as Mr. Beaumont cut the tape from her face, she told him and Ron that she asked you to do it. It was just a joke, she said, a joke on Ron. You'd tied her by the hands to one of the old rusted out car bodies near the dog run and left her lying there while you were out in the lot behind the plaza with everybody else, drinking beers and cursing Corey. When Ron asked where Sunny was, you pulled him away from the group and told him, "She's petting the dogs in the run out back." And you laughed.

Ron didn't want to go; he was scared and you knew it. But you knew he'd do it because he liked to be the hero. That's what you said, anyway. You didn't know Ron would get your dad first. And they found Sunny still there curled up under the car; the dog was pacing, watching her, and when he and Mr. Beaumont approached, it threw itself at the fence, snarling and growling.

You told me the next day. You said, "I did something

to Sunny. She didn't like it." And then you forgot about it. The others didn't know what you'd done until the next school year, and by that time it didn't seem so awful. That's the way it works, isn't it? After enough time goes by, and you've seen worse things, you realize it's not as bad as you thought it was.

When I finished the story, you said, "That's a lie."

29.

You jumped up and stalked over to the tracks and kicked at the rails, then turned back.

"Tell the truth," you said.

"I did."

"Did you?" Jericho asked me.

I nodded.

"How do you know it ain't the truth?" He said, turning to you.

Boxcar had waddled out to the end of his rope to get to you but he was only half way. He wagged his tail and whined a bit.

"I just know it. There's more."

"Ain't the way she said it bad enough?" Then the old man turned to me. "Why your stories all got to be like that?"

"Are you sure that's the truth?" You walked over to the dog and squatted down to pet him and rub behind his ears. "There wasn't something else?"

You were worried, confused. I wanted to tell you more then, honest I did. But I couldn't. I don't know if it was because Jericho was there, or if I just couldn't make myself say it out loud. I just know I wasn't able to.

"You tell her you want to hear something good," Jericho said when you finally came back to sit with us under the little oak.

"It's okay," you told him.

"No, it ain't. There ain't no way a boy could have that much bad in him. She's got to be making it up."

"Why would I do that?"

"Who knows? Maybe he done something to you and you're aiming to make him sorry for it. Maybe you're crazy."

"Don't say that," you said. "Don't say crazy."

"Well, it's got to be something. Nobody's got that much bad in his life. Nobody."

"How do you know?" I said.

"One bad thing," he said. "Maybe two. But bad after bad after bad like that? No way. Why you putting all that on this boy here?"

I grabbed two empty water jugs and left. I wanted you to come after me and tell me you'd make Jericho leave, make him move on. He had no business staying there. But you didn't. It was all wrong, you know. I'd known you all your life and Jericho was a stranger and even if you couldn't remember, it was wrong.

As I walked through the scrub I went over it in my head and after a while I realized the memory was blurred and soft like modeling clay, filled with possible outcomes, and I could choose how it would go. For a moment, like a sigh, I wasn't sure any more what was the truth and what wasn't. I wanted to tell someone I was right—it could be done. You just make it different—make the past go away.

I was still mad about Jericho when I got home. I

made dinner for Ruby and Celia, for when they closed up their shops–a tuna noodle casserole. And when Ruby came through the little door she could smell it cooking.

"What's wrong?" She said.

Tuna noodle casserole is our comfort food. We always have the ingredients on hand. Remember that time you stood me up for prom and took somebody else and when you came over at four in the morning, after you let Ruby slap you in the face, you asked me why was I sitting in my pajamas on the couch with a big bowl of mush and what was that awful smell? Those are the things I should have told you out in the scrub. Those stories. So we could laugh and you'd think you were very good, almost perfect.

But that wouldn't work; I knew it wouldn't. You'd remember someday. Maybe not everything, but most of it. And if I didn't give you at least a little bit of the truth, you'd never trust me again.

I told Ruby about Jericho–about how I wished he'd leave you alone so I could take care of you and help you get your head screwed on right. I told her how much I wanted things to be better, for you to be better. I knew you could be renewed somehow and made whole. She didn't say anything for a while; she just sat there on the couch staring at her hands.

"I'm sorry," I said. "I'm not trying to get back with him. Honest."

She got up and went to the little kitchen, pulled open the oven door and took a look at the dinner. "Soon," she said. Then she sat down again beside me. "Maggie, baby. It scares me sometimes, thinking you turned out like me. Celia warned me all the time to make sure you didn't."

"That's not nice, is it?"

"It hurt. When she'd say, 'Don't let Maggie be another Ruby,' I'd hear 'Why can't Ruby be more like Jewel.'"

"Is Aunt Jewel perfect?"

"Nobody on God's earth is perfect, baby."

"But Celia lives with us. I thought she loved us more."

Ruby laughed.

"Really," I said. "I thought we were her favorites."

"She came down here to keep an eye on my girls—your sisters first and then you. Said I wasn't fit. Not as long as I wouldn't give up on your dad."

"Could you have given him up?"

"Maybe. I always thought I had a line somewhere and he got closer and closer to it every year. But maybe I just kept redrawing it."

"Why?"

"Because he loves me." She sat up and took the pack off the coffee table, smacked out a cigarette and lit it. She stayed hunched like that, her elbows on her knees, smoking. "He still loves me. And he's older now; he's changed."

"But you said they never change."

She was filled with worry. "Don't tell Celia I said this, baby, but...if you love him, and if he loves you, you got to fight for it."

Don't tell Celia. There was something sinister about that. If it was the right thing to do, why couldn't I tell Celia?

"How old were you when your dad died?" I asked

her.

She took a long drag on the cigarette and let the smoke float out of her mouth. "Twelve," she said, and the rest of the smoke came out her nose.

"You guys never talk about him."

She leaned back on the couch and looked over at me. "My dad was a lot like Bishop. Handsome and easy going, but he had a temper."

"He didn't hit her?"

"No, no. He never hit anybody. But he could get mad. Hell, we all can get mad. But it didn't matter because he'd always say he was sorry and everything would be great again. And then he was gone. Just like that. One minute he's kissing you good-bye in the morning and the next they're telling you he's dead."

We sat there for a long time while her cigarette turned into a tube of ash. Then she sat straight up and said, "It's almost like love and pain are supposed to go together." She turned to me and laughed. "Ain't that the damnedest thing?"

When Celia came home, we ate our casserole, not talking. Celia was looking back and forth between Ruby and me, like she knew we had secrets, but she didn't say anything. She knew I'd tell sooner or later. I couldn't keep Ruby's secrets any better than Ruby could keep mine—not from Celia.

30.

I was better the next day, calmed a little and not thinking so bad of Jericho. It was good you weren't out there all alone. Heading over to the side gate with the water and some sandwiches and fruit for you and him, I saw Putty at his parents' trailer. He was leaning on the back of his truck chewing on his thumbnail and he pushed himself off to come over when he saw me.

"Here," he said, taking the water jugs from me. "I'll walk with you a ways."

"You going out to see him?"

"I haven't decided. You think I should? You think he remembers?"

"I don't know. The more I talk to him, tell him about himself, the more he looks...full. Like he has knowing in him. But he doesn't act like he remembers. It's just there, in his head, waiting for him to want to get hold of it."

"Kyle's mom told me about it–she looked it up. She says it's a fugue state. Fugue. I think that's what it was. Said it would wear off. And he might not remember what he did while he was in it."

"What would make it happen?"

"She says stress. Stress."

"So we're right. Something bad happened. Either he did it, or something died, or *someone*."

"Maybe."

We didn't talk while we passed by the junkyard. I always snuck past, afraid to have to see your dad again, see how sad he was. I think I was afraid, too, that he'd follow me out to the railroad tracks and try to drag you home. And I was afraid he'd see Jericho and say awful things to him. Putty turned to look through the fence a lot and I wondered what he was thinking.

When we'd taken the path out into the scrub he said, "I should tell you something."

But he didn't. So I said, "Well, go on then."

It was going to rain again, but the deep blue was far off in the west and there was still no wind to dry the sweat off our faces. I was glad Putty carried the jugs so I could reach around to my back and rub the trickles into my shirt.

"When he hit you last year," he said. "And you broke it off and you wouldn't talk to him about it. Ever. He tried to talk to you, but you wouldn't let him say anything."

"What about it?"

"He told me he was sorry."

I sighed a bit. "At least he remembered doing it."

"He's ashamed of what he said, how he told everybody what you did."

"I didn't do it by myself, you know. He took me there."

"I'm just saying. He said he'd spend the rest of his life making it up to you."

194

"You mean, he wasn't mad at me anymore?"

"He was hurt. And maybe he was mad then, but just because he was still working on it."

"So, he could still be mad about it, even now."

"I don't know. I only know he's sorry. He wants you back."

"Were we ever really together?"

"Yes," he said. There was an urgency in his voice and he kept turning to look at me and then to the path. "Maybe if you tell him you still love him. Maybe if you tell him you'll get back with him. Maybe you could say you'd marry him."

"Marry him?"

"That's what I'm trying to tell you. He was going to ask you."

I stopped on the path and gaped at him. He was still talking, going on in that nervous way of his, telling me all the things you said. Somewhere behind me, in one of the pines, a bobwhite called its own name over and over again and I tried to concentrate on it so I could keep myself from smiling. It was exactly like Ruby thought it would be—I was doing just what she was afraid of. As soon as you remembered it all, when you came back to being Jack, we'd be together again and even while I knew in my head, in that thinking part that tries to tell me the truth, that it could never be good, everything in my heart was dancing.

"You're saying he loves me?"

He was breathing hard, like the whole conversation took a lot out of him. He grimaced. "I don't know, Maggie. I don't know what he thinks love is."

"He doesn't love me?"

"I didn't say that, did I? It's just...if it were me. If I loved you. I wouldn't do you like that."

I let out a laugh. "You want me to marry him, though."

"I didn't say that, either. I want you to say you will. He needs to get his head on straight. He'll come around if you tell him—"

"You think he's lost his mind over me? Even I'm not that stupid."

"No, but if you tell him you love him, it'll bring him back." He looked all around at the ground and then at the saw palmettos and mounds of rosemary. Reaching up, with the water jug still in his hand, he pulled his wrist across his forehead and squinted up at the sun. "He needs something to hold him in place. To bring him back to us."

I started walking again, letting him follow. "Maybe he needs you," I said. "Not me."

"I don't think so."

"Why not? You know him better than I do."

"That's not true. It's always been you. Any time he'd done something, it was you he'd talk to after. He never wanted me or Kyle."

"Geez, Putty, if you can't figure that one out I don't know what to tell you."

"I don't think I'm the one he wants to see right now."

"He might not even know who you are. What harm could it do?"

"Can't you remind him? About you?"

"I can't do it that way," I told him. "I can't just say,

look at me. I was your girlfriend and you hit me, remember?"

"Why not?"

I turned on him and said, "Because there's a lifetime of Jack that he's forgot, not just in the past week but all his life. Stuff he might not let himself look at, even after he comes out of his fugue state or whatever. A lifetime of him not wanting to see it. But he remembered hitting me, Putty. After he did it, he remembered that. And he was sorry for it."

"What...you're telling him about what he did before?"

"I'm telling him who he is."

He shook his head. "You shouldn't be doing that."

"What did you think I was doing?"

He lifted the jugs wide in the air and dropped them again to his sides, shouting, "I don't know. Telling him where he lives, who his dad is, who we are, what he likes to do, his favorite foods. Jesus, Maggie, you can't be telling him the bad he's done. What would make you want to do that?"

I turned again to walk the path. "I don't know," I said. I should have told him the truth; if anyone could understand, it would be Putty. We both were always willing to forget the things that Jack could.

"Why would he ever want to remember himself if you tell him that stuff?" He said.

"He can't be sorry for doing what he won't even look at."

When we got to the big plot of cactus, Putty gave me the water jugs and said some other things before he went on back to Trailer Haven. It wasn't important stuff and didn't make all that much sense. Something about messing in things I had no business in and then saying he didn't really mean it and didn't know what he was talking about and maybe it wasn't anything anyway and I should forget he said it.

It was hard not to look at you differently when I saw you there under the little scrub oak with Jericho that day. Even though you looked less and less like Jack, what with the black scruffy beard on your face and neck, and the dark red of your skin from the sun, you were yourself, more and more, in your eyes. Part of me wanted to do what Putty said–tell you I loved you, I'd marry you, if you'd just come home. I tried to imagine you thinking it, sitting across from me at the picnic table that time when we sat and said nothing to each other. Were you waiting to ask me to marry you? It was absurd at that point, the thought of it, and that scared me.

I could feel the keys under my shirt and I almost took the rope off and handed it to you. Just to see what would happen. I'd tell you that you'd swallowed them and suddenly you'd remember everything and I knew somehow that you and me would be the least important thing at that moment.

As you all ate, Boxcar included, I watched you, waited for the times you'd look at me and then look away. You were starting to know me, I could tell, because you couldn't let our eyes meet for very long. You'd have it all back soon enough, I told myself. You didn't need me pushing you.

Jericho smiled at me and said, his mouth full of food, "He convinced me. He made me see the telling of the stories, they help him. Help him focus—find memories to hang on to."

"You're remembering, then?"

You nodded. But you still had that emptiness about you; you still weren't you. Not all the way.

"What's next?" Jericho said. "What year? What grade?"

He wanted to please you, I realized, and I could understand that. He was looking at you and his eyes were shining and happy. I wondered how long it had been since he'd had a friend, not that it would matter so much. It was you. Fully you or crazy you, Jack. You made people want to help you, to be near you, to love you. And you didn't do anything to make it happen. You didn't smile at us, or pet us, or tell us jokes. What was it that you did? Do you even know?

"Why don't you tell *us* some stories?" I asked Jericho.

"Pshaw," he said, spitting out bits of sandwich. "I'm as bad as Jack here. Can't remember a damn thing."

You smiled at him and turned to me and you were both waiting. So I told you about the ninth grade. I was so mad the night before, and confused, and wondering if Bishop still loved Ruby, if he ever really loved her at all, that I fell asleep before thinking about it—getting it straight for the telling. But the blood in the dirt and the buzz of the lazy flies was never so far from my mind that I'd have trouble recalling that year.

31.

Tucker sat with his chair balanced on the back legs, smiling at the picture of his sister on the table in front of him.

"She's been gone ten years?" I said. "Why?"

His smile deepened and his eyes got glassy with tears. He told me Jessica went off to see the world. She left home in the summer some ten years ago when he was fifteen; she'd been planning it since she was in high school. She said college could wait, adulthood could wait. What she wanted was to feel the world under her feet and see it all up close. Tucker said their parents wouldn't let her go, but once she turned twenty-one, she withdrew a bunch of money and set out on her own.

"I don't know why she did it," he said. "For a long time, I thought there must be a reason. Something bad must have happened, something I didn't know about, that made her want to leave us. But I couldn't find out anything. And when she finally called me, after she'd been gone a few days, I begged her to tell me why."

I waited for him to finish. He let the front legs of the chair hit the floor with a thunk and rested his arms across the table. I pulled another beer from the six pack and handed it to him. He twisted off the cap and drank.

"It's getting warm," he said.

I nodded and sipped from mine. "So, what did she say?"

He rolled his eyes and then rubbed them with one hand. "She said life was an illusion, and too short, or something. If you love me, you'll cheer for me. Stuff like that."

"You still think something bad happened to make her leave?"

He shook his head. "No."

"She just wanted to do what she said? Travel the world?"

"Yep." He drank some more.

He was angry. He folded his arms and laid his head down on them. "I don't know why I'm telling you all this."

"Is that what you meant, when you said she wasn't perfect?"

He sat upright again. "No."

He got up and started pacing back and forth in the small space between the foot of the bed and the television set, slow, like he just needed to move his body, to feel it passing through space.

"Do you have a brother or sister?" He asked me.

"Two sisters. I haven't seen them since I was little, though."

"Where'd they go?"

"They live with my aunt up north."

"Why?"

I drank my beer and looked over at the bed. "I don't

know—to get away from my father."

He stopped pacing and stood looking at me. I smiled as best I could and shrugged.

"Was your dad a good man?" I asked him.

He nodded.

"Are you sure?"

"Why do you say that?"

"I don't know, maybe I've drunk too much."

"Go on. Why?"

So I told him and I think you'd agree, Jack. I said somebody as nice as that, as smart and friendly, somebody who lived in a nice neighborhood with a nice mom and dad and a brother and they all loved her—well, somebody that happy really doesn't have any reason to walk away. It didn't make any sense to me. Not at all. My sisters left for a reason. Even Bishop left for a reason. You left for a reason; even when I didn't understand it, I knew there was one.

When he came to me, and pulled me to stand in front of him, and kissed me, I let him. And I'm not sorry about it at all. I know you've been with a few other girls, not just since we broke up, but even while we were going out. But that's not why I don't feel bad about it. It wasn't a revenge kind of thing. Tucker needed to connect with something and so did I and I thought it was the most natural thing I'd ever done.

He dropped me off at the side gate on River Front Drive later that night and I found most of the neighbors out at the picnic tables with Celia and Ruby. They had the citronella candles burning and their cans of mosquito repellent to spray themselves into a cloud. You knew there was something awful wrong when the trailer park sat outside after dark in the summer. I sat with them for a long time, letting Ruby rub Skin-So-Soft lotion on my arms and face. She was smiling at me, tears in her eyes. They didn't talk much, certainly not about you. We were all talked out by that point. Pat Dunn wondered, as she often did, if the combination of mosquito repellent and cigarette smoke could cause an explosion of sorts, but this time, instead opinions and wild speculations, the group just nodded.

After an hour or so, I followed Ruby back home to our trailer. I sat in our little kitchen while she made a sandwich, wondering if I should tell her about Jessica.

"You slept with him," she said.

I didn't say anything and I suppose that was enough.

"A bit fast, don't you think?"

"It wasn't like that," I said.

She stopped for a second to look at me, her knife poised over a tomato on the cutting board.

"Tell me," she said.

I tried to explain it to her. I thought she'd understand; I know you wouldn't. Or maybe you would, depending on how much of the old you is left and how much is new. I told her I felt empty somehow, and lost. Too much didn't make sense, and I didn't want to make sense of it. And it wasn't like Tucker wanted sex, so much as...and I didn't have the word.

"He needed to be close to somebody," I said.

"And you did, too."

I nodded. She was smiling then, like I'd told her a secret—the good kind.

"You remember I asked you and Celia a while back about so much bad happening in one place?"

"Sure," she said. She brought her sandwich to the table and sat down.

"I guess maybe you were right."

32.

The others didn't find out about you tying Sunny up in duct tape until the next year, when we were in ninth grade. Stories went around that you'd raped Sunny and the principal pulled her out of class to question her about it. He said he had to call the police if there was any truth to it, but Sunny swore it was a lie. Nobody ever figured out who started the rumors, but you decided it was Ron. You grabbed him one afternoon off the bus and started hitting him, telling him you'd kill him for it.

Putty and Kyle pulled you off him and wanted to know what it was all about, but Ron wouldn't say anything. He turned and walked off toward River Front Drive and I followed him. It took a while for everybody to forget it and go back to being okay together. But it would never be the same.

We were fractured. Ron was smarter than all of us and he spent more time at schoolwork. And Mary was suddenly popular. She never invited her new chatty friends to the trailer park, though, so she was gone a lot. She did invite me along more often, but I just wanted to be near you, so I stayed home most of the time.

You skipped school a lot that year. I hated it and told Ruby so—said I didn't want to go if you weren't there. She said if she ever caught me skipping, she'd ship me off to my Aunt Jewel's in Tallahassee; I knew that was a lie but it scared me just the same. I told you to come with me to school, but you still skipped as much as you could get away with. You'd take your dad's truck out into the scrub by the lake all by yourself. Sometimes you'd camp out there. Even Putty said you weren't around anymore.

It was in November of that year, when you came into Trailer Haven and dragged Brody Paulson out of the pool and started beating him up. We all climbed out of the water and stood there dripping, shivering, and watching until Mr. Haverty stopped you. You told him to leave you alone and ran off toward the junkyard. We followed you, let you walk on ahead while we whispered about it.

We couldn't figure out what Brody had done. We knew you didn't like him. He was Old Man Pinkerton's great grandson and didn't come around too often, but when he did, he'd call you names. He said you ought to be incarcerated; you should be institutionalized. But he hadn't done anything that day.

Putty said you took a lot of time with things; you thought too much and got madder and madder until you nearly burst with it. It was like a bruise. You get one, but you can't remember what you hit that made it happen. By the time you got mad enough to punch somebody, we'd forgotten what made you do it.

Ron said it wasn't right. You ought to give a person a warning. Otherwise, if you sit there and do nothing while they make you mad, how are they supposed to know they did something wrong? Mary said they should just know. And anyway, Brody was a punk, leastwise that's what Celia called him. He deserved it. But I reminded them he was only ten.

"A ten-year-old with a big mouth," Kyle said. "Whoever heard the words that kid says?"

And Ron said, "Just because *you* don't have a good vocabulary doesn't mean other kids don't."

Kyle grabbed Ron by the shirt and punched him, but not hard. They fought for a while, until they realized we'd all gone on ahead and then they stopped. I was never really sure why Ron came along with us at all but he told me once a few months ago that he always felt like he had to protect me and Mary.

"If there's a guy to pick on," he said, "the bullies tend to leave the girls alone."

I didn't believe him, to be honest. I think we were stuck with one another, somehow. And Ron didn't know how to *not* go along. We'd been friends for so long we couldn't quit, and we didn't want to. Not really. At least that's what I always thought.

We got out into the scrub and followed you to the lake and into the pines where you stopped. When we came up behind you, we saw the deer. You'd wrapped silver duct tape around its snout and tied its front and back legs together with it. Your rifle was lying a few yards away and Putty went to pick it up but you stopped him. You might have shot the deer, but we couldn't tell because you'd slashed at it with a knife, back and forth across its mid-section. The knife was stuck in the shoulder, and the animal's insides lay spilled out on the blood-soaked dirt covered with flies.

"Were you gonna eat it raw?" Putty said.

You said nothing. You were scared, so scared you couldn't get hold of a response.

Then Ron said, "Why'd you tape it up? Like you did to Sunny?"

"What?" Mary said.

That's when Ron told everybody what you did to her and they all just stood around, uncomfortable, trying not to meet your eyes, not wanting to look at the dead deer.

"We should leave it," Kyle said. And they all turned and started walking back. They were disturbed, you know. Maybe you don't know because you weren't all there that day. You were lost inside your own mind.

"Why'd you do it?" I asked you.

You shook your head and turned to leave and I asked you if you didn't want your gun and your knife and you looked back at me and said no. Do you remember what you said to me after that? You said, "I get it now." And you wouldn't say any more. I followed you through the scrub asking you about it but you told me to shut up and leave you alone.

I think I get it now, too. I think you had to know, even if it wasn't quite the same, what it meant to kill something beautiful and innocent. Whatever it was you learned that day, it changed you—just a little bit. When I found you out in the scrub that night I thought you would tell me about the deer. You'd say it with that faraway voice, like it wasn't real—tell me what you did and how you did it and that you had to forget. You'd press your fists hard against your head and say it again and

210

again and I'd know that it would be gone and we'd never talk about it again.

But you didn't do that. You didn't mention the deer. You didn't tell me how much you loved your dad so I could tell you I loved mine. You didn't want to talk at all. Instead you kissed me and didn't stop. We both undressed there, standing in the scrub, and you checked around for sandspurs and cactus and then pulled me to the dirt, and for a while we were breath and the stars and the soft earth of the scrub. I wondered when I was lying there watching you pull your pants back on, the air whispering all over me, calling me to lie very still, if you'd forgotten.

"Was that our first time, Jack? It was, wasn't it?" I reached out my hands and you took them, pulled me to standing.

"Yes," you said.

Forgetting is easy as that. I laughed.

"What?" You said, and you laughed too.

But I couldn't tell you why. I knew it could be done. I could forget, just like you. I could change the past, by retelling it.

33.

When I finished with the story, you were leaning against the tree, your knees up, with Boxcar between them, licking your face. I thought you hadn't been listening.

"The boys went out there a few times," I said. "Putty and Kyle, anyway. To watch the deer rot. One day they said it was covered with black vultures. They ate it clean."

You got up and said, "I'll be back in a while." You walked across the tracks and off into the scrub.

"That one didn't seem to bother him so much," Jericho said.

But I knew better. I watched you walking, your head down, your fists at your temples. I knew you were coming back to yourself. Soon we'd fix it all and start getting things right.

"I don't think I'm leaving here," the old man said.

"What do you mean?"

"I tried walking out with him yesterday. He wanted to show me the lake in the stories, but I got out a ways and told him I couldn't do it."

"You walk to the plaza every day."

He shook his head. "Only once or twice. Jack goes

for both of us most days, brings me food. Beer."

Boxcar let out a whine and put his chin on Jericho's thigh.

"Where will you go?" I said.

"I'm here."

"You don't mean," I said. "You can't die here."

"Why not?"

"In the scrub?"

"The black vultures can have me; I don't mind."

"Don't say that. It's awful."

And he said, "I came of this earth and yet I don't remember being the earth; why should I resist returning to it and forgetting once more?"

"Is that from your book?"

He nodded.

"But what does it mean?"

He smiled. "Death ain't no different from life; it is life."

"Say it again."

He got out his book and found the quote and read it to me three times and I liked the way it sounded in his voice. I understood better, then, why you liked Jericho and wanted him to stay. He was soothing, even if not everything he said made sense to me. There was an insistence there, under his voice, telling me that whether I knew it or not, his words were important.

Maybe Jericho really was a prophet. Maybe he was right that I shouldn't have told you all the bad stuff. But he was wrong about you. A person can have bad woven throughout his life, one thing after another. I might have changed a thing here or there, but the bad was in it, just

214

the same.

I went to work that afternoon at the bait shop and Celia stayed and did her books in the little office in back. We walked home together at seven and she was quiet. I asked her what was wrong.

"I wish you wouldn't worry," she said.

"Maybe it's time I did some worrying. Maybe I ought to grow up a bit now."

She lit up a cigarette. "You just keep your head with Jack. When he comes 'round, you got to leave it alone."

"I know that."

"Do you?"

When we turned down River Front Road, the rain started but we didn't run.

"It's Ruby, ain't it?" I said.

"I told you not to worry. Just let me..."

"Let you worry? What good will that do?"

"What good will anything do? I just don't understand it. I don't understand."

"Maybe you're wrong. Maybe he really has changed."

"You haven't lived with it as long as I have," she said. "You haven't had to watch her heal as often as me." She picked up speed and left me behind once we were in the trailer park. The door to our trailer slammed shut behind her before I got to the steps.

Together, we made baked chicken over rice, swamped in cream of mushroom soup and by the time dinner was ready, Celia seemed to have gotten hold of herself; she was even smiling, laughing a little. I realized how easy it was for all of us to go from pain to joy—much easier than the healing of a bruised face or a broken arm. Faster. It's

215

just that, once the bruises are gone and the bones are whole again, the physical pain is gone. But even when we're laughing, the heartache lingers, gnawing at us.

"Why is there so much bad here?" I said when I'd finished eating. "Jack's had a lifetime of bad. Mr. Pinkerton's son is in jail. Kyle's dad is in jail. The Old Twins, their whole family...killed in the house fire. And Bishop."

At that, they both put their forks down at the same time, little clanks on their plates, and looked at me, still chewing.

"And that ain't all, is it?" I said. "How can there be so much bad here? Right here?" I put my fingertip on the table by my plate.

Ruby wiped her mouth off with her napkin and shook her head. "There's bad everywhere."

"Not this much. There are places that are better. There are people who are better; probably most of them."

"It's true enough," Celia said. "But everywhere is touched by it."

"Evil is like a fairy ring," Ruby said. "You know, those mushrooms. And all them people say it's fairies. But it ain't. Underground, see, there's these spores or seeds. They grow out from the middle, fan out like, in a circle. Little fingers of evil, reaching out far and wide to find the good and infect it."

Celia and I sat for a minute thinking about it. Ruby said stuff like that a lot. Sometimes she made more sense than others. You remember, don't you? When she told you not to go into the pool after you ate three hotdogs because your stomach had to first separate the light buns out of the heavy dogs and send the light buns to the top so you could float? We didn't believe her, but she was so certain and serious we figured it must mean something else and we were just too young to understand it. I think there's a word for that. Ron would know it; I should ask him.

I thought about it a lot. Evil starts where it gets hold and it reaches out from its source, grabbing on to whatever it can, and the farther away the good is, the less likely evil is to reach it; but that doesn't make it safe. Suddenly I saw the world with spots of concentrated bad, and lines of it, like spider legs, reaching out, searching, seeing how far they can get.

But then I thought maybe Ruby was wrong. Maybe it was something else–poverty or hopelessness or fear–that let the bad seep in and take hold; it could reach out from our little trailer park all it wanted, but it wouldn't get far– the world was safe from us. I don't guess I believe that anymore.

When I went back out to the scrub you were pacing in a tight little frenzy and I thought it was over, but when you saw me, you stopped and while I could see some recognition there in your eyes, I knew you were still lost.

We ate our sandwiches and Jericho started asking me about the trailer park and the bait shop and Ruby. I told him my parents were still married even though they haven't lived together for years. I like to think I said it just because it was in my head, but sometimes we say things because we need somebody to pull the words out of us. Maybe we don't even know what it is we don't want to say until they start tugging at it.

"Where does he live?" Jericho asked me.

"A block or two down south, with my grandma."

"You see him a lot."

I shook my head. "I haven't seen him in about a year."

The old man winced. "He lives right down the road and you ain't seen him?"

"It's complicated."

He sputtered and bits of bread flew out his mouth. "Ain't nothing that complicated."

I knew it then. I had to go see Bishop. I'd been waiting for him to come to the trailer park, to be brave and come begging forgiveness. But maybe I was the one who needed to ask for that. I knew I never would. I guess I don't need forgiving for loving you any more than Ruby needs forgiving for loving him. But there was something I needed to know for sure–I never thought to ask about it, or to look for it, because I just assumed it was there.

"You going to tell us more?" Jericho asked.

The telling would be easier from that point because Sunny was gone after ninth grade. Nobody ever talked about her anymore, nobody dared.

34.

By tenth grade you'd stopped struggling. The fear in your eyes had hardened right up into a resigned hatred of anything good. I stayed, following you and Putty and Kyle around, and you knew I was yours for the taking. But sometimes I'd find you looking at me with your eyebrows pulled in, like you were trying to make sense of me. I liked to pretend you were protecting me from yourself and I suppose you were.

We spent more time out in the scrub, you three always drinking or smoking or both. You smiled more and even laughed sometimes. You told stories whenever Ron wasn't around about breaking into houses and cars down in my dad's neighborhood or farther out and getting chased by dogs. Kyle told us he caught you looking in some girl's window; he snuck up behind you and started making grunting noises and the two of you ran off laughing.

Just after school started that year, we had the hurricanes. You remember, don't you? When Frances hit, everybody in Trailer Haven, except Mr. Reynolds, the guy we weren't allowed to speak to anyway, huddled together like refugees in the bait shop and laundromat. You were sitting with Putty and Kyle behind some of the machines where we couldn't see you. I went over and asked you about your dad and you wouldn't speak to me. And when we all came out to wind and gray, the world looked like it had been turned upside down and shook out. The trailer park was flooded and Mr. Haverty's roof was peeled back. He stayed with Doc Fred for a long time.

Then a few weeks later, Jeanne stormed over and took what was left, and even Mr. Reynolds came with us to the plaza. But you weren't there. And when it was over the lagoon was dotted with half-sunk and capsized boats. We rode with Old Man Pinkerton down south to see a catamaran, kicked out of the water and deposited on dry land just west of the highway. The power was out for too long and everybody ran low on food, so Mr. Peterson opened the convenience store and we ate granola bars and cans of Vienna sausages.

The Sluce's trailer was tipped and two oak trees were decorated with strips of aluminum siding wrapped up in them like ribbons. Mrs. Bentemyer said Barefoot Bay was wiped off the face of the earth; it was the apocalypse, she said. And you'd just come up from the junkyard in waders and said there were worse things. Everybody stared at you, kind of knowing like, and numb.

One night in October you had a handgun with you and I told you to put it away because it scared me. Even Kyle wanted you to hide it.

"You're taking too many risks," he said. "You want to get caught?"

"Or shot?" Putty said.

Kyle said you broke a window the night before and

woke the whole house.

"I got the money, didn't I?" You said. "Sitting on the kitchen table, pretty as you please."

By January, Putty and Kyle stopped going around with you at night. But we all still sat around drinking in the scrub until early morning listening to you tell stories about it. You said you were so good at it, you could get into a house and take whatever you wanted out of the bedrooms while people slept.

"I'm telling you," you said. "I was standing right there in her room watching her. I could have stayed there all night and she'd never have known."

"There's no way," Kyle said.

We all acted like we didn't believe you, maybe because we didn't want to. And a few nights later, I woke to find you standing next to my bed. I jumped at first, before I realized it was you, and you put your hand over my mouth and whispered in my ear.

"You want to go out to the lake?"

We snuck out of my trailer and walked out into the cold, damp scrub behind the junkyard. We were surrounded by quiet and you took my hand and didn't let it go until we got out onto the pier and sat at the edge.

"You want to hear a story?" You said.

I nodded. I thought you were going to tell me another one about Sunny and I tried to imagine what it would be, but instead you told about another girl named Jessica. I could tell you were making it up because you had to stop every few sentences to think about it, figure out where to go next. And when you finished you said, "How'd you like that?"

"How does it end?"

You shrugged and pulled a pack of cigarettes out of your shirt pocket and lit one up. You offered me one and I said no. "How do you think it ends?" You said.

"He kills her?"

You rocked your head to the left and then the right and said, "I could see that."

"You should write it," I said. "It's scary."

"You're the one who writes stories."

I laughed, short and quick, and shivered. "A couple of stories in fifth grade don't count."

"I wouldn't be able to write that one anyway. It's not believable."

"People like that kind of thing, though. Horror stuff."

You stood up and took my hand to pull me up and we walked off the pier and you kissed me and pulled me down to the sand and when I started shaking you asked me why. You asked if I was okay and I said I was and I kissed you back and we made love by the lake and you smiled at me after because I was crying and you kissed the tears off my face. I was confused but I didn't say anything.

Just before school ended, you put on a ski mask and broke into a convenience store after hours in the next county over. When the clerk came out of the back room into the darkened store, you shot him. You stood there staring at him while he bled on the floor and begged you not to kill him, and then you ran away.

The first place you went was my trailer. I found you standing by my bed in the dark, breathing heavy, and I woke Celia. By the time we got you over to Mr. Haverty's, you were shaking and struggling to breathe and we could barely get the story out of you.

The five of us were in on it. Celia, Pat Dunn, Mr. Haverty, me, and Doc Fred. We sat up late watching the news with you trembling on the couch between Celia and Mr. Haverty. I remember the chill in my body at seeing it. Watching you cry. I didn't know if what you'd done was the reaction to something bad, or the something bad you'd have a reaction to.

The clerk wasn't hurt bad, just shot in the shoulder, and you didn't end up stealing anything. So it was agreed we'd keep quiet. We'd say nothing. And nobody came by asking questions. Not for a long time. When the cops showed up nearly a year later, we five stood together, and Celia put her arm around me, squeezing my shoulder, like a warning. *Don't you say anything*. Not one word. But they were asking about some girl who went missing out on the highway. Not you. The clerk couldn't describe you. You left nothing behind. You weren't going to be found out.

You never told anybody else about it, so far as I knew. Not even Putty. And you never told any more stories about breaking in to houses or cars or stealing or peeping into windows. I don't know if you stopped, or if you just stopped talking about it. But the rage seemed to have left your eyes. They were dull after that—as if you were lost inside your own mind, thinking.

35.

I'd seen Jericho making faces when I was telling the sex part, but I didn't care. I was going to tell it real. And anyway, it wasn't my fault the old man was there; it was yours. But by the time I got finished, he'd forgotten about the sex and was looking at you, worried, and you nodded, like you remembered it all. I had to go to work so I left you both with Boxcar to talk it out. I figured Jericho had something in his book about lying and stealing and all that, and you two could try to make it okay.

Your dad came by the bait shop again that afternoon. I knew he only wanted to ask about you so before he could start, I told him you were the same. He drew in a breath and forced it out fast and he got that look in his eyes that usually came with yelling at somebody.

"He's got to come on home," he said.

"He will. I promise."

"This is out of hand. What the hell's going on out there?"

"Honest, he's just trying to figure it all out."

"How hard is it? You told him didn't you? Where he belongs? It's gone on long enough."

"If you try to force him to come home, he'll run. I swear. We'll never see him again."

I felt bad for him, but I was glad he was being sensible. I knew if it were me out in the scrub, Ruby wouldn't put up with it at all. She'd march right out there and drag me home; she'd chain me to the trailer if she had to. Then we'd have to spend months and months working our relationship back to something good. But your dad got it; he saw that you were an adult; you had to work this out by yourself. He was doing what a good father would.

That's when I knew I would go see Bishop. My dad was the same; just like yours. He was giving me the space I'd asked for a year ago. He was treating me like an adult who could make her own decisions. I should have realized it months ago and gone to see him.

Your dad sighed and nodded. "Well," he said. He pulled a small gold ring out of his pocket and handed it to me. "Give him this. It was his mother's. Tell him I need him to remember. I need him to come home."

My eyes welled up with tears looking at it. I couldn't say good-bye when your father left, I just lifted my hand. The way I saw it, your father was desperate and lost without you. I could hear it in his voice—years and years of struggling together, each of you dealing with the loss of your mother in a different way. You were causing him so much pain, I felt like I had to help him. I was helping him by helping you. That's the way I saw it then.

I was determined to push you a little bit, so the next morning when I took sandwiches and water out to the tracks, I gave you the ring first thing.

"Hold out your hand," I said. And when you did, I dropped the ring onto your palm and waited for a reaction.

You looked at it for a long time and then picked it up and turned it over and over.

"Your dad gave it to me. He said it's your mom's. He wants you to remember."

You closed your fist around it, stood up, and walked away from us, across the railroad tracks and farther until you turned into some shrubs and disappeared. Boxcar got up and went out a bit, his tail wagging, whining.

Jericho and I ate our sandwiches in silence. Every now and then we'd peer out across the scrub looking for you to come back. When you did, you were coming up from the south, along the tracks, with two six-packs. We didn't talk about the ring. We drank beer and listened to Jericho tell us about his family in Texas.

He told us stories about his wife, Lettie, and their two kids, Cozzie and Ervan. Cozzie was ten and Ervan was eight and he and Lettie taught them to swim in the pool at the park. Cozzie took to the water like a fish, he said, but Ervan needed more help. He told us they went to church on Sundays and Ervan always wore a white button up shirt and a proper tie and Cozzie had a closet full of Sunday dresses and Lettie wore pretty hats. They ate dinner out once a week and Ervan got ribs and most of his shirts were stained with barbeque sauce, but Lettie was as calm as could be–never raised her voice, never had to. It was the perfect life, he said. There was a hazy beauty to it, a softness around the edges, all the sounds muffled in his memory almost like it wasn't real.

I wanted to tell him it wasn't. I wanted to say he'd created it in the time he'd been away, telling the story over and over again. His family life had probably been harsh, too sharp and too easy to walk away from, and over the years he'd changed it into something only a madman would leave. And his children weren't small anymore. He was an old man now and they must be grown. But he never wanted to imagine what happened to them after he left because that would make him feel bad. And I wanted to say, see? I told you so. You can change the past. And if you've done a good enough job, you won't even know you did it.

And I wondered if he hadn't muted the whole thing just to make himself out to have sacrificed something–martyred himself, somehow erasing the stain of what he said he'd done to make him leave them. And what he'd done, too, in reality had been much clearer, brutal–not the bland story he'd convinced himself of since it happened.

You caught me staring at him and my face burned hot because I knew I was looking at him like I hated him. You'd think I was jealous, because I said Jericho shouldn't interfere with you and me, he should move on. But that wasn't it at all. I just didn't want to be like Jericho, that's all. I could see myself in forty years telling stories and making it all sound...pleasant. I wondered if I'd know it, somewhere in a little spot in my mind. Would I know I was lying? Did Jericho know?

The old man had stopped talking, his story trailed off into his own head.

"Is there more to tell?" You asked me.

"Some."

"Bad?"

"No," I said. "Not so much bad left. But Jericho might be embarrassed by the next story." I smiled at him.

"I'll take a walk, then." He said. He pulled a few beers off one of the six-packs for us and got up with the rest of them and his little book. He and Boxcar walked up a ways and found a spot against a small pine tree and I watched as he popped the tab of a beer and opened the book to read.

You turned back to me and smiled. I felt like I was melting and blushed again.

36.

I saw Tucker again the next night; you'd been gone for nine days and I was starting to believe you weren't ever coming home. This time when he came to pick me up he parked in front of the trailer and let me take him out to the picnic tables to introduce him around. They were all expecting him, so they'd practiced not looking worried or sad or horrified. They were determined to make him feel like he was wasting his time there and the news for him would be good. But as we both turned and walked away, I could hear the silence behind me. Their fears stayed with me all that night and I wondered if I could hide it as well as they did.

We ate at a little diner up north, tucked into another plaza, with a bar and booths with ripped fake leather upholstery, and he made me tell him about Ruby and Celia and my dad. I knew he didn't want to talk about his sister and that was okay with me. But as I was talking, I could see the tension in his face. He was trying to listen, trying to be distracted, but it wasn't working well enough.

I told him about Bishop helping me learn to ride a bike out on River Front Drive when I was six. He'd run me down toward Beaumont Road and then back up to the side entrance to Trailer Haven, and there would be Ruby with his beer. He'd guzzle the whole thing and then run me back down the road again. If he let go of the handlebar, I'd scream and he'd say, "I've still got you; I've got you." But I'd scream just the same. He had hold of the seat and never let me fall and by the eighth or so trip down and up again, he said he couldn't run anymore. It'd have to wait until another day. And I told him I didn't want to learn to ride a bike; I wanted him to run me up and down the road like that all the time. There was nowhere else I wanted to go.

As we left the diner, Tucker said, "I thought about asking you to a movie, but..."

"That's all right."

"It's not a good time to be going to the movies."

I nodded. "I don't think anybody would say anything. I mean, we need to take our minds off it."

"Did you want to go see one then?"

I told him no. I told him we should get beer and go to the motel like we did last time. So we sat at the little table again and we drank without saying anything for a long while. He'd left all the lights in the room off and only the dim flickering bulb over the walkway outside the window outlined his profile. The air conditioner clicked on and the curtains, pulled far over to one side, billowed out and bobbed.

Then he said, "It's my fault."

I shook my head. I knew what he was talking about, even if it made no sense. "It's not." I said.

"It is."

"You said she was a free spirit. She did what she
232

wanted to do."

"I could have stopped her."

I almost laughed. "How?"

He looked up at me and said, "I just should have, that's all."

We sat there looking at each other, the air conditioner humming all around us, the light outside flickering.

"People are going to do what they're going to do and you can't stop them," I said.

"It was a dangerous thing to do."

"Kids hike all over Europe, you know. I've heard about it. I'm sure they do it here, too."

"Why don't we hear about it, then?"

"Because it's here."

He laughed. "That doesn't make any sense."

"It does. Europe is foreign and mysterious and it has all those castles. We always talk about doing things far away. But you know there have to be people who want to walk across America. Your sister was one of them."

"That doesn't make it not dangerous."

"You were fifteen. You expect a grown woman to listen to you?"

"She was only twenty-one."

"That's grown. Plenty grown."

"I should have..." He didn't finish. I thought maybe he knew he wasn't to blame. He must have known it. It was honorable, blaming himself a little. It was...what is the word? The word that means he's a gentleman who treats a lady like she's special. That's what he was being, acting like it was his job to protect his big sister, when it really wasn't.

"It's not your fault." I threw it out there again to be sure it stuck.

We started on our second beers and I was trying to find something I could say to him to make him feel better, but I didn't think there was anything for it. He'd come around in time and realize he couldn't beat himself up any more. It wasn't doing anybody any good.

"Did you know Jack Beaumont?" He said.

I was startled. I must have looked like a rabbit caught in the light.

"You did, didn't you?"

"We grew up together. Him and all of us at the trailer park."

"You think he's going to come back?"

I didn't answer.

"They'll have to catch him?"

"I don't know."

"Some of the others, they're saying he's still around here, that he hasn't gone far."

"They think someone's hiding him?"

"Maybe." He was peeling his label off, not looking at me. He said, "Nobody saw anything? Suspected anything?"

I drank some of my beer and then drank some more and he'd pulled the whole label off and looked at me, wanting an answer. "They're two different things," I said. "Seeing and suspecting."

"So, you saw something."

"We won't know what we saw until the whole story comes out."

He pushed his chair onto its two back legs, one hand

grasping the edge of the table. "You either saw something or you didn't."

"We didn't know what we were looking at." And I wondered if that was even true. I wondered if we just didn't want to see what was right there under our noses.

"Did you see my sister?"

"No."

"I'm not blaming you," he said. "Or anybody else around here."

"Aren't you?"

"I don't mean to. I just don't understand how something like this happens, how it goes on for years, with nobody noticing."

"I don't know," I said.

He uncapped another two bottles and handed me one. He got up and went to his suitcase, sitting on a stand in one corner. He unzipped it, dug inside it, and pulled out a sleek black handgun. I stood up, scared.

"It's not loaded," he said, coming back to the table.

"How can you tell?"

He rubbed his forefinger along the side of the gun. "You can't tell. But I can." He put the gun on the table and sat back in his chair.

"Why do you have it?"

"Safety."

"Why are you showing it to me?"

"I don't know," he said. "Maybe I just want you to see what a big man I am." He smiled and chuckled a little bit. "Sit down. I swear I'm not going to shoot you."

I sat down and guzzled from my beer. "You're going to shoot him, aren't you?" I said. "That's why you came down here."

"I'm not going to shoot anybody."

37.

We started dating in the summer of eleventh grade. You never said anything and neither did I; we were just together one day and that was that. Ruby hauled me down to the free clinic to get birth control pills and Mary thought that made her the worst mother ever.

"She's encouraging you to have sex," she said. "That's irresponsible."

I tried to defend my mom, but there was no reasoning with Mary. For her, sex wasn't something you planned for, because planning for it meant you were a slut. Sex for Mary was something you accidentally did because you couldn't help yourself. She was hanging out with the homecoming queen and her court, all the girls in school who had sex but didn't admit it to anyone.

That year at Christmas, Bishop came around again and he and Ruby started planning to get a trailer together on one of the open lots. Ruby told me not to hang on you when Bishop was around, not to kiss you or let you touch me except to hold my hand. She said my dad was like a guard dog and he wouldn't want to imagine you and me doing anything serious. So whenever Bishop was at the trailer park, sitting out with everybody by the pool or at my trailer, we had to cool it.

"You think he wants to kick my ass?" You said once, when Bishop was staring at us while we tread water in the pool.

And I said, "I don't know if he hits men."

When I said it, I wasn't being funny, but you and Ron and Putty laughed and then everybody at the picnic tables wanted to know what was so funny and none of us would tell. I knew my dad wouldn't like that and sure enough, when we got out of the pool, he called us over to where he and Ruby sat drinking beers and smoking cigarettes, and he said, "What were you all laughing about?"

"Nothing," I said.

We were still drying off with our big ratty beach towels and he grabbed hold of mine and yanked me over to the table.

"You tell me what was so funny."

You stepped over to us and said, "Leave her alone."

My dad leapt up and off the picnic table to hit you, but he tripped over the beam that held the bench to it and fell on his face.

"Run," I told you.

Putty pulled you away and you two ran off and spent the day out in the scrub. My dad didn't remember it the next day.

I thought everything was going to turn out all right that year. You were changing–relaxing. You didn't run off and get into any trouble and spent most of your free time working with your dad. You were doing okay in school. It looked like we were all going to be normal and I was starting to think of our future. We could live at Trailer Haven and I could run the bait shop while you ran the junkyard. I started writing *Magnolia Beaumont* in my notebooks at school and imagining the little Beaumonts we'd have and you let me write Always Magnolia on the back of your hand whenever I wanted. We'd become so corny it was heaven and I was giddy with it.

We went out into the scrub once, without the others, and I asked you if you'd carve us into a tree and you did. JB + MH. Then you said it would be our tree and we could bring our kids out to see it and our grand kids, and our great grand kids, and then you stopped talking–disappeared for a minute or two. I thought you were thinking about it–picturing it all in your head the way I was doing. But when you looked at me, your forehead was pulled tight and your lips curled with the hint of a sneer. I didn't ask you why.

During Christmas break, we found the graveyard. We were all together again. Ron, Mary, Kyle, Putty. All of us. The half-dozen. We spent our days riding around in your dad's truck, with Mary, Ron, and Kyle in the back. You drove out into the scrub, up to the mall, to the theater. And we went down south to the inlet and fished. And once, we let you drive around exploring on the way home and we passed by this old cemetery, down a dirt road, out in the middle of nowhere, up against some woods. It wasn't too far from home, but we'd never seen it before. We walked down there a lot after that and sat among the graves drinking and talking and telling ghost stories.

One night you and I went over to Melbourne to watch a movie and afterward you drove us out to the cemetery and you wanted to have sex on the graves and I didn't really want to.

"It's disrespectful," I said.

You already had me on the ground, pulling off my pants, and you said, "It is not. We're just putting a little life in death." You laughed at that. And as we made love, you kept talking about it. "Why should we keep the dead separate from the living? Why do we leave them all alone? They should be right here with us all the time. This is how they enjoy life. Through us. Watching us. Watching us do this." When we were finished and I was wriggling into my pants, you said, "Try to relax a little next time."

"There won't be a next time."

"You mean ever? Or just here?"

"Here."

"Are you afraid of ghosts?"

"It's disrespectful," I said.

You were mad at me then and you took me right home and dropped me off at the side gate at Trailer Haven without even saying good-bye. I didn't hear from you for the rest of the week. You didn't call me. I went over to the junkyard but your dad said you were busy. I asked Putty if he'd seen you and he said no. School was about to start again and we'd wasted a whole week of Christmas break just because I didn't like having sex in a graveyard.

I was out in the field behind the plaza one night after dark with Ron and Mary. I watched you drive out to U.S. 1 and turn south. I was angry, I guess. Angry that you were going out and doing things without me—punishing me. So I told Ron and Mary I wanted to go to the graveyard. Ron got us some beers from his parents' fridge and we walked south through the woods on the little path we'd found and they talked about school the whole time. Ron was on his way to being valedictorian and Mary said when he got rich and famous, he had to come back here and buy us all houses and cars. He didn't say anything to that and it made me smile.

"Listen," Ron said.

We were quiet then and somewhere in the trees we could hear high-pitched fluttering sounds, like the neighing of a tiny horse, with a trembling warble in between.

"Screech owl," he whispered. Ron was thrilled; it was only the second time we'd heard one.

The first time, we were thirteen, I think. Ron and I stayed out by the pool late one summer night after everybody else had left and he asked if I wanted to go out into the woods down south to find one. He said a bird watcher spotted one nearby the day before. So we sprayed ourselves up with more repellent and hiked into the woods south of the junkyard.

I doubted we'd hear one. What were the chances we'd find what we were looking for? Any time I started to talk, he'd shush me and smile. We tiptoed like thieves through the shrubs and bushes along a path, Ron pointing the way with his flashlight, until I got this crazy idea that it was all a trick and Ron would turn and run at any moment, leaving me out there in the dark.

But then he heard it. A throbbing whinny above us. We stood looking at each other for a long time until I'd forgotten about the owl.

"They're monogamous, you know." He told me on our way back home.

"What does that mean?"

"They find a mate and stick with her, pretty much, forever."

He walked me all the way to the door of my trailer and I told him I thought he might leave me out in the woods by myself.

"I would never do that." He was insulted. "I'm not Jack, you know."

This time, when he heard the screech owl, Ron kept walking. He didn't look at me and smile and I wondered if he even remembered that night in the woods.

When the three of us came out into the back of the cemetery we saw your truck across the way on the little dirt road and walked toward it. I heard the sounds, before I saw the bodies—a few yards in, we'd come upon two naked people, on the ground behind one of the tombstones, having sex. I turned away, embarrassed. Ron was pulling at my arm trying to get me back into the woods, when I realized it was you. Scrambling to your feet, covering yourself up, you said my name. I heard you calling me as I hurried after Ron to the path.

"Maggie," you were saying. "Magnolia."

Ron, Mary, and I didn't talk at all on the way home and the screech owl seemed to follow us the whole way, laughing at me.

38.

When I finished telling you the story you said, "Is that all?"

I thought it was plenty; but I suppose the things that were important to me weren't for you.

"I didn't shoot anybody or rob anybody or hit anybody?"

I turned away and watched Jericho, curled up on one side on the ground, his hands pressed together under his cheek, and Boxcar at his feet keeping guard while the old man napped. I didn't want to look at you then because you'd finally talked about yourself as if you knew who you were and I wasn't sure what I'd find in your eyes.

"You spent more time working at the junkyard," I said. "If you did any of that, I didn't know about it."

When I got home I found Ruby sitting at the little kitchen table with a swollen face, one eye closed up, her hands wrapped around a mug of coffee. I stared at her, all the usual feelings flooding through me. First is fear—like I'm living through it even though I didn't see it happen, not that time—then relief because she's alive, then anger at her and at Bishop, and a sick remembering of all the times past, and finally resignation. You can't stop it, the inevitable. It keeps at you until you accept it.

"Please don't say anything," she said.

I got a soda out of the refrigerator, popped it open and took a seat at the table. "Can I say hey?"

She smiled. "Hey."

"Has Celia seen it?"

She shook her head. "I asked Pat to keep an eye on the laundromat for me today."

"What are you going to tell her?"

"I'll go back to work tomorrow. No big deal."

"You can't hide from her. She's going to find out."

"You remember I told you to go see your father? I'm not sure now is a good time."

"No kidding."

We sat at the table and I drank my soda; she never sipped her coffee. She only wanted the feel of it–the heat searing through her hands up her arms into her head. She wanted to suffer in the trailer in July and sweat it all out like a cleanse.

"I never liked the smell of coffee," I told her.

"Really?" She smiled a crooked fat smile. "When I was young, I loved the smell. It was the taste that got me."

"But you like it now."

"It grows on you. The bitterness."

"Well sure," I said. "You put enough cream and sugar in it."

"The smell of it reminds me of Celia and Dad. We'd get up in the morning and the house would be filled with
244

it—this earthy heady aroma. Dad would be in his boxers at the table behind a newspaper and Celia would be flipping pancakes, standing in the kitchen in her nightie and her lacy robe, and her slippers with the feathers at the toes."

I smiled. "Like home, huh?"

"What does it make you think of?"

"Dirty laundry and sweat and body odor with some skunk added in."

Ruby laughed and reached up to put a finger to her cheek, wincing. "So you never tasted it?"

"Once. It was awful." I shuddered, still remembering.

"You get used to it."

"I don't see how that's possible."

She shrugged. "You can get used to anything if you do it enough."

And of course, she was right.

A terrible argument raged that night when Celia got home, one of those family fights—maybe you don't know about those. They involve the usual screaming—always the same words—maybe some slapping, and a lot of crying. It started out well enough. By that I mean it was just between Celia and Ruby and it was the same fight they'd been having for years about Bishop and when was Ruby going to wise up and stay away from him, so I figured I was safe. But once we sat down to eat at the little table, it somehow got turned around to me.

Celia said, "How can you expect Maggie to be strong when you won't even try?"

"I have tried." Ruby was already crying by that point and that only made it worse. "I've done all I can but it's no good. The man's in me, part of me."

"Oh, for crap's sake, Ruby; when are you going to see it for what it is? You want him to do it. Yes, you do. You want a man to make you feel like shit and for the life of me I can't figure out why. Why? And now look at Maggie. Your own daughter, your flesh and blood. Look what you've done to her?"

"She didn't do anything to me."

"You shut up and stay out of it. You're telling your daughter–you've been telling her since she was born–that love is punishment. It's torture. By God, Ruby, are you going to tell her it's murder?"

I pulled Ruby's plate away as she covered her face with her hands and dropped her head to the table, bawling and snorting. You had to feel for her. She'd been caught between Celia and Bishop forever and there was just no pleasing either one of them. I can still remember a summer day when I was nine and there had been a fight that morning like this one. Later that day, Ruby was pushing me in a swing, I'm not sure where it was, and she was telling me–like I was her best friend in all the world, she was saying, "I want to do what my mom wants me to do. I do, I do. But I want to do what Bishop wants me to do, too. I want them both and I can't have both; it's got to be one or the other but I can't choose."

"But you do have both," I said to no one in particular. Neither one of them heard me over Ruby's sobbing and Celia's cursing.

The rest of the evening I got lectured by Celia on all the reasons I didn't want to end up with a man like Bishop–a man like you. I didn't bother to argue; there wasn't anything I could say. When she was tired and ready for bed she asked me if I was still going out to the scrub to see you and I said I was. I said I would keep going out there as long as it took and she couldn't stop me. She walked to her bedroom heavy and slow.

Ruby was on the couch with her head back, her eyes closed, and the trailer was so quiet I could hear her breathing. A light knock hit the door and she popped up and looked around. She thought Bishop had come over; she got up and pulled the door open and I saw her shoulders relax.

39.

I t's Ron," Ruby said turning to me, trying to cover her face with one hand.

He and I sat out front of my trailer on the lawn chairs and I told him what happened. He'd heard it all before.

"She thought you were my dad," I said. "She wouldn't have opened the door if she'd known it was you, not with her face like that. The funny thing is, when she jumped up, I couldn't tell if she was happy to see him, thinking he came to apologize, or scared he'd come to hit her again. It's all the same emotion in her."

"Love and fear," he said.

The sky was lit pink beyond the trailer tops and the park was awash in a pale blue haze. Nearby a mourning dove cooed, 'dear lord, why, why, why?' I remembered the time Ron showed them to me, pointing. "Those are the birds you heard last night when you were crying." We were seven, I think, sitting outside Trailer Haven against the fence on River Front Drive. The doves perched above us on the telephone lines asking, 'dear lord, why,

why, why?'

"Make them stop," I said. "I'll cry again." No other bird sounds as hollow and tormented as a mourning dove.

"Let them coo," he'd said. "If you were as dumb as a dove, you'd be sad, too."

I tried to recall then, why I'd been crying that time, but looking back on it, there were a lot of things to cry about. Suddenly, I felt a rush of guilt and gratitude.

"You remember the mourning doves?" I asked him. "That one time I was crying out by the fence and they were up on the telephone pole?"

His head moved slightly, back and forth; he didn't remember. He said, "There were a lot of times we heard them cry."

We sat for a few minutes listening and a wind picked up and I could feel the wet in the air.

"Rain tonight." I was thinking about you and Jericho, hoping you were wrapping yourselves up in the tarp.

"Maggie."

I realized he'd come to talk to me. I'd forgotten, I suppose, that he didn't live there anymore; Kyle was the only one left. It used to be one or the other of us was always at another's door, come just to sit outside, or to walk around. But we weren't the half-dozen anymore.

"My parents are moving."

"Where to?" We didn't see the Wilson's much anymore; they lived over in the corner lot, at the back, remember? Not the sociable kind, never out at the pool, except when we were all very small.

"A few miles north. They bought a house."

"Well, that's nice." It wasn't like I knew them all that well, but I did try to sound interested.

"It's just that I won't be coming around anymore."

I looked at him a bit too long because it didn't hit my mind at first. But then I figured it out. "But, why not?"

"What's the point?"

My eyelids fluttered, I can still feel them, at the shock of it. What was the point? I was going to say that Putty and Mary still came over; I still saw them. But then I remembered that they came to see their parents and, of course, Putty wanted to see you.

"You don't want to come over to see me?"

"And do what?"

I was going to say swim, ride our bikes, eat ice cream, and I chuckled and shook my head. "Talk?"

"About what?"

"I don't know. Our lives?"

"You mean Jack."

"I don't mean Jack."

"But that's your life, isn't it?"

"That's not true," I said. "This is awful."

"What's awful?"

I got up and started walking around, kicking at the little rocks that escaped Celia's flower bed. "We're fading away," I said. "The half-dozen. I thought we'd be together forever and nothing would really change."

"You remember my brother?"

"Tim," I said.

He nodded. "You know how he was always fighting with my parents? Pissed off all the time. He left as soon as he could and hasn't come back. I asked him about it and you know what he said?"

I sat back down in the chair beside him. "What?"

"He said our parents were worthless—said they ruined him. They verbally abused him, treated him like a servant, demeaned him. He doesn't know how I can stand them. He doesn't care if he never sees them again."

"Is that what they're like?"

"That's the thing, see? I know they weren't perfect, but I don't remember it like that. My experience was almost the opposite of his. And I don't know if it's because they treated me better or not; it probably was. But the result is that my brother and I lived two very different childhoods while sharing a tiny bedroom in that trailer full of cats."

He was looking at me, waiting for me to understand, and I think I did, but I couldn't say it exactly.

"Maybe it was the cats."

He laughed. "You've always tried to make things better by pretending they were."

"So?"

"It doesn't work."

"It does," I said. "You just take the best parts and grow them, work some of that good over onto the bad, that's all."

"But it's an illusion. The bad is still there."

"Not if you only remember it with the good you've put on it."

"Yes it is."

And I knew it was true. Maybe I knew all along. Of course I did. "You're saying Putty and Kyle and Mary...and now you—you don't want to come around

252

anymore? Even if you could?"

"Something like that."

I shook my head. "Why?"

He sighed in that way he does when he thinks I'm dumb. My dad sighs like that. You do, too.

He said, "Putty wouldn't care if Jack was the only friend he had; Jack's the only friend he's ever needed. It was always him and Jack–we were extras. And Kyle. Jesus, Kyle's had another life beyond us since his mom sent him off in middle school. Maybe before that and we just didn't see it."

"Kyle's just Kyle. I mean, he's a drunk, sure and he spends a lot of time at the bar, but he works there."

"He spends a lot of time away from us."

It was my turn to sigh, big and deep, but not at Ron so much as at the truth. "It's normal. I was just being, what's the word, you know...over emotional."

"Melodramatic."

"Yeah, that. I knew we were going to grow apart and move on. I just thought we'd keep in touch. Reunions, or something."

"I'm trying to tell you," he said. "We don't like each other. None of us. Mary can't stand any of us. Kyle only loves Jack. Putty only loves Jack. And I only–"

I could hear him then. Like when your ears pop open after you come out of a loud party...they might stay clogged into the next day and then you turn your head and everything's louder and you wonder how long it had been muted and what you might have missed. It was like that. Just like that.

"But I'll miss you," I said.

"You know where I live."

When he stood to leave, I got up and tried to think of something to say. It seemed like we'd forgotten something in all the years we'd known each other, but whatever it was, neither of us had hold of it. He was ready to say good-bye, but he had a question on his face. Before I realized what it was, he'd reached out to my neck and grabbed the rope, pulling it out from under my shirt. He held the keys in his fingers and looked at me.

"What's this?"

"Keys," I said. His brows lifted like they always do when he's perturbed with me. "You remember Jack vomited at the lake that day?" He nodded. "There were keys in it."

"You picked through his vomit?" He dropped them to my chest and took a small step backward.

"He swallowed three keys and then vomited them up. You don't think that's, I don't know, important?"

"If they're important, why are you wearing them around your neck?"

"I'm waiting for the right time to give them to him."

"When's that going to be?"

I shrugged. "I guess I'll know it when it comes around."

He stared at the keys hanging from my neck for a while, chewing on the inside of his bottom lip. Then he nodded, his head bobbing up and down like a float in the ocean. "I admit, that's the strangest thing I've ever heard. Swallowing keys."

"You see why I'm worried about him?"

"You should be worried about yourself."

"It's okay. Honestly, he's different."

"Now he is. But when he remembers..."

I lifted the keys and dropped them back under my shirt. "I'll be fine."

For a moment he stared at me, like he didn't see me at all. Then he stepped close and hugged me. He kissed me, a little one, on the lips and said, "Give my best to Jack."

I carried the two gallons of water and a bag of sandwiches out into the scrub the next morning to tell you about our senior year in high school and I knew I had only one story after that—a story I didn't want to tell. Both you and Jericho sat hunched and weary under the tree, stroking your beards—his long, scraggly and gray, and yours still stubby and black.

It didn't rain the night before, after all. I felt baked by the heat and there was no wind to ease it; I felt like I was taking in fire with every breath. Only the insects could stand to move and talk in the heat and by afternoon even they would shut up.

"I told him he should move," Jericho said when I sat down and tried to catch my breath. "He can't remember nothing by sitting here staring at the railroad tracks."

"He should go home," I said.

"Maybe he's got to get farther away before his psyche feels safe enough to remember."

"You can stop talking about me like I'm not here," you said.

"Well, you're not."

Jericho laughed so hard he started coughing and Boxcar whined at him. You smiled a little bit, nodded. I

255

think you knew a lot more than you would admit to. You can tell me when you come home if that's so or not. But I was pretty sure you'd remembered enough to know you needed to go back home and let your father help you sort the rest out.

"Did I graduate?" You asked me.

"Yes."

"Was it a good year?"

I looked out across the tracks to the shrubs, the palmettos, and the weak little oak trees. "A year's too long to be good or bad," I said.

40.

We knew you had guns; you'd had them your whole life, but it was rare to see you with one. You had the rifles but you didn't hunt so much anymore. You had a handgun, a slick black thing that looked fake, that you liked to take out to the scrub and shoot at trees once in a while. And one day, you told the boys your dad showed you all the hiding places in the junkyard. You rattled them off.

One gun was stashed in a stack of tires by one of the back sheds and another under the seat of the junked Plymouth in the far corner. There was one by the first shed on the left, behind a row of rusty fans, tucked up inside an old umbrella. Several stuffed in nooks all over both the trailers, the one you lived in and the office.

You weren't bragging when you told us, that's the weird thing, no matter how much Putty and Kyle thought you were the luckiest guy in the world. I think you were trying to tell us it was wrong, somehow.

"A person only needs one gun," you said.

Putty said that wasn't true. You need a rifle for hunting and a handgun for protection.

"It only takes one bullet," you said. "And for that you

only need one gun."

Kyle asked you if you were on something. "Shake it off," he said. "Let's go to the lake."

It had been forever since we'd been out there, but none of us wanted to go. We felt old already. But as the school year passed, things changed. It's a funny thing about that last year in high school. You're getting older and the future is looming and you ought to be scared because you have no idea what you're supposed to do. Ron was the only one who had a plan to make things better. Putty never talked about it—he was just going to keep doing what he was doing, mowing lawns and landscaping. You and I had jobs, but Kyle and Mary had nothing. But even with a job, or a plan, life outside school was like a big open book and we'd be expected to fill it up with stories. So we were scared.

But as the end of the year got closer and closer, a surge of expectation, like electricity, passed through us, stronger than fear—freedom. We could smell it. As if the summer was calling us, telling us it would last a lifetime if we could just make it to June. We'd wear the stupid cap and gown and sit through an agonizing ceremony with sweat pouring down our backs and it would be the last crappy thing the school could make us do. Then we would be free. And we started to feel young instead of old.

One day in April, we all skipped school even though the principal had been yakking every morning all week during announcements that seniors would be suspended if they didn't have a written excuse for not showing up that day. Celia said she'd write every one of us excuses that said we had an epidemic of food poisoning in the trailer park. She didn't do it and she didn't have to.

I went to Mary's the night before and we sat on her bedroom floor painting our toenails and I told her she had to spend Friday with us, not her friends.

"You are my friends," she said.

"You know what I mean."

And she did know. Her friends were all going to the beach. One of their parents had rented a pavilion. They'd have food and probably alcohol and games and races, like it was a national holiday. But she couldn't go. She just couldn't.

"We've been together since kindergarten," I told her. "You have to do this with us. And you have to go out with us after graduation."

"I guess," she said.

In the end, Mary gave us only a little of her time, and I've wondered if that Thursday night before skip day was our last chance with her and we failed. We'd snuck out before–as a group, I mean. When we were in sixth grade, the year Kyle was gone, we all agreed to meet out at the picnic tables at two in the morning and most of us made it. Ron had set his alarm clock and woke his whole trailer up so he wasn't there. And when his dad couldn't get back to sleep, he went out for a walk to smoke a cigarette and heard us talking, stomped over and made us all go home and back to bed.

We did it again in seventh grade and we all made it out and walked to the field behind the plaza. Sitting out there in the dirt with the weeds, surrounded by the dark and the cold of December, we were separate from the world somehow. At one point, our whispering stopped and we listened—the dogs at the junkyard had launched into frenzied barking. You said it must be a raccoon or possum, and then you had to go home.

This time, we gathered on River Front Drive at the side gate and crossed the field on a diagonal, making our way through the woods to avoid walking past the junkyard. We got out into the scrub and hiked in silence to the railroad tracks. The night wasn't hot enough, or wet enough, for mosquitoes. Still, some of us had come smelling of repellent. Kyle brought two bottles of rum. "The only repellent I need," he said, and both you and Putty brought beer. We sat on the tracks drinking and talking.

We reminisced about the good things. Even when we remembered somebody getting hit or teased, somebody running off crying, or getting tossed in the pool, we were laughing about it. It was just like our parents told us—the past gets blurred over time, softened and sweetened. But we danced all around the edges of the dark—those things we'd all forgot by some kind of secret, unspoken agreement.

A train horn echoed from the south—soulful and off-key. We all froze, our heads turned toward it, listening, and I wondered if we were all thinking the same thing—about the time you held Sunny down on the tracks. Mary got up first, and then Ron. I followed them off the rails, headed for a safe distance. But you stood up and faced the south and said, "I see it." Putty staggered to his feet behind you and the both of you stood there, waiting for the train.

You turned to us, your face nothing more than shadow in the night, and said, "Chicken. Last one off wins."

It was stupid, you know. Was it because we were drunk, or because we realized we might never be the half-dozen again, or were we just foolish? Whatever the reason, Kyle and Ron ran over and joined you and you all started hollering and jumping up and down.

Mary looked at me and sighed. "Come on," she said.

So we went over, too.

Standing between the rails, we could see the light of the engine. The horn echoed—reminding me of the mourning doves. The train was thunder and getting closer and I could feel the slight vibration on the rail and lifted my foot off it. Putty was ahead of me, shifting his weight back and forth from one side to the other and I got it in my head somehow that he was making sure nothing would stick; he was preparing to jump off the tracks.

Closer and closer, the thunder of it overtook every other sound and we started to move off, but you grabbed me, turned me back to face the light, and held me close. I tried to pull away but your hands dug into my arms. You put your mouth to my ear and said, "Wait for it."

I thought I heard Putty laughing and Mary screaming and everyone was yelling at you to stop it, to let me go, to get off the tracks and the train was nearly on us and you said it again—you shouted in my ear, "Wait for it." Then you let go of me and you had a gun, aimed at the train.

In that split second before you pulled me off the track with you, I laughed. And I could hear myself saying, "You're going to shoot the train?"

We lay in the dirt with the train rushing past us like an angry hornet. You were face down with Ron on your back, bent over, pinning your hand to the dirt, shouting. Putty was there, then Kyle, wrestling the gun out of your hand and Putty was the one who came up with it. When you staggered to your feet, Mary slapped you in the face and pummeled your chest until you pushed her away. Sobbing, she helped me up and we all stood there staring at one another while the train roared northward and when the track was clear and we heard the despondent dinging of a crosswalk south of us, Mary pulled at my arm and walked me home all the time saying, "It's enough, isn't it? Isn't it time we stopped this? We can't do this anymore."

And I was still laughing about it. You were going to shoot the train.

The next day you came and got me at the trailer for senior skip day and I waited for you to say something about the night before, but you didn't. We spent the day at the pool and cooked hamburgers on the grill and the adults pretended not to notice when Kyle brought the keg over. Mary came by and sat on one of the lawn chairs for a little while, before she left for the beach.

At graduation the next month, Mary posed for pictures with us and was nice about it, before she went off with her friends. Your dad was so proud, Jack. He couldn't stop smiling; he kept slapping you on the back and laughing and saying you did it. You'd gone green around the edges, trying to smile, and we all thought it was the heat. Celia wet a paper towel and put it to your forehead and made you take the gown off.

We all started toward the cars. Ron and I walked

behind you and I heard your dad say, "You're a man now. My boy's a man. Time to act like one, if you know what I mean." He put his fist in your ribs and twisted it, laughing. Ron groaned, embarrassed for you. You stopped, bent over, and vomited your breakfast in the parking lot.

You didn't come to the party at Trailer Haven. Even Mary showed up for a while. They had a big cake for us and everything. Everybody got presents. But you weren't there. Putty said you were sick, but I thought there was something else, something out of place. I snuck off and walked over to the junkyard, but I couldn't go in; I didn't think you were there anyway. I walked around and out into the scrub, out to the tracks, out to the lake. I stood on the pier listening and heard the high-pitched wheezing laughter of the osprey and the little blue heron croaking just like Celia in the morning before her first cigarette—throaty and dry. It was four o'clock by then and you weren't anywhere. I walked back to Beaumont Road and took the path over to the cemetery and stood looking at the dead people, but you weren't there either. It wasn't right that I wanted to find you and you couldn't be found. It just wasn't right.

41.

I thought it would turn out worse than that," you said.

"You thought maybe the story would end with the reason you're out here in the scrub?"

You nodded.

"Graduation was seven years ago."

You were startled by that. "Then there are more stories."

"No."

"And us? You said before that it was over. Was it because I made you stand in front of the train?"

"No. It's been off and on forever. And we're off right now."

Jericho said, "The heart is made true when it battles an angry sea."

"Your book?" I said. He nodded. "What's it mean?"

He looked out over the tracks. "Trouble has a way of making you realize how much you love somebody, that's all."

"I'd like to know what happened between you and

me," you said.

"That's another story."

"So tell him," Jericho said.

I said no. Maybe next time.

"What I want to know is why you was laughing about him shooting the train," he said.

"You don't think it's funny to want to shoot a train?"

"All due respect," he said to you. "It's a touch crazy."

You didn't say anything. You didn't tell him to not say crazy. You looked at me, but didn't see me and I think maybe you remembered it. You knew why you were trying to shoot the train and why I was laughing.

"Maybe it wasn't so crazy," I said. "I mean, if you look at it like a lesson in your little book."

"What lesson would it be?"

"Sometimes the bad is so big and we're helpless in the face of it," I said. "But the strong never quit fighting, no matter how small they are against the enemy."

We all took Boxcar for a walk through the scrub and Jericho told us the truth. He said he'd been in jail a few times and he'd always tell people it was because of the party, because of what he'd done to that girl. She didn't kill herself; that was a lie. A lie he told himself a lot, trying to reason out why he'd turned out so wrong.

"In the end," he said. "I guess it was just growing up there in the heat and the dread of poverty where none of us ever felt like we had enough to eat. Mending our rips and tears over and over again didn't make the fabric stronger so much as it made us meaner."

He and all his friends, he said, did nothing good for nobody. He got married because she was pregnant, same reason as everybody else he knew. And he left her two years later because she was pregnant again. Same story, same ending.

We'd stopped while Boxcar sniffed at the base of a pine and lifted his leg.

"When I was out about a year," he said. "Going town to town, working odd jobs, drinking and smoking off what I earned, it hit me. It's not for money a man should work, but for the wealth of his soul. I couldn't get it out of my head, so I wrote it down in my book. And I tried to live it. Told myself I'd be made whole by it; and when my soul was wealthy, I could go home and find Lettie and the kids and make it right."

"But you never did?" You asked him. "You never went back?"

"I realized going back would have been for me, for my salvation. But it could only bring more pain to Lettie."

We walked again, Boxcar pulling Jericho along to another odor in the bushes.

"Leastwise," the old man said. "That's how I reasoned it. We'll always wonder, those of us who are thinking creatures, when we're telling ourselves the truth and when we're lying like thieves."

"Lying like thieves," you said.

I understand that now, how the lies are cheating us out of our own stories, the truth of who we are. We're stealing from ourselves.

When I got back to Trailer Haven, Putty was sitting in one of the lawn chairs outside my trailer. He saw me and stood up. He was antsy, having trouble looking at me. He shoved his hands in his pockets, took them out again and

267

ran them through his hair and then cracked some knuckles, and into the pockets they went again.

"What's the verdict?" He said. "He remembering?"

A tiny tremor fluttered in my gut. Putty was scared. Like your dad was scared. I got the feeling there was a story I couldn't tell you, something I didn't know about, and that same question came back to me. What did you do, Jack?

"Some, sort of. I think." Maybe it was just me wishing it was so.

"I should go see him," he said.

I nodded. "Maybe you should. Maybe you'll jog the rest of it back into place."

He sat down again and I took one of the other chairs. His knees bounced up and down and he started pulling at one of his thumbs like it needed to come off.

"What happened?" I said. "Before he took the bike off the pier. Was he mad about something?"

He shook his head. "Not that I know of. We're not around so much anymore. None of us. Something could have happened. But it's been years since he went nuts like that."

"Except last year," I said.

Putty winced. "Yeah, that. But that was different. Wasn't it? I mean..."

We sat quiet for a while. He glanced at my trailer behind him and then said, real quiet, "You would take him back. Wouldn't you?"

I looked at him, saw in his eyes the same old struggle. Loving you, fearing you, hating you. Maybe he always thought he was like you and had trouble deciding if that was good or bad. But he wasn't like you. Even when he tried, he couldn't do it.

"If you knew somebody who never lied to you," he said. "And then he told you something that you couldn't believe. I mean, you just could not believe it."

"Like he was abducted by aliens?"

"Sure, like that. Unbelievable. What would you do?"

"What do you mean?""

"Would you believe it? Would you act like it was true? I mean, you know, tell the proper authorities and what not?"

"Will the authorities believe it?" I was smiling at him then, glad he'd changed the subject.

"I don't know. And then what if they do and it was a lie and then you get that person in all sorts of trouble. You know, they're in the paper now, and everybody's mad at them for telling such a lie."

I chuckled. "Do you have something you want to tell me?"

"No, I was just wondering."

"Putty," I said, very serious. "Did they probe you?"

He laughed and jumped up from the chair. "Cut it out."

"Are you going to see him?"

"Maybe. I got to get to work now."

When I went back out into the scrub the next morning, I asked you if Putty came out and you said no. You asked me if I had another story to tell and I said there really wasn't anything left, and anyway, I'd decided to go see my father down south a ways. I asked if you wanted to come with me and you said yes. I don't know

269

why I asked you. Looking back on it, I think it was a test. For all of us. For you, to see if you were lying. One last bit of doubt had to be erased from my head and when you said you'd go to my father's house, I knew for sure you didn't remember.

And a test for Bishop. That was the test I don't understand. Why would I do such a thing?

42.

You'd been gone for twelve days when I saw Tucker again. I was dreaming every night of waking to find you standing over me in the dark, but each morning I had to remember you left me in the scrub with Jericho.

Ruby said I should leave Tucker alone, let him feel what he needed to feel without me getting in the way. I told her I wasn't doing any such thing but she didn't believe me.

"You telling him stories?" She said. "About Jack and the junkyard?"

"No." I couldn't think about you any more without holding my breath and getting dizzy. I couldn't hear your name without wanting to cover my face and weep. The last thing I wanted to do was tell stories.

She was getting ready to leave for the laundromat, sitting on the couch tying her sneakers. The news was on still, it was on day and night since you left us, on whether anyone was in the trailer to watch it or not. I was at the little kitchen table eating toast, moist with melted butter.

I said, "I didn't tell you I went down to see Bishop."

She put her foot down to the floor and sat up to stare

at me. "When?"

"Not two weeks ago."

"And?"

"Do you think a person has to love himself before he can love someone else?" I thought maybe Ruby was wrong about my dad. Maybe he didn't have a demon, maybe he was just mean. Maybe he wasn't capable of real love–but is there real love and fake love? Is one love better than another?

She lit up a cigarette and breathed in deep. When she talked, her words were smoke. "Fractured people are as capable of love as anybody else. Maybe more."

That was the very thing Jericho said, but I still struggled with it. "Why would somebody hurt a person he loves?"

She chuckled. "We hurt the people we love all the time."

"I don't mean everyday hurt."

"I know what you mean," she said. "But pain is pain. It's not like there's a line to draw somewhere that says if you do this awful thing you love them but if you do this, you don't. We hurt each other. On purpose, on accident, because *we're* hurting, because we're messed up and don't know what else to do. It don't have anything to do with the love. That's separate."

She had to be right–I needed her to be. My dad loves me and he hurt me plenty, so she had to be right.

After Ruby went off to work, I found some of the neighbors out at the picnic tables waiting. Before I could sit down, Mr. Haverty said, "We saw that boy of yours this morning."

272

"What boy?"

"Your blond boy, Tucker." Doc Fred said.

"He came through the front gate," Pat Dunn said. "Walking."

"Where is he?"

Mr. Haverty pointed to the back of the trailer park. "He don't look too good."

"None of us look too good," Doc Fred said.

I walked through Trailer Haven to the back gate and I could hear the news through open windows. We were all waiting, just waiting, and I wondered how long it would go on. There would be news and hearings and juries and trials and I was exhausted thinking about waiting and watching through it all. I remembered what Mrs. Swanson said on one of the first days, when we were all still stunned and quiet and wondering where you'd gone to and when you'd come back. She said, "This will be our lives for years to come."

When I came up to the back gate, I saw Mrs. Swanson had chained it shut. She'd hung 'no trespassing' signs along the fence to keep the reporters out. I climbed over and saw Tucker, sitting cross-legged in the dirt in the middle of Beaumont Road facing south. Beyond him, I could see the barricade and one or two police cars down by the junkyard.

Tucker didn't turn around when I came up behind him. His little black gun was on the dirt in front of him when I sat down.

"How much longer?" I asked him.

He shrugged. "They said it could take weeks."

"It's been weeks," I said.

"Just feels like it."

"Why did you bring the gun?"

"Stray dogs, wild hogs, bears."

"I don't want you to shoot Jack," I said.

"I told you I wasn't going to."

"Then put the gun away. It scares me."

He reached for it, slid it around to the other side of him so I couldn't see it.

"Thank you," I said. "You want to go get some dinner tonight?"

"Let's get a pizza and eat it in my room."

"Why don't you go to that hotel where the others are—the other ones waiting for news?"

"I don't want to be around people."

"You want me to leave you alone? Ruby says I should."

"No. You're not people."

"I'm not people?"

"You're Magnolia. Not people."

I chuckled. But I understood what he meant. "What'll you do when you get the news?"

"What do you mean?"

"You'll go back home to Georgia."

"Yeah. I guess I will." I didn't say anything to that and he said, "Sorry."

"It's not your fault. None of this awful thing is your fault. I should say something."

"You just did."

"No, I mean, something deep. Jericho would have a quote to make you feel better. Something from his book about blame or...I don't know."

"He just makes it up, doesn't he?"

"Yep."

"So make something up."

He turned to smile at me, finally, and I said, "Okay." I thought a long time. Tried to make my brain work the way Jericho's does, trying to teach himself the entire lesson of life in a tiny book of lined pages.

"Well?" He said.

"I can't think of anything."

"Maybe because it is my fault."

"How could it be?"

"She asked me to talk her out of it."

Everything stopped, even though nothing really did, and I held on to it. Things start to make sense when you get tiny pieces to put together to make a picture. I knew I should grab hold of that piece and keep it until I had more.

"But she didn't mean it," I said.

"She told me she'd stay if I wanted her to. All I had to do was say so. She wasn't even sure she wanted to go. I told her she was only nervous. 'It's an adventure. It's normal to be nervous.' And I told her she should go."

"It's not your fault."

"You can keep saying that all you want but it won't make it true."

"If your sister is in there—and we aren't even sure she is—you can't say you killed her. You can't say you did it."

"There's plenty of blame to go around. It doesn't have to be just me or him. I'm partly to blame. I should have told her to stay."

"You couldn't have known."

"I should have known."

"That's crazy."

"I don't care." He grabbed his gun and stood up. "I don't care if it's crazy or stupid. I just know I'm wrong. My parents wanted her to stay home. I wanted her to stay home. She even wanted it. But I sent her away."

I stood in front of him, ready to say different, tell him he couldn't do it to himself, but I had no words for it. And then I knew what Jericho would say. He'd say you can't talk a man out of his own self-loathing. You can only love him despite it. I was afraid of the gun, but I stepped into him and wrapped my arms around him. He rested his head against mine.

"Please don't shoot me," I said.

"It's still not loaded."

Relief flooded through me and he laughed—or he was crying. I held on tighter, thinking either way he needed me to.

43.

We left Jericho and Boxcar at the little oak with your backpack and the supplies and headed south along the tracks and I asked you if the stories helped–if you were remembering. You said you felt like you were standing in front of a door and all you had to do was open it. But you couldn't do it; there was something stopping you.

"Don't you remember anything at all?" I was sure you did.

"Yes," you said.

"Tell me."

"I can picture the junkyard. And the dogs in the runs. I remember my room. My mother–she's cooking, cleaning, dancing. You and Putty, Kyle and Mary, and Ron. I see us at the pool and in the scrub and at the bus stop. But when I see these things, I don't know them. I know what they are and what they're supposed to be, but they're foreign and strange. It's like I don't belong there, in my own life–if it really is my life."

"But do you remember doing the things I told you about?"

"Some. But they're different. Twisted up, somehow."

"It'll come back," I said.

"And then what?"

"Then you go home. And you decide."

"Decide what?"

"Who you want to be."

"You would forgive me? For what I did?"

"Of course."

"And Sunny. Would she forgive me?"

"She already has."

"How do you know?"

I chuckled. "She couldn't help it. None of us could."

"What happened to her? Where did she go?"

"That's something you're going to have to remember on your own," I said.

On the other side of the woods we were in my dad's neighborhood. We walked over to Wycoff and turned west and passed by all the little houses, dogs barking at us from behind fences, kids in weedy front yards spraying each other with hoses, cars up on blocks with young men standing around them covered in grease, drinking beers.

"This is my dad's," I said, stopping in the road. "You stay here. I'll just be a minute or two."

As I walked up the little driveway, I saw my dad at the front window. He was glaring at you and I turned to see you kicking up dirt. When I got to the door, it opened and my dad came out and didn't even look at me.

"Daddy," I said.

He pushed past me and started toward you.

"Dad," I called.

But he didn't hear me, I think. You saw him coming at you and you just stood there, with this blank look on your face. I called your name and if you'd understood–if you'd remembered–you'd have run; but instead you let him walk up and punch you in the face. You fell backward to the ground and I screamed. Bishop leaned over, grabbed you, and picked you up only to throw you down again.

My dad was smaller than I remembered him, and darker, like he'd been left in the sun. But he still had those arms that pulsed with strength, always ready to beat something back down to where he thought it ought to be.

"Stop it," I yelled and I was at him, but someone grabbed me and pulled me away.

My Grandma Hanson had come out to get me. You were lying on the dirt road with your hands up in front of your face and my dad got a couple of kicks in before the neighbor got hold of him. Everybody was yelling except you, and the dogs behind the fence had gone mad. My dad called you a lousy stinking piece of shit and my grandma wanted to know what I was thinking bringing you over there, and you stared up at us like a wild animal.

The neighbor got my dad to go inside and I called back to you to wait for me as my grandma pulled me to go with her. You were up by that time and looking at your hands.

My dad was in the little kitchen at the little round table wiping the spit off his face. He grabbed his can of beer and guzzled it.

"Maggie, what were you thinking?" Grandma Hanson said.

I sat next to my dad. "I'm sorry."

He leaned forward and put his head in his hands for a

few seconds, then he sat up and slapped the table.

"Tell me you ain't seeing him again," he said.

"It's not like that. He's troubled is all. I'm helping."

"Troubled?" Grandma Hanson said. "I'll say."

My dad wouldn't look at me; he was staring at his hands on the table and he balled them up into fists.

"It's all right," he said.

"What do you mean?" Grandma said. She was standing in her little kitchen with one hand on the counter and the other on her waist. She'd got fatter and grayer in the year I'd been away and her mouth pulled much deeper into the frown she always wore. "She had no cause bringing him here."

"I said it's all right."

My grandma shut up then and started wiping down her counter tops, muttering. The fan at the open sliding glass door oscillated side to side and between the irritating hot breezes, sweat trickled down the sides of my face. Two Rottweilers outside, in the dirt of the backyard, could have been dead for all I knew; they lay still in a tiny patch of shade on one side of the doghouse.

"It's good you're here, Sunshine," my dad said. He tried to smile and lit up a cigarette, pulling the ashtray across the table toward him. It was then I remembered how beautiful he used to be. He still was, under the lines and gray stubble, behind the scars on his face and neck from bar fights. "Good to see you. How's your mom?"

"You know how Mom is."

He turned his head slightly and eyed me, smirking. He nodded. "And Celia, the old witch; how's she doing?"

"I came over to ask you something."

"What's that?"

Suddenly I felt stupid–like I had no business in it. It was always between Ruby and Bishop and no one else. I knew that wasn't true, but that's the way everybody tried to see it–it's personal between them and it doesn't have anything to do with me. I couldn't just blurt it out and I didn't know what to say instead. Pictures started coming at me, in my head, and I thought that must be what you felt–confused and grasping at things as they rush past. I found one and hung on.

"Remember Easter Sunday when I was eight?"

He took a drag on his cigarette but didn't answer me; it wasn't one of those questions that really needed answering. But in the kitchen, Grandma Hanson said, "I remember."

"We were living at the trailer park and they had an egg hunt for the kids out in the big grassy field behind the plaza and you went around with me and you'd whistle and wink and nod to help me find the eggs. You carried my basket and held my hand and walked with me back home. You carried the sliced turkey in that flimsy aluminum pan and it was so full it buckled and you almost spilled it. And everybody at the trailer park brought food and we all ate at the picnic tables, swatting at fat flies. You remember?"

My Grandma had come to sit with us at the table and they both looked at me, sort of sad and worried.

"When are you going to stop doing that," my dad said.

"Don't you remember?" I was urgent by that time, insisting on it.

But he shook his head. "You can't make it better just by telling it better."

"Yes you can."

"Don't be ridiculous," Grandma Hanson said.

"You can't," he said.

"*You* do," I told him. "Don't you?"

My grandma let out something like a laugh and choke together.

"You do," I said. "Every time you hit Ruby, you'd tell it later, and it wasn't the way it happened."

"I didn't lie."

"You did. You left out so much."

"What? What did I leave out?"

Me, I wanted to say. You left me out. I sat for a second or two wondering if Ruby was right. He was older. I could see it in and around his eyes and in the way his middle jutted out and his chest sank in. He was drained; maybe he was tired of himself. I said a little prayer in my head then. *Please God, make him grow tired of himself.*

"Look," he said. "Maybe I tried to make it out like I wasn't so bad, like I couldn't help it. But I can't change the past or what I did. Nobody can."

"But you loved Ruby, didn't you?"

He thought a bit and said, "Would you call that love?"

"I don't mean that—I don't mean what you did to her."

"People what love each other," my grandma said. "Don't treat each other like that."

"Don't they?" I looked back and forth between them. My dad was shaking his head and smoking; he took a big sip out of the can of beer and it slid across the table when he put it down.

"I love her," he said. "God Almighty knows how much."

The outer corners of his eyes were shiny wet and I got a hint of joy inside me because I had my answer. And it wouldn't matter what anybody ever said after that—not even you.

"And I'm sorry. Sorry for what I did to her and to you. But that don't make me a better person."

"Course it does," Grandma said.

Bishop glared at her and she turned away, her head first, then her shoulders, and finally she rose out of her chair and went back to wiping the counter tops in the kitchen.

On Easter Sunday, when we were eight, we had an egg hunt out in the big field behind the plaza, but I didn't find any eggs. I stood with my basket, waiting. I had a new dress, sunny yellow with tiny white tufts of thread like dots all over it. I followed everybody back to Trailer Haven and they dug through their baskets, popping open the plastic eggs to see what they got. Ron gave me some of his eggs and told me to open them, but I didn't. I was waiting. Later we all had a big turkey dinner out at the picnic tables and I told Ruby I wasn't going to eat until my dad showed up. He promised he'd be there. Ruby made me a plate of food and said I had to eat it, but I sat and waited. Everybody was in the pool and I still waited. They were eating pie and I waited.

Finally my dad showed up. He was drunk and Ruby was yelling at him in front of everybody, telling him he missed the turkey dinner. So he picked up the tray with the leftover turkey in it and threw it at her and stalked away. I'd been crying since the egg hunt and I didn't think I could cry any more. But tears never get used up.

When I left my dad's house, you were gone and I ran to the railroad tracks, scared that you'd pack up and leave me for bringing you to my dad's. But I found you waiting for me, pacing back and forth. When you saw me, I knew somehow everything had changed, even before you said it.

"You lied to me."

44.

I just stood there, looking at your eyes–endless and deep again, the way eyes are supposed to be, and filled up with everything I knew and more.

"You lied to me," you said again.

"It doesn't have to be a lie."

You shook your head and chuckled, angry, like I was stupid, and everything in me sank like the earth was pulling at me. It would all go back to the way it was before. I told myself it didn't matter. I had my answer and that was all I needed. We could fix it, now. You and me together.

"You remember everything?"

"Not everything." You turned and started walking up the tracks and I chased after you. "But I remember you."

"It doesn't have to be a lie," I said.

"You can't change a person by pretending they didn't do what they did. You can't just say it was somebody else–that I hit someone else, stabbed someone else, raped someone else. It doesn't work that way."

"It did before."

"What did you think was going to happen when I remembered it all? You thought I'd believe I did all that shit to some made-up person?"

"Yes."

"Why would I do that?"

"You did it before."

You stopped and turned on me, your mouth twisted up into an angry smirk, disgusted. "What the hell are you talking about?"

"*You* did it. Not me. You didn't remember any of it. Why do you think Putty still says none of it happened? He was right there when you stabbed me with the pencil and he still says it never happened. They all saw you try to drown me in the ditch, but Putty says it didn't happen. Why is that, Jack?"

You flinched.

"Because you said it didn't happen," I said. "Nobody could do anything about it. Nobody could help me, because you'd come after them if they told the truth. Jack, you invented Sunny, not me."

I saw it in your face for a fraction of a second–the sudden impact of the truth. "Your dad calls you Sunshine," you said. You closed your eyes and your face scrunched up and you put your hands over it and bent over like you'd been punched in the gut. When you stood up again, you mumbled, saying oh God oh God oh God. And you hit your head with your fists. "I have to leave," you said. "I have to get out of here."

"But why?"

You started walking again.

"I'll come with you," I said.

"What's wrong with you?" You yelled it out into the scrub, like an answer might rain down from heaven and

286

we'd both understand. "What's wrong with us?"

"There's nothing wrong with us. Nothing wrong with trying to make it work. To fix it."

At that you turned on me again, came at me, grabbed my right arm and squeezed hard.

"Look at it," you said. "I fucking stabbed you with a pencil. You can still see the lead."

"You were little—"

"Look at it," you screamed at me and twisted my arm, grabbed the hair on the back of my head with your other hand and forced me to see the mark. "And when I took you out into the junkyard and raped you by the dog runs, what was I then? A little kid, Maggie?"

"It's okay, Jack. It's okay."

You pushed me away and started walking again. A sound escaped you, with each step you took, something like a whine, or a cry. You wrapped your hands around your middle once and looked up to the sky and said, "oh, God," and then you stopped, doubled over and put your hands on your thighs and I thought you were going to vomit, but you didn't.

"You didn't know what you were doing. You never remembered any of it the next day. It was stories is all. Stories in your head about Sunny."

You laughed then, that mean laugh I should have been used to. "That doesn't change anything. It doesn't change me."

"You've done bad things. We all know you must have done something awful and it's messed you up. But we can fix it."

"You don't fix things by pretending they didn't

happen."

"You can. It's like forgive and forget."

You started north again, quiet for a long time, and all we could hear was our footsteps in the sand and the cicadas shrieking. "Not this," you said.

I followed you all the way back, toward the tree where we'd left Jericho, trying to think of something to say and all I could manage was, "It's okay now. We can move on from it now."

But you said no. You said I had no clue, no fucking idea what I was talking about and then you ran away from me and at first I thought you were trying to leave without me. Then I heard Boxcar yelp and scream and I stopped and my mouth opened, but no sound came out.

45.

I still don't know how much you remember, Jack. I don't know if you'll ever get this or if you want it. The truth is Jericho was right, wasn't he? It's my story really. Not yours at all. Maybe I've been telling it for myself all along.

You'd been gone for sixteen days. I was alone in the trailer. Celia and Ruby were working and I was supposed to call them as soon as I knew anything. But when I saw her face, her picture, on the television I panicked. I realized the police had already contacted Tucker and everything fell into place. I knew why he was here. I left the trailer and ran north all the way to the motel and banged on the door to Room Six. I screamed at him to open the door. I begged him to let me in.

"Tucker, please," I said.

A man came out of one of the rooms down the way to look at me and I was crying. Finally the door opened and Tucker was standing there. I rushed in and grabbed him, held him tight. I told him it was okay. Everything was okay. He broke down then, fell to the floor; I went down with him and we stayed like that for a long time, leaning against the bed.

When he stopped sobbing, when he'd wiped his face and nose with the tissues, I got up and took the gun off the table and put it back in his suitcase. We lay on the bed, wrapped up in each other, and I told him he couldn't do it. He couldn't do it to Jessica; she wouldn't want it that way. And he couldn't do it to his parents. And he couldn't do it to me.

The motel telephone rang and he sat up to answer it and I listened to his half of the conversation.

"Mom," he said. "Yes. Yes. Okay. I'll be there."

After he hung up, he sat on the edge of the bed for a while, his head in his hands. Then he lay back down beside me.

"Thank you," he said.

"For what?"

"For everything."

"How did they know?"

"That day I saw you at the police station, I was there to file her dental records." He was quiet for a long time and then he said, "I was going to kill him first. But I knew I'd never get close enough. So it was just going to be me. But...today, when my parents called and told me they'd heard from the police, I got the gun out and I sat here with it and I realized I was waiting for something."

He stopped, so I said, "For what?"

"I was waiting for you to come and stop me. I told myself I'd wait ten minutes. After ten minutes, I told myself I'd wait an hour. I didn't have to keep telling myself."

"I ran over as soon as I heard it on the news."

We walked down to the little store and got a six-pack;

290

Tucker handed me his wallet and let me pay because he was shaking all over. We sat at the little table with the curtains open so we could watch for bums and prostitutes and he drank like it was a drug to make him forget. He remembered that his phone was off and went to get it.

"My mom was worried," he said and scrolled through all the messages he'd missed. "They're flying in tonight. They'll be here for a while, one or both. Until we can take her home."

"I don't want to meet them."

He looked up at me, a sad half smile at his lips, and nodded. I got up and closed the curtains and we made love and he went into the bathroom after and stayed a long time. Then he got dressed to go to the airport. He wouldn't look at me.

"I'm always going to be here on this day," I told him. "When you think of me."

He wrapped me up and held me tight and said, "No."

I took the gun, even though he promised he wouldn't do anything with it. I carried it home in a paper bag.

46.

You were ahead of me, so you saw it all before I knew anything was wrong. You ran toward a man I'd never seen before. He was behind your stubby oak with a bat, swinging it downward into a patch of rosemary and Boxcar was yelping. Before you got to him, he tossed the bat aside and fell to the ground, his hand stabbing at something in the scrub and I wouldn't let myself think it was the dog. He didn't see you coming, but his friend did; he kicked Jericho up against the oak a few times and ran off north, carrying a bag and I remember wondering what he could have stolen from a bum. Jericho had nothing.

By the time I caught up, you had the bat and swung it; the man fell forward to his hands and knees and turned, panicked, one arm raised, to look up at you. Swinging again, you caught him across one side, leaving him stretched out at your feet. He shrieked when you raised the bat over him.

I screamed then. "Jack, no," I said. And you stood frozen, the bat above your head. The man put both hands over his face, begging you not to do it. You dropped the bat and kicked him. He got up and ran, limping, his arms wrapped around his middle.

Boxcar was wriggling in the dirt, bloodied and warped, whining. Jericho tried to get to us, crawling, his nose dripping blood. He was saying, "No, no, no."

You pulled him up and took him back to the tree. I watched you dig a towel out of one of the backpacks and hold it up to his face. You put your hand on his head, Jack, and you said something to him I couldn't hear. I saw it. I saw you lean forward and kiss him on the forehead. Boxcar let out a long shuddering whine and I kept my eyes on you; I was afraid to look.

"Go get a shovel," you said to me as you approached and picked up the bat.

I was dazed, still. None of it had quite come to rest in my head. "What?"

"At Doc Fred's trailer. There's a shovel in that little shed he has out front. Go get it."

My eyes fell on the bat in your hand and then I forced myself to look at Boxcar; he was still whining, but not as loud, and twitching in spasms. He'd been stabbed, his middle slashed open. He'd be dead soon. And you wanted a shovel. I looked again at the bat.

"Go," you said. "And don't look back. Just go."

I could make all kinds of judgements about it now. I could say, isn't it funny how I did it? I turned and ran into the scrub toward home and I didn't look back. I didn't want to see it. None of us wanted to see it, did we? And there you were the whole time trying to show us. But we closed ourselves off from it.

By the time I got back, you'd put the bloody towel over Boxcar and Jericho and I watched you did a big hole and put him in it. Jericho told us what happened. They came down the tracks and asked him for money, drugs, whatever he could give them.

"I said, 'I'm same as you, I ain't got nothing.' But they took our packs and dumped it all out and Boxcar, he'd been out doing his business and come across the tracks, growling, baring his teeth." Jericho sucked in a ragged breath. "That one boy hit him. Slammed him with the bat and Boxcar yelped but still he leapt at him."

You were shoveling the dirt back in and the old man stepped forward and looked down into the hole and said, "Poor old dog."

You told me to pack up all of Jericho's things and as I did it, you went over to a good sized scrub pine and started whacking it with the bat. I heard it. Thwap thwap. Again and again and I started crying. A loud crack echoed around us and you kept at it, until the bat was broke in two and you flung the pieces away.

You started shoving all your stuff into your backpack. "I want you to take Jericho to the trailer park," you said. "To Mr. Haverty and Celia. Get him to a shelter. Maybe the C.I.T.A. mission up north."

Jericho said, "No, I'll stay here," but you didn't hear him.

All those pieces to your puzzle were left scattered in the dirt after you'd packed away the big stuff. The heart locket, the dog tag pendant, the journal, all of it. You were on your knees, taking each thing, holding it for a second, like it meant something to you and you almost knew it. Then you had the gold wedding band. You held it up to show me.

"He told you this was my mom's?"

I nodded.

I don't think I've seen rage like that before. Not on you, not on Bishop, on nobody. You stood up and let out a roar, like an agonized final breath, and then you walked over to the tracks and set the band on the rail. I was starting to understand.

You put the rest of the pieces into the front pocket of your backpack and then started gathering up the keys. You examined them, one by one, turning them, tracing the cut edges with your trembling fingers and I thought you were trying to find the right one.

"Are you looking for the keys?" I said.

You didn't hear me.

"You swallowed them."

Your breath rattled in and out in a jagged sort of way.

"Jack." You looked up at me. "You swallowed them and then took Ron's bike into the lake. You vomited them up on the sand after. You remember?"

I pulled the black rope off my neck and held it out to you. "Here," I said.

The life drained out of your face when you saw them, but you took the rope and ran your fingers over the keys and then pulled it over your head. You stood up and grabbed your backpack, leaving the rest of the keys in the dirt.

"How long have I been out here? How long?"

"About two weeks."

You put your palms to the sides of your head and squeezed. "Two weeks," you said. "Jesus Christ. I have to go."

296

"Where?"

You swung the backpack over your shoulder and when you turned to me, I saw it was all there again, the fear and the rage, loss and secrets. You shook your head and glanced behind you up the tracks.

"Why'd you swallow them, Jack?"

A shudder escaped you, and something like a whine. You put your hands to your face, pressed your fingertips into the flesh and I thought you were trying to pull it off your head.

"I've been stopping myself forever," you said. "There's always a way to keep yourself from doing what you know you have to."

"I don't understand."

You dropped your hands and looked at me, weary and pained. "Listen to me," you said. "If you see my dad, tell him I'm sorry."

"But Jack."

"Tell him I tried not to do it. But I had to. I *have* to."

"Jack."

"I love my dad. You know that, right?"

"Wait," I said. "You can't go yet. There's one more story." And I started talking before you could say anything to stop me.

47.

It was last summer, I said. After school got out and we had a new batch of graduates at Trailer Haven. I was pregnant and you drove me over to Orlando, to the clinic, on Saturday morning in your dad's truck and waited all day. On the ride home you asked me if I was okay and I said yes and that was all we said to each other.

On Sunday afternoon they had the graduation party out by the pool with a cake and hot dogs and we were all there, the half-dozen. Even Mary, and she was drinking beer with the boys. After a while we all walked over to the field behind the plaza and sat in the dirt and we talked about the time we all buried something important, a part of us, and nobody mentioned that it had all been dug back up and stolen from us.

We weren't laughing, but we were smiling, like we'd made it through a trial. As if childhood and youth at Trailer Haven was a torment to be survived and we'd done it and come out changed and not quite whole. If we were whole we'd have been laughing about it.

It started out innocent enough.

"Why don't you have a beer?" Kyle said to me,

holding out one of his extras.

"No thanks."

"Why aren't you drinking?" Mary said.

"I don't feel like it."

I could see your chin set rigid and your eyes go blacker like the trigger had finally been set.

And Mary said, joking, "Are you pregnant or something?"

I laughed. "Right. I'm pregnant."

And you said, "Shut the hell up."

Ron got up and said, "Leave her alone."

"Just shut the hell up," you said.

Ron took a step toward you. "We're not going to do this anymore, Jack. Why don't you head on home."

You stood up and got real close to him and said, "What's it to you, anyway?" You turned to me. "Is this what you want? You want this jerk-off running your life?"

I got up and was telling you to stop it, but you kept going, on and on about how you'd seen us looking at each other, you knew we'd been aching over it for years, and why didn't we just do it already. And then you said it.

"Then you can kill his baby like you did mine."

We were all stunned, even you, but it only took a few seconds before Ron hit you. You shoved him off easily and came at me, punched me in the face. I fell down and you stood over me, picked me up off the ground and hit me again. The guys jumped on you then, pulling you away, and Mary got me up and we ran toward home, across the field to the side gate. You followed; the boys tried to stay ahead of you, to keep you off me.

We'd got almost to the picnic tables inside the trailer

park when you had me again. You slapped me hard across the face, cursing, and I could feel your spit on my neck. Before I knew it, my dad laid you flat and started kicking you, and the whole trailer park was up and pulling you two apart. My dad was screaming at you. He said to stay away from me—said if you ever laid a hand on me again he'd kill you, rip your heart out and feed it to your dogs. Finally, Mr. Haverty took you away, walked you to the junkyard.

Then my dad started in on me. "That's it. You'll never see that fuck-up again. You hear me?"

I told him to leave me alone. Told him he had no right to tell me what to do or who to see. Told him if anybody was a fuck-up it was him and I never wanted to see him again. And then he slapped me across the face, back-handed, the way he always did my mother. As I ran off to the trailer, I heard Ruby behind me screaming obscenities at him.

And later that night, after they'd cleaned up from the party, I went out and sat with everybody at the picnic tables and Mr. Haverty said, "What happened?"

I looked over at Mary and Kyle and Putty and Ron and Mr. Haverty said, "We already asked them and it did no good. Somebody tell us what happened."

I said, "Nothing."

And then they knew, I guess. That it was you. All those times I was hurt, when they found me tied to a tree with my clothes in shreds, when Celia had to cut off all my hair because duct tape was stuck in it, and she suspected something awful because I wouldn't get out of the shower—whenever Mary would run me home crying.

301

You did it. And I think they finally understood that they'd known it all along. But it wouldn't be until Putty told them that they'd be able to let themselves really see it.

When I finished telling you all that, there in the scrub by the spindly little oak, Jericho watching us, sorry for us, you just nodded.

"You don't have to go because of me," I said.

You chuckled, an angry kind of cough and said, "It's nothing to do with you."

"But I love you," I said. "I don't care about the past."

"You're not hearing me."

"Don't you love me, Jack?" I knew you did. I had my answer and it was yes. What you did wasn't mixed up in love—what you did wasn't what you felt.

You looked around, at the train tracks, at the way north, at Jericho—him standing there, his eyes pleading, like we were all he had left in the world and we were leaving him. When you turned back to me, you said, "I can't say it. Don't you get it?"

I shook my head no.

"I didn't honor it, Maggie. I trashed it. I was driven to it, because I...never mind why. It's not important why."

"Just tell me you love me."

"I'm not going to cap a lifetime of hurting you like that. It's not right."

You put your hands on my face and kissed me. I was going to tell you that you were *there*, right then. That was the good in you and if you held on to it everything would be okay. But I didn't say it.

"You'll come back, won't you?" I said. "You'll fix it and then come home."

"I'll fix it," you said.

Jericho and I watched you walk away, up the tracks, for a long time, waiting for you to look back but you didn't. I expected to see your fists hit your temples, and I'd play it all out in my head. You'd say, "Forget, forget, forget." You'd tell me how much you loved your dad and I'd say I loved mine, too. Then we could keep going and not let any of the bad hurt us. Until next time.

As Jericho and I headed through the scrub to the trailer park, I asked him if he didn't have something to say—a deep and meaningful verse from his journal that I'd want to understand, but probably wouldn't. He laughed and pulled his little book out of his pants pocket and handed it to me.

"I don't want to take it with me," he said. "I want you to have it. I want it safe."

And then I leaned in and kissed his cheek.

48.

In the middle of that night after you left, a girl ran around in Trailer Haven screaming and banging on doors. Doc Fred caught her. We all saw the police take her away, wrapped up in a blanket, and Doc Fred told us later she didn't have a stitch of clothes on—skin and bones—and could barely stand once inside his trailer. They'd brought over a special policewoman for her. It was so dark, even the dim porch lights that all flickered on when the screaming started couldn't show me her face. But I could hear her crying, gasping. She was still afraid.

They took your dad away an hour before dawn. We were still awake, most of us, shaken, when the blue flashing lights came down River Front Drive and shut off before they got past the side gate. We counted a dozen cars and a van. Standing out back near the dead end, where we could see down Beaumont Road, we thought we'd hear something—shouting, gunshots. But there was nothing. We didn't even know what happened until the news the next day.

Coroners' vans came and then detection dogs and backhoes and it was all there on the news every day.

People started showing up at the convenience store—families with missing girls—and the police told them to go home and wait. But they didn't. We got to see the trailer park and the junkyard on television, from a helicopter with a camera on it, and it sometimes spun around in a slow circle and made us dizzy. We could see them searching, gutting the ground near the sheds by the dog runs in the back.

The whole country, maybe even the world, was watching us and every night a horrible woman on television glared into the camera, peered right into our trailers, and said awful things.

"Somebody there had to know. There's no way this went on down there all these years and not one person saw anything. These people have blood on their hands, mark my words." She paused just to sneer at us and nod. Then she said, "Where is Jack Beaumont, this monster's son? Why isn't he behind bars, too? If not for the safety of girls everywhere, for his own?" And we sat there, all of us, watching when she said, "I wouldn't be surprised if a father somewhere has found Jack Beaumont and dished out some vigilante justice."

Reporters knocked on our doors and shoved microphones at us, asking us what we knew. They wanted to hear about Digger and about you. They asked us stupid questions like, "How do you feel?" and "Were you surprised?" Until Mrs. Swanson closed and locked the gates and put up signs and we all agreed we'd ignore them.

One day, I was told to close up the bait shop and come home. When I got there, Putty was sitting on the couch, his legs up on his toes, jiggling, twitching. He was hunched over, his hands clasped together and held hostage between his knees. What's worse, he was crying. He looked at me and shook his head and sobbed.

Doc Fred was there and Mr. Haverty. And Celia and Ruby. They all gaped at me like they couldn't believe I was alive, so I knew Putty had told them the truth about all the things you'd done to me and they had no more excuses, no more barriers to put up to keep from seeing it. But it was more than that. Doc Fred got up and said they had to take Putty to the police.

"What is it?" I said.

But they couldn't tell me. They didn't have the words. They sat there, shaking their heads.

"Tell me."

"You tell her," Mr. Haverty said. "Then you come on out and we'll go down to the station."

Once they'd gone outside, Putty shook his head and said, "I don't know if I can tell it again."

I sat next to him, put my hand on his leg. "You told them about what he did to me," I said. "Why?"

"They asked me about it."

It all fell out of him then, all the stuff you told him years ago. When we were fifteen the two of you went out into the scrub and got drunk and you started crying and Putty wanted to know what was wrong and you told him. You said you saw everything. At first you weren't sure it was real. Your mom would be sitting on the couch watching television, or standing in the kitchen making a sandwich and your dad would just walk up to her and stab her. With an ice pick or a steak knife or a screw-

307

driver. In the legs, in the arms, in the hands. And he'd bandage her up and kiss the wounds and then burn her with a cigarette. And your mom was numb, you told him. She wouldn't scream, or even cry out; but sometimes you'd find her weeping. When we were all eight, he stabbed her to death. A million tiny wounds all over her body, you said. And your dad cried because he couldn't stop the blood. There weren't enough bandages. And he told you how much he loved her. He hurt her because he loved her.

Putty said your dad told you that if you told anybody what happened, they'd take him away and strap him down to a bed and poison him to death. He made you promise you would forget what you saw. He gave you your mom's gold heart pendant and you buried it that day in the field because you knew you couldn't forget if you kept it.

You told your dad you would forget. You had to. Because you loved him.

"I didn't believe him," Putty said. "And I told them that. I thought it was a story, like the ones he'd always tell about Sunny. And Celia asked me what I meant and I told them how he'd stab you or tie you up or hit you and then he'd talk about it like he'd done it to somebody else—like it was just a story he was telling."

And they thought that was all there was to tell.

"So, he was hurting that girl...his new girlfriend?" Ruby said.

"The girl what come through here the other night?" Doc Fred said.

Putty said no and told them the rest. Your dad picked girls up off the highway sometimes. He took you with
308

him when you were little—tell you to smile at them, let them sit in the middle of the seat between you and him. He'd make some excuse. Say he could drive them up north a ways if that's where they were headed. But let him stop by home first to pack a quick bag and you and he would visit your uncle once he dropped them off. But they never got dropped off, you said. They never got out of the junkyard. One of them had on a ring and your dad stole it from her and then married her with it. He married them all, you told him. And he made you talk about them like they were your mother until he took the ring off their fingers.

Your dad would make you dig the holes and he would roll the barrels into them and you'd both cover them up and he'd show you what he got. He'd pull a pendant or an earring out of his pocket, or a lock of hair. He kept the souvenirs on his dresser in your trailer and you'd spy on him—watch him stand there naked touching them. And when he'd turn and see you, he'd tell you that he loved them and he loved you, too, and you had to forget.

And when you were fifteen, he brought home another one and you tried to help her. You told Putty you went to the shed with the keys and tried to unchain her from the wall but your dad caught you and he shot her—right in front of you, before you could say anything. Then he cried and told you he was sick and couldn't help it. It was partly your fault, he said. If you weren't around, he could really get married again and he wouldn't need to find these girls to take it all out on. But he would never get married again because he loved you too much. It was just the two of you—best pals—and he told you if you ever told

309

anybody, they'd take him away and strap him into the electric chair and fry his brains. You had to forget all of it–it never happened. You didn't see anything. And he promised he would never do it again. And you loved him and feared him and you had to forget.

"Jack said he was doing the best he could to put it somewhere else and not look at it."

Putty stopped talking and I sat beside him for a while not knowing what to say. I could see you, every age at once, smacking your temples with your fists, rubbing them raw, muttering, "Forget."

"Why didn't you make him tell?" I asked him. "Why didn't *you* tell?"

"I didn't believe him. I thought he was nuts. Nuts."

It wasn't too long afterward that they started identifying the bodies and showing the girls' photos on the television and the entire trailer park sat inside their trailers watching with their mouths open but no words to speak, and shaking their heads. It was like a dream–confusing but too real–and we all knew we wouldn't wake up from it so much as walk slowly away from it day after day for years.

49.

When we were sixteen, in the middle of tenth grade, I woke one night to find you standing next to my bed in the dark. You remember? I was startled at first, but you put your hand over my mouth and whispered in my ear. "You want to go out to the lake?"

I can still hear the vibration of silence in my ears as we snuck through the living room. Once we slipped out of the trailer and into the chilly night air, I thought the world was alive with nothing but the moon and the ground under our feet. It was January–cold and damp and quiet. You took my hand and didn't let it go. We didn't speak as we snuck through Trailer Haven, out the back fence, down Beaumont Road and far beyond the junkyard so the dogs wouldn't see us.

Once out in the scrub, I asked you where everybody else was and you said you didn't care and I could feel the want of you like I was on fire. If Ruby and Celia only knew–if they knew who you were in the dark with just me. Quiet, gentle, and sweet. If they could see the outline of your shoulders against the moonlight and the curve of your mouth in a cautious smile, they'd understand.

All the way to the lake, we whispered stories about the half-dozen. You told me that Putty was getting on your nerves; he wouldn't let you alone. It was like being married, you said, and we laughed and tried not to wake the scrub. And I told you that Mary was in love with one of the junior varsity football players and she let him put his hands inside her pants but then she changed her mind and he called her a cunt. And you said we should do something, maybe stash a joint in his locker and then report him. You said Kyle was mad at you all the time now and you went over to his trailer to ask him about it but Putty showed up and Kyle told you both to get the hell out.

When we got out onto the pier, we sat at the very end, on the edge—you cross-legged, smoking a cigarette, me with my feet dangling over the water, swinging back and forth.

"You want to hear a story?" You said.

I thought you were going to tell me about Sunny because those were the only kinds you'd ever told before. But instead, you told me about Jessica. I could tell you were making it up because you had to stop every few sentences to think about it, figure out where to go next.

"Let's say there's this old man," you said. "He's bald and looks like he's going to give birth to a keg and he's flat-footed and likes to go around his place naked."

I giggled. "All the way naked?"

"All the way. He likes to be ready."

A shiver swept through me and I knew, somehow—maybe it was the razor edge in your voice—this wasn't a funny story. "Ready for what?"

"He likes to keep girls. On his property. Only one at a time. One at a time is enough."

I tried to smile but my upper lip wouldn't stop twitching.

"He keeps them chained inside his tool shed. And he has to be ready...to go out there whenever he gets the urge to—" You stopped and looked at me. "You know."

I nodded.

"His place is out in the middle of nowhere," you said. "But he keeps tape wrapped around the girls' mouths in case they scream. Not that anyone could hear them, because he's also got these giant rabid dogs and if anyone ever came near enough, they'd hear nothing but barking. Once, when someone came along and shot his dogs, and he knew the girl might scream and bring the law down on him...he went to see her and wrapped her shoelaces around her neck really tight so it wouldn't happen. Then he went and got more dogs."

I rubbed the cold away from my arms and tried to get you to look at me, thinking maybe you'd smile and remind me this was fun and you weren't going to do something bad. But you were looking out across the lake into the dark.

"After a while, the man got another girl. And this man has a son. He's fifteen, say. And one day, the old bald man gives his son a set of keys and tells him to go on out to the tool shed and check on the girl. The son is scared, real scared. His hand shakes when he fits the key into the lock. The dogs are barking and he can hardly breathe as he slides open the door. He's hit with the stench of shit and piss and he has to back up and keep

313

himself from puking before he looks inside. At first, he doesn't see much; it's dark and the shed is filled on one side with a lawn mower and hoses and tool boxes. But then he sees her there, huddled in a corner, crying, choking, struggling to breathe against the thick silver tape wrapped around her face."

"Jack?" I said.

"She's red, from the heat, and wet with sweat. And he sees that she's wearing the wedding band his father gave her; all the girls wear the band before the old man rapes them the first time. The son cuts at the tape, but he can't get it out of her hair. Her name is Jessica. She tells him she wants to go home. And the old man thinks it's funny so he lets his son go back but he has to cut the tape off each time. Jessica asks if she can write something and he puts a pencil in her hand and holds a piece of paper to it, even though her hands are tied together at the wrists, and chained to the mower. And she asks the kid to help her. After that, the old man tells his son he can't go out to the shed anymore. He's done with her and it's time to stop feeding her."

"Jack," I said.

"A few days later, the man tells his son to go see if the girl is still alive. And again he's terrified and struggles with the lock. The door slides open, loud and creaky, metal on metal, and the smell of shit and piss is still pungent. The girl is lying on the ground inside, her legs spread wide, her feet chained to the back wall, her face covered with silver tape, arms stretched out behind her head, locked together at the wrists to a chain pulled taut from the other wall."

314

You sat very still for a while, not saying anything. You took a long drag from your cigarette and shook your head. I didn't want to hear any more.

"He sits beside her," you said. "She's naked. He's ashamed because he's staring at her—he wants to touch her, feel her skin, put his hands on her breasts and between her legs, but then she turns her head to face him and he sees in her eyes that she is now prey and he is a predator. Realizing what he is, the son staggers out of the shed and slides the door shut, locks the lock, and knows he's done this before. With a different girl. In a different time. At a different age. But it always turns out the same."

You tossed your cigarette into the lake and smiled at me. "How'd you like that?"

"How does it end?"

"That was the end."

"That wasn't an ending."

You shrugged and pulled the pack of cigarettes out of your front pocket and lit another. You offered me one and I said no. "How do you think it ends?"

"He kills her?"

You rocked your head to the left and then the right and said, "Yes. In a way, it's the son who kills her."

"You should write it," I said. "It's scary."

"You're the one who likes to tell stories and anyway, it's not believable."

"People like that kind of thing, though. Horror stuff."

You stood up, tossed your unfinished cigarette to the water, and took my hands to help me up and we walked off the pier and you kissed me and pulled me down to the sand. You straddled me, took my arms and put them on the ground behind my head, held them together at the wrists with one hand and dug behind my back to unclasp my bra with the other. When I started trembling, you covered my mouth with yours and then asked me why. I shook my head; I couldn't say. You told me to leave my hands where they were and I did and you pulled my jeans off and yours too and you put your mouth on every part of me until I couldn't leave them there anymore and we made love on the cool, damp sand by the lake and you smiled at me after because I was crying and you kissed the tears off my face. I was confused but I didn't say anything.

50.

Jack.
Jack.

It is my story, after all.

So much time has passed. I haven't been able to write in weeks. Ruby found me sitting on my bed with the pages and she started to read some of it and told me I should finish and be done with it. I told her it was for you.

"Except some parts," I said. "I'll have to tear up some parts before I give it to him."

She pulled me into a hug, the kind she used to give me when I was four and I'd scraped my knees. "Baby, baby," she said. "You know you can't do that. It's too late."

"I know."

"Maybe you could burn it up. We'll build a fire out by the picnic tables in one of the grills and you can watch it turn into ashes and fly away. Would you like that?"

I nodded. She said it would be like giving it back to God. You give it all to Him and He'll take it from you. That's what it's all about, she said.

"That's what Jack did," I told her.

They are calling them 'remains.' They aren't people or bodies anymore. I was with Celia one morning, early, still dark outside, and we had the sound on the television turned down so we could barely hear it to keep from waking Ruby. I think they said they might never find them all. Nine so far. Nine women–remains.

Then they started showing a scrolling list of young women who'd gone missing in Florida; women who might be buried in the junkyard. Celia stood up and shouted, "Oh, my dear Lord in heaven."

I shushed her, but she fell to the floor in front of the television and turned the sound up and when the pictures and names started at the top again she pointed.

"Josiekatellen," she said. "Josiekatellen. Josie, Kate, Ellen."

Ruby came out from her room bleary eyed and frightened and we all sat cross-legged on the dirty carpet, the glowing screen on our faces, reading their names and capturing their images in our hearts. We'd scooted so close I could hear the television hum, and for some reason it brought to mind the toad song and the cicadas shrieking and the rumbling of a million frogs all night long. I used to think they sang lullabies, even after Ron told me it was mating calls. It's a lure. Like everything else. Creatures want to be heard, but how much of the noise is distraction before the strike?

We found out you'd come home, from the news. Mr. Haverty came running over to our trailer and we all–he, Celia, Ruby, and me–sat staring at your picture on the screen. You were in police custody they said. We watched all night and into the next day and nobody wanted to go to work, but we had to, and we took turns. Somebody would run over to the plaza and tell if there was something new, but there wasn't. All day and into the next we waited. All your friends came through our trailer, wanting news. Pat Dunn, Doc Fred, Mrs. Swanson, Mr. Pinkerton, Putty, Kyle, Mary. Ron drove over to the police station to find out more but they wouldn't tell him anything.

By the time we heard they let you go it was too late. We scrambled to find you. We looked all over. The junkyard was still locked up and nothing inside it moved. We stood at the gate, all of us, the whole trailer park, our fingers locked into the chain-link fence looking into what we had worked so hard not to see, and we turned away.

Henrietta Cleary and Celia went north and south along U.S. 1, asking at all the little stores and the motel. Ron, Putty, Kyle, Mary, and me—we walked out to the railroad tracks, up and down them, then to the lake and out onto the pier where we called your name. Our voices echoed through the scrub and quieted down the cicadas and we'd stop and listen and wait for them to start back up again, slow, just a few, then more and more and faster and faster and higher and higher until the air was filled with the screeching again.

A reporter found you at the junkyard. She'd gone looking, like we had, and the gates were locked up, police tape still hanging off the fence. But you were there now, lying just inside, like you were almost out, almost free. Or were you looking out and knowing you'd never be?

Everybody waited for the coroner, debating whether

you'd done it yourself or whether your dad had somebody do it or whether it was all a big mistake and it wasn't you at all, until we learned that you shot yourself in the head–but we knew that all along. It seems we're well practiced at looking away from what we know, because we don't want to know it.

You killed me, Jack; I've been dead. I imagine you believe you saved me but you're wrong. I'll always think you're wrong about that, but there's nothing I can do about it now. I was so angry at you for doing it, I wanted to go down to the junkyard and shoot myself in the head just to show you that you'd wasted your time.

I didn't eat for days and Ruby kept coming into my room begging me to get up but I didn't want to. I knew the first thing I'd do was walk down the road, wrap my fingers in the chain link fence and stare at your blood in the dirt inside the gate and so I had to stay in bed until the rain washed it away. I couldn't understand why it wasn't raining.

After a while, Tucker came over, all the way back from Georgia, he said, just for me. We lay on my bed for a long time and I asked him if he'd brought his gun.

"I don't have a gun anymore."

And then I remembered I hid it under my bed in a paper bag–it had been there for me the whole time. I started laughing and he laughed too. I sat up and wiped the tears off my face and saw Ruby standing in the doorway, looking at us like we'd gone crazy. The smell of tuna noodle casserole baking in the oven started my stomach howling.

Your father's lawyer is saying it was you all along–that

you were the one who kidnaped the girls, raped them, starved them, murdered them, and buried them. You were the one. But you should know that nobody believes him. Not even that awful woman on the television—she's found something else to talk about, but she'll be back when the trial starts. And anyway, the girl who came into the trailer park the night you left says otherwise. We hear she told the police that you unlocked the shed, unchained her, set her free. Your dad is going to die, just like he told you he would.

Jericho came into the bait shop yesterday—said he had an epilogue for his book. I told him he could have it back but he didn't want it. He said he had no time for that now. He got a job over at Putty's nursery and Mr. Haverty gave him a spare room in his trailer and he had plenty of years left in him. His life would be different from now on, he said. And anyway, he had it all in his heart.

I gave him the book and he opened it up to the back and wrote in his last thoughts and then said he'd see me at the trailer park. This is what he wrote:

"I spent my life chasing after the fog, and any time I'd find some I'd wrap myself up in it trying to forget; but it was fleeting. It was only mist. Now I know some things are too dark to turn away from. Some of us can't blind ourselves, can't rest in the fog, or dance in the rain. We are the ones who remember."

I've decided I won't change any of what I've written, Jack. If I owe you anything, it's the truth. And some of that truth can change, like the way we feel or what we think is true. But mostly the truth stays the same.

Somebody else's evil changed you; it's not your fault. You didn't get to be who you were born to be. So, I'll finish our story, and then I'll sit at your stone in that little cemetery down the road and read it to you. And together, we will always remember.

Jericho thinks I should add an epilogue. He says there's usually something more that should have been said and if you add one little bit, you'll feel just full enough to let it go.

Ron says the epilogue is for wrapping up all the things you left out. I didn't leave out anything but a few words. And anyway, I found them; Ron helped me. They are: vulnerable and vulnerability, intimacy, metaphor, and chivalrous. Ron says those are good words to know.

But Tucker says there are no such things as epilogues. He says the story never ends. People are woven in and out of it, but when they're gone, it keeps going. And if the story ever did end, there would be no one left to write an epilogue and no one left to care. And he says to thank you for giving Jessica's journal to the police; it's meant a lot to his mom.

As for me, I think an epilogue is the good-bye that you don't really want to say. So, why say it?